I KNOW
WHAT
WOMEN
WANT!

I0641287

I KNOW
WHAT
WOMEN
WANT!
...Story of an Indian Pick-up Artist

Harpal Mahal

Srishti
PUBLISHERS & DISTRIBUTORS

Srishti Publishers & Distributors
N-16, C. R. Park
New Delhi 110 019
editorial@srishtipublishers.com

First published by
Srishti Publishers & Distributors in 2013

Typeset by EGP at Srishti

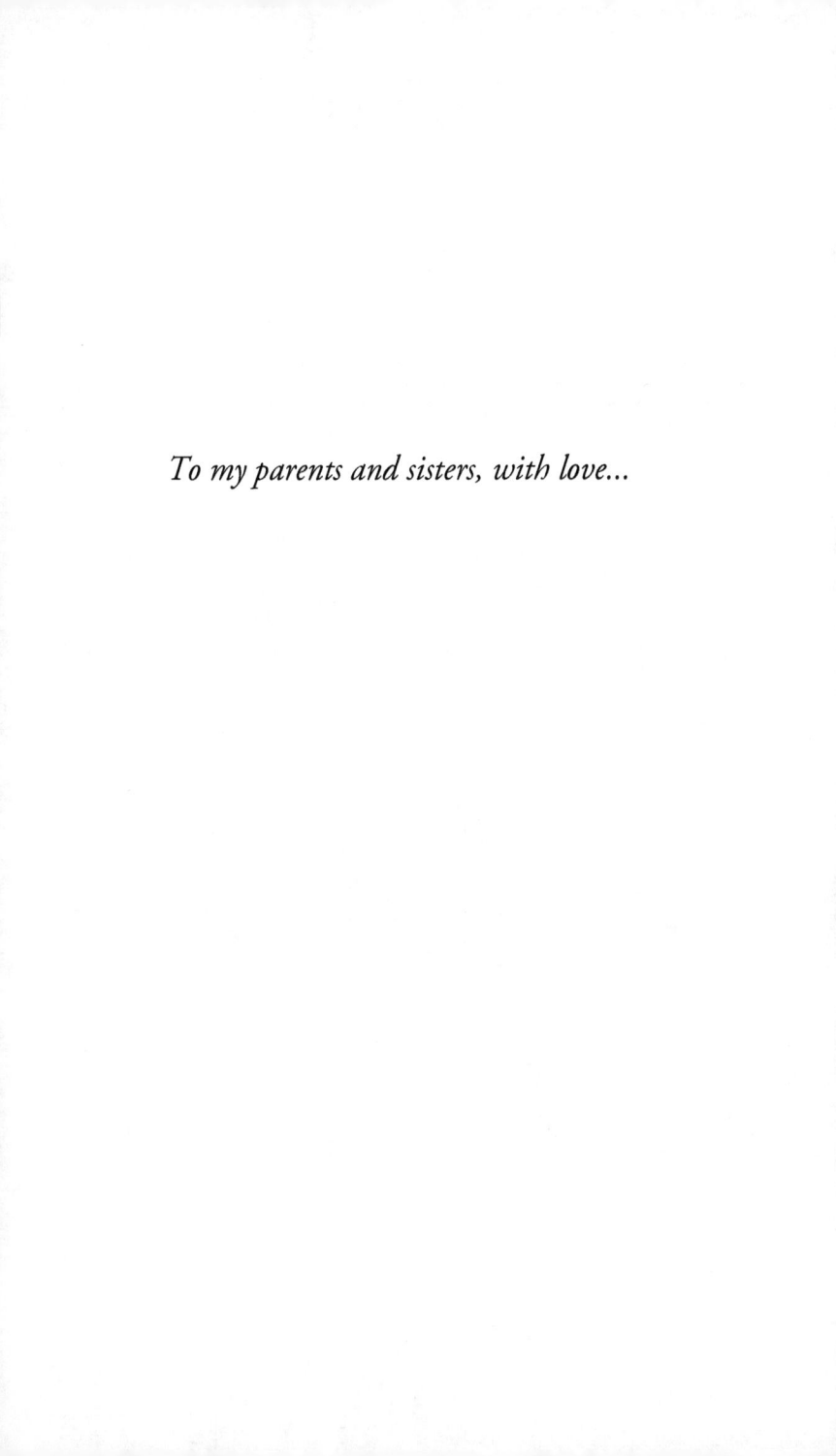

To my parents and sisters, with love...

ACKNOWLEDGEMENTS

I would sincerely like to thank the following people for making this book happen.

First and foremost, Nidhi, for being the sole reason this book could be written. I started writing this, you made me finish it. The only person who was willing to read this and guide me at every page. You were my motivator and my first unofficial editor. Thanks for taking this journey with me and helping me make this book less graphic.

And to my friends. You know who you are. Although this book is a work of pure fiction, if I hadn't taken 10 percent of you and put it in every character modelled on you, the characters would have been life less.

And finally to my family who thought I was just staring at my laptop for hours and yet were patient.

As we walked towards the entrance, I saw a long serpentine queue. I walked past the Mohawks and the cleavages straight to the main door. The bouncer bent forward in reverence as my three friends followed me into the pub. We could sense our presence being felt in the pub.

We sat in the bar and the bartender instantly gave us our drinks. He had prepared them the moment he saw us entering. A Bloody Mary with a tinge of extra salt for me, Long Island iced tea for Mohit, a Pina Colada for Aman and a Strong beer for Anthony.

'Guys remember, we have just come to relax. I am tired and a little put off with so much action lately,' I said in a weary tone. It had been a long week for all of us.

'I never knew even this had a saturation point. But we have come to the right place the music is awesome here', Aman said taking a sip from his glass.

Y….M…C….A…., was the song being played. The crowd sang loudly along with it. I hated the music here. They played the same songs every day. One almost knew what the next song would be. My eyes gazed at a couple dancing close by. They looked into each other's eyes incessantly, with passion galore. They danced with beautiful synchronisation and every time the dance movements brought them close, the guy had a nervous smile. Maybe this was his first dance with the girl he loved. He appeared anxious for her approval. Strangely, I felt warm looking at them and for some reason I kept on watching them for a while. The song changed to *'pretty woman, walking down the street....'* And the guy sang along for his girlfriend while she blushed. *The innocence, silliness and anxiety of love*, I thought. The feelings seemed distant and alien to me. I wondered whether I too could one day look into a girl's eye and sing for her as if I meant it.

I looked at the colossal size of the place which meant a lot of unoccupied spaces even with so many people around. There was a lot of wood used everywhere and I liked the classic look of it. I didn't know whether it was just a personal opinion but it seemed like only people with some class came here. My eyes fell on two such classy girls. A part of me wanted to talk to them and make them mine tonight but the other part was just too fatigued. I had already had enough this week. More than most guys in a decade. I decided to turn around and look at the bar instead. I knew what it was, a curse. Camouflaged as a blessing.

Aman and Mohit said something to each other and walked towards those girls. The girls immediately took to them and I could only gasp at my friends' never-ending appetite. *We want to makeup for the lost time,* they would tell me.

What has it changed? Are we really happy? I thought as I felt a powerful streak of emptiness run through me.

I looked at them again and now one of the girls was on Mohit's lap and the other one kissing Aman. My eyes met Aman's and I could see his eyes devoid of any emotion. He looked away instantly, maybe he was embarrassed. My body cringed in disgust at our own helplessness. It was only when I saw Anthony quietly texting away on his phone sipping on his beer that it eased my discomfort a bit. He had remained loyal to his love. But the other three of us had let ourselves go.

We had thought of it as a skill. Then we realized it was a power and by the time we could get out, it had overpowered us. We were helpless. But I knew it was all my fault. It had been never like this before and it wasn't meant to be like this now.

It all began two years ago......

'Come on, Anuj ,hurry up.' she said and immediately my heart rate increased.

'What do you think about this new page I have added in the presentation?' she said once I was seated next to her.

Rita was told to make a mock presentation on our company ITL, a facility management organisation. She was a new joinee in my team and it was her first day. An hour earlier my boss had asked me to help her in anything that she might need and that had kick started my anxiety. I realised that from up close she looked more beautiful and hence more intimidating. I saw the PowerPoint presentation she had prepared. The first page had a photograph in the centre and some pointers below it. My mind could not really process the information I was looking at.

'It's good, umm..' I said, my thoughts scrambled.

'It is? What about this picture? Do you think I should align it to left? and also I am not really sure about the point at the end?'

I tried to read '*ITL will invest further in systems and methodologies. A "Corporate Solution", i.e. a standardised IT-business solution, has been further developed and implemented in a number of countries'.* I read it but couldn't comprehend a single word. I saw her looking at me eagerly for my reply. I was her senior and one of the best employees in the company. Although, it was only my third month, word had spread about a new guy who was very creative and efficient at his job. *My son you have it in you. You are made for bigger things!* My CEO had told me when I had cracked a big deal for the company on my own.

I looked at her and realized she was saying something to me but I couldn't hear it. I realized that the back of my shirt stuck to my skin with sweat even in an air conditioned office. My heart beat increased further and my breathing became laboured.

I was sure now. I was having a panic attack. It had come back to haunt after months and I dreaded it. My visits to a shrink had helped to a degree that I hadn't had a major problem for four months now. I was finally happy and had made the mistake of thinking that my life would be absolutely normal. She looked baffled by my silence and clumsy breathing.

'Its ..its good…..er just give me a minute , I need to go to the washroom.' I managed.

I walked fast and accidentally kicked a small dust bin and then dashed into a cubicle ahead of me. I saw every one staring at me as if time had paused for a moment Or maybe it was just a figment of my imagination. I walked as steadily as possible towards the loo. I saw my boss inside combing his hair looking in the mirror.

'Anuj, I just received a call from Mr Banerjee, we have to leave in an hour's time.' he said.

'Yes sir.' I said and went straight into the toilet. I sat on the floor and unfastened my tie which seemed like it was throttling me. I tried breathing deeply and thinking of pleasant things as my shrink had told me to but it didn't help. I put my head in my legs and sat there for eternity.

God, what is that you want from me? Why me God? Why do you keep on messing with my life? I thought and didn't bother to wipe the trail of tears which had reached my lips.

I came out during the lunch break. I could see only one guy from the audit department in my bay and he was talking on the phone. He had recently got engaged so maybe he was talking to his fiancée. And he didn't seem nervous. I found that strange.

'Hey Anuj, where were you? Had lunch?' he asked me interrupting his conversation on the phone.

'Yes.' I said and walked past by him. I switched off my computer and slowly took my bag.

'Where to?' he asked.

'Meeting.' I said and paced outside the door.

I knew I wasn't coming back to work. I was the one who was strange.

I had quit.

'Anuj wake up! Its 9.30 already! Aren't you getting late for work?' I heard my mother's voice ring in my ears, 'Get up, your dad is leaving for his office, he will drop you on the bike.'

'Mom it's an off day. My boss's daughter's wedding. They have told us its okay if we don't show up today.' I said and hid my head under the pillow.

'Okay, but anyways get up soon. It's better if one doesn't change ones time table. If you wake up now you will sleep early in the night and wake up in time for tomorrow'.

'I have heard this a thousand times; don't keep on repeating it every morning.'

'Oh! If you don't make big money, who will marry you? I say it for your own good. Time is money. What about us! We have lived our lives; we just want that you do well. Look at Suhaan, he has come back on leave from merchant navy and his parents are getting him married next month. You know how much he earns? He is six months younger….',

'Ma!' my thunder interrupted her 'It's 9.30 am and you are giving me all the stress possible at one go. I can't even see properly, I am still sleepy. At least give the tension in instalments. Does it occur to you that one can have his own stresses?'

'What stress can you have at your age?' she walked away dismissing my statement completely.

'You know what I wish?' I screamed so that my voice reached her in the other room, 'I wish I were born in America where parents discuss their kid's problems maturely and not like you Indian parents. Giving tension all the time.'

'Oh yeah?' I heard her voice from the kitchen, 'They would have kicked you out on your 18th birthday. And you, who never had a proper job, wouldn't have had a roof over your head'.

That statement frizzled my steam away.

'Yeah whatever.' I said although I agreed with her. 'Ma One day Anuj will be the King of the world. And your Suhaan Vuhaan will bow in front of me' I said and immediately wondered I had said it. I was absconding from my current job. This was the third job I had left in one year. But still I knew there was nothing which could stop me from achieving big things in life except for one little problem. Women. They gave me panic attacks; I had zero confidence with women. I have always been like that with women. All kinds of women, even cousins. My shrink had told me that there is a word for it; it's called gynophobia, abnormal fear of women. The fear had its inception in me when I was a young boy in school. I tried not to go back to the painful memory.

'Maa, where is my....', before I could finish the sentence she entered my room with my bed tea. I noticed a tinge of smile on her face. I looked at her and wondered whether there was anything to be fearful of women.

'Slow down, slow down, now!' Mohit yelled

Aman was puzzled, 'Why?' he asked.

'Look at that.......'

'What?'

'Girls!'

'Where?...Oh yes…Why only slow down? I will stop the bike.. let's smoke and watch them', replied Aman.

Mohit and Aman got off the bike hurriedly to drink tea while smoking cigarettes on the roadside, watching a couple of girls having sandwiches close by. Not that they were lechers but you never know when a girl gets impressed by a guy smoking 12 feet away from her and decides to be his girlfriend out of the blue. Yeah, that was their level of optimism. Mohit tried every Shah Rukh Khan expression he had seen in a movie the day before. Aman had put on his shades and was giving the girls a cold stare. He was trying out the intense John Abraham look from an action movie. Suddenly two other bikes came and halted next to the girls who sat on them and zoomed away. Not only did the girls not look at them, they hadn't even noticed their presence.

'Mohit sir, see there another group of girls.' Aman said with a gleam in his eyes.

'Oye, Mr Gone Abraham, let's go, I have to take the gas cylinder also.' Mohit said and they left.

They believed in doing this; walking past women, lingering around them, rushing to a chemist's shop to buy Anacin if they saw a girl there.

'The chemist's store is where you see the hot girls of your locality.' Mohit had once observed.

When an ex-roommate Salabh had got a girlfriend he had casually remarked 'You guys don't work hard. You have to the make an effort. Use, marketing strategy. Tell me, in shopping malls why do they keep their products on display? So that at least a thought enters a potential customer's mind to buy it. It makes the customer visualize himself using the product. The logic is the same. The girls need to know that you exist. Therefore whenever an opportunity arises, display yourself, show yourself to the girl.' He had won over a girl who worked at a nearby PCO booth and hence had become the self-declared love Guru to all the single guys in the vicinity.

And Aman swore by his tactics. He believed he needed a strategy. He stood 5'7" tall and a reasonably average looking guy. He always kept a beard to hide a weak chin and a very low self-esteem. He would often say that he felt naked without his beard.

Salabh had convinced Aman that he had come up with a new fool proof strategy. They had even gone out to field-test it.

They saw a girl at a chemist's store. As per his friend's advice Aman went and stood right behind her. He slowly took out one of the last hundred rupee notes from his pocket and dropped it on the ground.

'Excuse me ma'am, is t—t—this- this your money?' and he pointed towards the note.

The girl looked at the note and said politely 'No.'

' hehe, so if-if it's not yours then...' before Aman could finish the sentence a guy standing next to him picked it up, 'It's mine.' he said and looked at Aman, 'Thank you!'.

'You-you are welcome', Aman said grinding his teeth in rage. A hundred rupee note meant full three square meals for one whole day for a guy living alone in Mumbai.

Aman looked out for Salabh. He had disappeared.

Later however a sweet girl started showing interest in Aman. The girl was Aman's co-worker and she really liked his sweet nature. She adored his shyness regarding women. Until Salabh decided that he needed to take the game a notch higher and made Aman declare to her that he was actually a part of a gang who robbed banks and he kept a gun with him. Salabh's logic was that girls like the dark side in a guy. Aman gave it a shot.

The girl had got scared and spoke to her parents about Aman's involvement in a gang. Her parents in turn informed the local police and gave Aman's details. Aman was arrested and kept in custody.

'Tell us! Give us all your partners' names and every robbery you were involved in.' the constable pulled Aman's hair as he sat on a chair with his hands tied take up. He could feel his face burning under the strong light.

'I am not involved, sir, please understand!' Aman said barely able to speak. It had been half an hour since the thrashing had begun. 'Have mercy! Have mercy!' Aman pleaded.

'Mershy paieje tula? Haan re? he ghe mershy! (you want mercy? Take this!) the constable said and began hitting Aman on his legs with a hot iron rod.

'Salaaaaaaabh Maaaaaaadarchood!' Aman screamed.

'Who is Salabh?' The inspector shouted.

'I—I will tell you everything.' Aman had taken enough, 'I just know the gang leader, Salabh Shrivastava. He introduced me to the gang. I know no one else.' If he was going down, he wasn't going alone.

An hour later Salabh sat next to Aman in the lock up and it was his moment of glory now.

It was only when a friend's uncle who was an ACP intervened and vouched for them that they were let off. But the damage was done and Aman had made it to the newspaper. '24 year old lies to girlfriend that he is a bank robber to impress, lands up in jail.' It had a smiling passport size photograph of Aman next to it. And Salabh became an ex-roommate.

As time passed Aman got over this painful episode. But later he was involved in the biggest problem in his life. Her name was Vinita. He had met her through a common friend. The moment he laid eyes on her, he knew he was born for her. He knew she was 'the one'. After a month of hanging out with her Aman had finally confessed his feelings to her. To Aman's disbelief she had reciprocated his feelings. He was on cloud nine.

'Come to meet me no, I am feeling very lonely.' she said and a bright smiled appeared on Aman's otherwise exhausted face.

'I have just come home from my night shift, and it's 5.am. We will see if we can meet tomorrow.' said Aman faking a tantrum although from within he was ready to be awake forever for her. But the night shifts as an I.T guy in a five star hotel do take a toll on you.

'You want me to continue with this friendship, no?'

'Where should I come?' Aman hurriedly interrupted her. He could not take any chance even if she said it half seriously.

'Meet me outside my college'

'But can't you come a little ahead; I mean we can meet at a centre point. Your college is walking distance for you but I have to travel for almost an hour to reach there. Meet me a little ahead, please.' Aman genuinely pleaded this time.

'No.'

'Okay baby, see u at 8.am.'

'Okay but if you make me wait even for a minute, I won't meet you.' she said nonchalantly.

Aman immediately knew that it wasn't an empty threat. 'No Vini baby I will come.'

Aman didn't reveal it to anyone but he was seriously considering his future with her. And she loved him a lot too. A lot!! That's what she would tell him on the phone. And Aman would float hearing those words.

This would happen with Aman almost thrice a week. She would tell him on the phone that she loved him and was her girlfriend. Then she would insist on meeting him .But strangely after meeting she wouldn't even make eye contact with him and gave him the cold shoulder. Her phone would be busy most of the nights. Aman started getting suspicious.

And one day he did what he thought was the best thing to do at that point of time. He hacked her e-mail account and read her chats with a lot of other boys. It was pretty evident that she was dating two other guys and had regular physical relations with one of them. His world fell apart and he confronted her. She eventually decided to meet him in the presence of the other guy she was sleeping with. That day after her confession, Aman grabbed a newspaper from a passer-by in fury and hit Vinita on the head several times. When she started abusing him he caught hold of her hair and slapped her twice on the face. A crowd started to gather and a heartbroken Aman decided to walk away. As he turned around to look at her for the last time in his life, he saw her crying in that other guy's arms. He looked at that guy in confusion wondering how he could accept a two timer like her back. But that guy just looked back at him and winked. In that moment Aman realised that the guy was in it just for sex. Emotions had nothing to do with that affair. She was sleeping around with a guy who felt nothing for her but never let Aman, who could even die for her, touch her. As he walked towards the railway station with thousands of people around, he felt that he was alone in this cruel, manipulative world. There no thing such as love.

'What time did he say he would come?' Aman asked

'He comes in late every time man.' I quipped in frustration.

Aman and I were standing staring at the long empty road behind a jungle of call centres from where our friend was going to show up.

After waiting for some more time in frustration, we finally heard a sound coming from far off. A very faint but peculiar sound of the engine roared in the distance. We saw an indistinct pale shadow gradually growing in size against the yellowish orange horizon. Bike clocking at 100 kmph, swaying like a Grand Prix bike and the coolest helmet! It had to be him! The bike came to a screeching halt right in front of us with a drift creating a small cloud of dust. From the cloud appeared Anthony D'cunha.

As he walked towards us he took his helmet off and shook his head to push back his long hair. I swear it was always in slow motion like in the movies when he got off from his bike, every time. He came and still looking away, he shook hands with the both of us.

'What's up, guys?' He asked in his baritone. The guy had

everything going for him physically except his height. He was 5'5"

'All good, man! What made you so late?' I asked, my mind still in awe of his entry.

'No dude, I got lost actually...forgot the way and shit! I went too far ahead, like four kilometres ahead and had to come back. Hey guys hear me out..any of you got five bucks ? I think I need a smoke man, too confusing these roads of Mumbai!'

That was Anthony for you. Whenever he arrived it looked like a dude had arrived. But almost always the first thing he would say would be the lamest thing one could hear. When you met him for the first time, something about him would keep you in his awe. Until he spoke. He would just give himself away the minute he opened his mouth.

And sometimes he wouldn't need words.

Once it was raining heavily and he met us. His stopped his bike at a distance from us. He arrived with his signature entry. He lit his cigarette in the rain and walked towards us looking away and a group of girls standing close by couldn't help but lech at that man with tons of attitude and a body language oozing with sex appeal. He squinted and looked at the sky while walking, the cigarette hanging loosely from his lips. Even we had to stop and look at our friend walking towards us but suddenly something bizarre happened. In a split second Anthony vanished from our sight. In one moment he was walking towards us and in the next, he disappeared as if the earth had swallowed him. We ran to have a closer look and realized that a gutter had swallowed him. The rain had made the gutters overflow and one couldn't tell where the gutters were. It took six people to get him out and he was stinking terribly. 'I am telling you guys, this is some black magic shit', he said when I noticed his teeth had become red with blood.

He believed in demons and that someone was reading his mind all the time. He was awfully absent minded and almost always broke after the 3ʳᵈ of every month. The only gift his parents gave him was a fixed deposit of couple of lakhs for a rainy day.

He used it to buy a low end sports bike. He was that kinda guy.

And yet he was a friend. Because he was a genuine person who cared for all. He had a clean heart and conscience. And he would give us the funniest moments. His famous quote….. *'arre tu toh mera bhai hai'* (*oh! You are a brother to me)* mostly after getting drunk, in some weird Hindi accent unique only to him was quite popular. He had told this to almost every guy he knew after getting drunk. So much so that on his birthday his Facebook wall would be full of wishes like 'Happy birthday bro, tu toh mera bhai hai'.

'You have to do it, now!' I told myself as I looked at her standing with her group of friends.

It was a Saturday evening again. A day I waited for the moment it got over. It had been fourteen months now since I quit my last job. I had found solace in alcohol and friends who had lots of alcohol. I had decided that I would stop worrying about my phobia and it had actually eased my problems a little bit. It was all about being an aimless bum and partying on Saturdays. I still had problems with women but I left the problem as it was. Besides, there was a sensational development in my life. A very hot girl had shown interest in me for the longest time. She was my hope. Maybe if I could spend time with her, I could get cured of my disease.

Recently hordes of new cool places had suddenly appeared in the suburbs. The once poor sister of south Mumbai was catching up fast, if not over taking over. There were pubs, lounge bars, restro-pubs and so on.

But I loved The Hell. It was a new pub which had one of the best bars in the city, perfectly lit; not too bright not too dim, excellent music; mostly hip hop and pretty spacious dance floors. Although it did leave a hole in my pocket and indirectly in my dad's every Saturday I couldn't care less. I mean, it always seemed cool if you told a friend you were hanging out in 'The Hell'. Besides, it was the only place I knew where I could see her.

This place was also famous for more girl presence than that of guys. And that was rare in Mumbai. All guys hoped they would catch a prize chick, make out with her, brag about it to friends and climb a step up on the guy social ladder. Most girls hoped some guy would like them, so that they could give him mixed signals, make him chase and approach them so they could snub him and feel good about themselves.

This Saturday I found myself again in 'The Hell' staring at an angel from the heavens.

'Anuj ,man!!Why don't you talk to her …asshole'? My new friend whom I had met 30 minutes back told me. The fatso , whose name I don't remember or maybe I don't want to remember, probably had the hidden intention that if I scored with the drunk girl , maybe for a change, even he could have the blessing of actually talking to a girl. Or more maybe.

'Dude, are you fucking mad? She's in the smoking zone right in the centre of her gal gang…I don't wanna make a joke of myself'. I couldn't tell what I actually feared more, her or myself!

I had seen Richa for the 21st time in 7 months that night. Yes, I had kept a count. We had made eye contact numerous times on several Saturday nights .Once we were even in the same lift. Only the two of us. An uncomfortable silence had pervaded the empty spaces in lift. No words were spoken but our hearts were pumping so hard that it was almost audible.

One day we will be making out in the same moving glass elevator, I thought, *like in the movies.*

I remember it was only some days before the lift episode that she had noticed me. The weekend after, she had looked at me for 4 seconds continuously and that was the first time I started considering myself a little attractive. Well, others did find me reasonably good looking but I never really believed them. After all one does seek validation only from the opposite sex. I am around 5'9 inches, fair, boyish looking. Although my nose is a little pudgy and hair messed up but my puppy eyes, a lot of friends tell me, are my best feature. My eyes make me likeable instantly. And I love to believe that.

Richa on the other hand was a perfect 10. Dusky skin, kohl laden deep soulful eyes, sharp nose, long flowing hair, 5'8" tall. Damn, she was perfect. God! I madly loved her! But my friends thought that actually what Richa's cleavage and long bare legs did to me was limit the supply of blood to only my two parts: heart and dick. That I had more lust for her than love. I didn't agree but guess my bathroom floor did.

'So when are you gonna talk to her? When she is there on the floor with blaring music...just go now.'

'But what will I tell her? That hi I am Anuj, wanna be friends?? She will either make a joke out of me or snub me... I can't go now. Maybe next weekend.'

After a lot of convincing from the fat bastard and psyching myself up, I finally managed to approach Richa. Now, I couldn't care less about my attacks. Nervous or not nervous. Alive or dead, I had to talk to her tonight. This was my moment of truth.

After a truly awkward and mechanical walk inside the smoking zone I approached her. She had smashed the cigarette under her stilettos and was about to leave. It seemed kind of less dangerous now that all her friends had gone out and she was the only one, about to leave.

'Errr..Excuse me…'

Richa turned around and looked back at me so sharply that my balls went numb and I swear I couldn't locate them.

'Yeah…' the voice so sexy, so rich and now that she was close to me her scent made me romantically dizzy.

'Err..hi..you know wot. err..' I now knew where my testis were….in my mouth. And about to pop out with the next word.

'Yeaahh..tell me..??' she was getting irritated. I was making a mistake by stopping a hot walking girl and then fumbling by projecting verbal constipation. They walk (especially when walking alone) with so much focus and single mindedness, even while going to the loo, that it almost seems a sin stopping them.

I took a deep breath and opened my mouth to speak, hoping that the words would come out in one go. 'Hi my name is Anuj and I really think you are pretty and err I was wondering if I could be a you know a kinda friend to you and sorts ..hehe..i mean if you don't mind..and also…we have been looking at each other for a long time.. hehe.' Luckily, I hadn't panicked. I gave alcohol the credit.

'Are you done? Dude what the fuck is your problem you asshole! Don't you have anything better to do then lech at girls? You have been staring at me for ages now! Losers like you see a beautiful girl and start stalking her!'

It was a bolt from the blue.

'No..what? I don't understand….'

'Just fuck off. Just look at you, even my maid won't date you.' she said loudly. A crowd began to gather.

'What happened Richa?? Any problems?' A tall huge guy, probably a friend of hers suddenly appeared from nowhere. A bouncer stood behind him. Instead of intervening and controlling the situation, I thought he rather enjoyed this.

'No, just a regular loser stalker, let's go nothing to worry.' Richa said.

But her friend couldn't waste this opportunity to stamp his machismo over a guy who looked like he could be easily scared. He came very close and was almost breathing on my neck. I could feel the heat of his breath. Disgusting, Yes, but more scary.

'Any problems kid?' he asked slowly.

Kid? I thought, *Dude she can hear this! Don't call me a kid, man! Hit me all you want, but don't 'kid' me man.*

I looked around for my new friend. He had vanished.

Before I could reply, he pushed me so hard that I fell down some distance away. It didn't hurt physically at all.

But mentally I was wrecked.

I saw his giant figure come close to me. He picked me up by my collar and I felt weightless, 'The last time I am asking, is there a problem?'

'No sir, no problem.' The word 'Sir' just popped out of my mouth on its own. And I hated myself for that. On second thoughts maybe my mouth was trying to save my ass.

He gave the most condescending smirk and walked away with Richa.

I felt that God had an issue with me. Maybe it had to do with some bad karma in the previous birth. So far, nothing had worked out in this life for me.

I saw the bouncer laughing at me. The manager appeared and asked the bouncer, 'What should we do with him? Should we ask him to leave?'

'No, it's okay. He is just a harmless little kid. He won't do anything would he?' the bouncer said, all the time smiling at me. He appeared very amused. I felt naked in that place .The girl had given me all the right signals by making eye contact on numerous occasions…looking at me shyly, the way girls look at you when attracted to you. I knew even her girlfriends were teasing her about me. So what happened now? What was *that* all about? I felt confused, insulted, embarrassed and my self-esteem went so down in the flash of a second, that it could have touched the basement of the building. All around me I heard hushed smirks, laughter, smart remarks… I felt ashamed of myself.

You are right Richa! I am a loser! Why would you even talk to someone like me?

Richa had crushed the self-esteem she unknowingly had developed in me.

I hadn't felt so depressed in years. Not even my phobia attacks had made me feel this shitty.

Then I saw a shadow of a man giving me a cold look, standing in the dimmest part of the room, smoking away, looking at me with deep thought. Just a haze of orange light fell on his eyes. He wore a denim shirt with jeans.

I saw the man's lean frame coming directly towards me. When he entered the more brightly lit part of the room I noticed this guy had a mean look. Long nose, clean shaven, and sharp glued in eyes. Although he seemed like a very regular guy but something about him was very tough. Maybe his cold expression or his alpha male way of walking. He looked fearless and intimidating.

Damn it!! Shit maybe Richa's boyfriend or brother, or an ex-boyfriend. Wow, this is getting better by the minute .Surely, this time I am getting seriously hurt! ..Thank you, god. Why do you mess up my life so much?

As he inched towards me, my body stiffened. Suddenly I saw his arm coming towards me and I shut my eyes expecting the worst.

But to my surprise he just put his arm around my shoulder and said those words. The words which would change the course of my destiny,

'If you don't want to feel like this ever…follow me'.

His voice was devoid of any emotion. The man started to walk away towards the staircase.

I stood there watching him go away. I was unmoved, my thoughts were frantic. *Of course, I am not going with this guy anywhere,* I thought.

Then, a question suddenly managed to enter my already frizzled mind.

Could it be him? The Artist Guy, whose name is just doing the rounds in hushed voices in the city for almost 2 years? Who very few had actually met! I dismissed the childish thought. *He is just a figment of imagination of guys like me with no life and girls…,* I thought.

But something about the man's voice was so sincere that my feet began moving towards him, mindless of whether there lay any danger ahead. I wanted to be brave and more of a risk taker. Maybe I wanted to prove to myself that I didn't chicken out every time. Maybe I had nothing to lose. I had decided to follow my gut instinct. As I walked behind the enigmatic man I knew that now I could do anything not to feel like this anymore. Anything. The flight or fight response had taken over. Now I wanted control, to feel empowered and live a life I always wanted to. I was angry with myself, with the world and with God. I wasn't going down without a fight.

Yes, I don't want to feel like this ever, I said to myself and began following him with complete clarity of thought.

I left with the man in his chauffer driven sedan. The night was still young and I had no clue what lay ahead.

We passed from under a flyover and I saw a family of urchins who stayed there. There were more kids than adults. I saw a boy of around 10 years old wearing a dirty and torn school uniform. Maybe some rich kid's parents had given it to him. My mind wandered to my school days. I remembered that day and thought about what happened today.

In life, I am still standing at the same spot, I thought and tears swelled up my eyes.

As much as I avoided, my mind took me to that painful childhood memory, again…..

'Stop doing that….please Anuj, Ouch!!' the girl who sat in the bench in front of me said.

I was pulling her pony tail and all my friends were laughing hysterically at my act. Her girlfriends looked at me with disgust in their eyes but couldn't do anything about it. We were in the fifth standard and were all around 11 years old. I was the cool dude of my class. I would tease the teachers, rag the younger students and make little girls of my age cry.

Then one day tall Pandey ma'am with a nose of witch Griselda come to our class and announced, 'We need nine girls for a song for the annual function. The song is 'Itni Shakti hamme dena daataa…'. During the selection which took roughly three minutes, some volunteered and some were told to participate by the stern teacher.

'We would also need a boy, who would stand in the middle of all the girls', she thundered and her evil eyes started scanning for the right boy.

Please god! Not me, please god! I prayed to God and hid under the desk. Although I was very confident of performing on stage as I had done so on numerous occasions and I was also more than happy with participating as I would get to bully nine girls at one go, I was scared of the fact that Pandey ma'am was supervising this act. She had picked on me lately after she found out that it was me who had put chewing gum in a girl's hair who had to get her head shaved. She had hit me mercilessly that day and on many occasions after that, finding even the smallest mistake to have a go at me. She had even tried her best to have me expelled from the school but fortunately I was given another chance.

'Where is that pest, Anuj? Is he absent today?' she asked and nobody dared reply. I smiled, still hiding under the desk, at the fear I had put in other kids hearts.

'He has come, in fact he is hiding under the desk,' the girl whose hair I had pulled blurted out. I had no choice but to come out from under the desk and reveal myself.

'Anuj you are participating!' Pandey ma'am growled and told the monitor to write down my name in his list of participants. I knew why she chose me. To get an opportunity to kick my tiny ass. I had to participate in the dumb act or face the wrath of the most feared teacher in the school. When Pandey ma'am left I poured the contents of my water bottle on the girl's head.

The rehearsals would be for one week before the final performance on the day of our annual function. Gradually with every passing day I realized that I was, in fact, enjoying myself during the practise sessions. Pandey ma'am had only been a bit strict with me and nothing more and even at that adolescent age I thought that maybe she just wanted to channelize my infinite energy towards a more creative activity. Maybe she didn't really have an agenda against me. Meanwhile I had a gala time torturing the girls rehearsing with me, whenever I found an opportunity.

'C'mon Anuj, c'mon', my group of friends were cheering me. We were having the water competition. The rest of the class was out in the school ground for the P.T. class. Whoever emptied more water bottles by drinking all the water from them, would win. I defeated my competitor again. I felt like the king of the world. I began punching the air in excitement and celebrating my moment of victory. Suddenly I saw every kid around me go cold in fear. As I turned around I saw the tall figure of Pandey ma'am at the door. In the excitement of the competition we hadn't realized her presence. She had watched it all along. After feeling a healthy dose of her long flexible stick everywhere on our bodies, we were made to stand outside the class with our arms raised as a punishment. I felt the most scared among my friends as I had to face her again during the practice sessions. A peon came and asked me to go the rehearsal room as Pandey ma'am had called for me to practise. I teased the rest of my partners in crime and went away singing and whistling. For them, I was above the law. However, the display of happiness was just an act of bravery and from my insides I was scared even to take the next step towards the rehearsal room.

As soon as I entered Pandey ma'am gave me her meanest look, 'Anuj, don't think you have got away with the punishment. See what I do after the rehearsals,' she said and I was stunned to silence. She was the only teacher I feared. The practice began and as usual I was in the front row on my knees with two girls each on my either side and five girls standing behind me.

We began singing, '*Itni Shakti humme dena data, mann ka vishwaas kamzzor ho na….*' and with that I realized I had to go to pee. I had drunk too much water. But I thought I should ask the fiery ma'am only after the song got over. The girls took their sweet time finishing the song displaying their talents to impress the teacher. A stanza finished and there was a pause for 10 seconds before the next. But I couldn't wait that long and I started before them and realized I was singing alone. The girl next to me burst into laughter and I instinctively gave a hard tap on her head with my knuckles. She started crying deafeningly and immediately I knew she was over doing to get my ass whipped by ma'am.

'Anuj, you stupid boy, come here and bend down holding your ears. Now!' she roared.

'Ma'am I need to go the bathroom first, it's urgent', I pleaded but she didn't budge thinking it was a trick and I could run away. I had to bear the punishment and did exactly as she told me to. To my horror the bending of my knees put all the pressure on my stomach. I was scared for the worst.

'Ma'am please..', I begged.

'One more word and I will thrash you so hard that you will cry in agony for days. Just be quiet'.

'Ma'am I am serious', I said and at that very moment she lashed my behind with her stick. I lost control. Soon a pool of my pee had gathered and began traveling towards the girls in front of me. They let out a roar of laughter and I looked at Pandey ma'am and she too was laughing uncontrollably. My heart sank and I was fearful. I refused to stand up in embarrassment. The girls didn't stop laughing and neither did ma'am, I knew they wanted to rub it in. I sobbed but they went on laughing forever. A House keeping bai came to clean the floor and she got rid of my half-pants and the underwear, all the time cursing me. I stood there naked and scared. The girls ran away laughing more loudly. I knew now that everyone in school would know about it in the next half an hour.

I was in shock for days after that incident. I became irregular at school and the life in me was taken away. I could still handle the boys, but it was the girls who constantly reminded me of the incident with their smirks and giggles. I avoided any interaction with women in coming years which made my situation worse. And whenever I had to, I just made a fool of myself, fumbling and messing. In college too I avoided any interaction with women and kept to myself and some guy friends. I never shared the problems with family. That incident changed my life. I didn't fear death as much as dealing with women.

Mumbai really looked much better at night. The illuminated roads with the cool air and the fact that there is very less, almost negligible traffic on the roads just slows down the pace a bit. Strangely, my re-visiting my past had made me calmer. I felt relaxed but didn't understand why. Maybe there was a sudden surge in my courage. I wanted to face my demons to get over them.

I decided that I would have a peek at the guy sitting next to me and see what his expression was, without him noticing, of course. I was wrong. He had *no* expression on his face. The quintessential poker face! Suddenly I felt a strong chill running down through my spine.

What the fuck am I doing? Where am I going? Who is this guy? Was I hypnotised?? Just because a girl didn't entertain me, I decided to go with a random weird guy to some place I didn't even know?? Wait, is this guy gay? Oh fuck!! From trying to do a girl to being done!! What if he was some kind of pyscho murderer??

I should go home man!!

'err..excuse me sir, where are we going by the way?' I asked.

After thinking hard and gazing at the sky for a minute or so, slowly he turned his head to look at me. I think that movement of turning his head took another half a minute.

'hmm..so you don't know who I am...'

It seemed more of a soliloquy than a question.

'I am extremely sorry sir, buh-umm but I haven't really recognised you, have we met before?'

Again he made me wait for the answer. Everything was slow yet captivating about this guy. He managed to hold your attention even though he hardly seemed to try.

'I understand kid, I do. You are scared. And I don't blame you', he said casually.

My mind began processing that information. And a minute later I realised that he yet hadn't answered my question! Then suddenly he looked deep into my eyes, 'If you are ever gonna trust someone in your life; trust me.'

To my utter-surprise it made me feel at ease.

'Sir I hope you don't mind me asking, but what's your name? Who are you and err where are we going?' I didn't know which one was my most urgent question.

I was hoping for a quicker reply this time but no, this time he went a step ahead. He did not answer at all.

He kept looking outside the window in deep thought. I decided to give up and began to look outside myself. Our car stopped at a signal. I saw a group of youngsters having tea from a chai-wala whose shop was built on a bi-cycle. Next to them a poor, old-looking drunk man had collapsed on the footpath. He lay there with his mouth open. I thought maybe he was dead but then I saw his abdomen move while he breathed, indicating life. Nobody around gave him a second look. *People don't want to focus on a miserable man's life,* I thought and looked at the man sitting next to me. *Why would he want to help me? What could be the catch?*

We crossed the plush and pleasantness of the Bandra – Kurla complex. And then I realized that we had entered the ugliness of the biggest slum in Asia, Dharavi.

This aint good, man! I thought.

I tried my best but my mind just couldn't associate pleasing things with the place. Although it had hordes of thriving legal businesses, it was known more for its all kinds of anti-social elements. But how could a guy who looked so dapper and sophisticated and who owned such a luxurious car, live here?

He definitely doesn't live here. Then where was he taking me to? The fear returned.

I need an answer, now.

I mustered up enough courage and asked the man a little assertively this time, 'Sir, I don't mean to offend you, but where are we going and why are we in Dharavi?'

And what he did next staggered me.

He smiled.

'Don't worry kid' and looked at me for a second or two, 'You are very lucky, you will know.'

'But shouldn't I know where we are going.'

'School', he snapped back, 'now, be a little patient.'

I didn't ask him more because I had already gathered that he was a little allergic to simple straight answers.

The chauffer stopped the car and we got down. He turned the car around and went away. We began to walk and I had a hard time matching his slow elegant pace. .He seemed to have all the time in the world for everything. I on the other hand, was always in a hurry. I walked fast but soon realized that I had left him behind and slowed down for him to catch up. When he reached me, I again strode at my natural pace and realized he was left behind a second time and had to slow down again. I was the one supposed to follow him. He must have found me awkward.

Now, the suspense was killing me. We were walking through the small claustrophobic alleys of tiny dingy houses, with gutters overflowing, mosquitoes attacking us with gusto. There were houses on top of houses with minuscule iron stairs everywhere. The lanes became narrower, the stink more unbearable until we reached a dead end. Or so I thought. On looking closely I realised that there was a path ahead. Between the two walls of adjoining shanties there was space enough for one person to pass. On the inside of the wall I could see a small image of a werewolf. He entered through the opening sideways and started to move in. I followed him, with a little fear and maybe with the thrill of impending adventure. The opening took us to a small shanty. I realized that there was nothing around this shanty except for the back walls of the other houses. He knocked on the door thrice, waited for a while and then knocked for the fourth time then pushed the door open. *Oh a code*, I thought! A very old man was lying on a cot. As soon as he looked at the mystery man besides me, he stood up and smiled.

'Chacha.' he said and handed over a hundred rupee note to the old man.

Yup, right! This is the school and this frail old man is the teacher! What an anti-climax, I thought.

Then the mystery man went to the corner of the room, shifted a wooden cupboard which had small wheels. Suddenly from under the trolley appeared an opening that led to a basement. I was dumbfounded.

This can't be real man!! This is surreal. Am I fucking dreaming?

He opened the lid and started to walk down the metal stairs. I had no choice but to follow him. The stairs clanged under my feet.

If you ever are going to trust someone in your life, trust me.

I was hanging onto these words.

'Let's have one-one beer more.'

Anthony would always need more alcohol. Money or no money, he would declare his needs to the universe. The guy had no qualms asking for what he wanted. He was like a baby demanding more milk. Aman, on the other hand, always played it smart. If anyone asked Aman whether they should all buy more alcohol or not, he would always say, 'not really, whatever you guys say. I will give you company!' He knew that most people would anyways buy more alcohol and this way he didn't have to shell out the money because he hadn't really asked for it.

Mohit was always game for more alcohol. The only problem was that he had to be the sponsor every time. He earned the most. Had the best job. And this is when he hated it.

I had asked them to party with me in the club that night but they preferred drinking and chatting at home. So did I, but that chick mentally pulled me towards that particular pub every Saturday night. Besides, Mohit was terrified of a very strong possibility of paying for everyone's entry charges. So he had dissuaded Aman and Anthony from going pubbing, citing lame reasons.

'Yup Lets order for one more round…Anthony how much do you have on you brother?' Mohit was hoping for a miracle.

But Anthony was staring at the ceiling indulged in profound thoughts.

'Anthony!!' Mohit almost shouted

'Yeah dude.'

'Bro do you have some cash on you for the next rounds?'

'No man, I just have like sixty rupees and I have to survive for the next six days until my salary comes.'

'So why one-one beer more? Why did I even bother!' Mohit fumed and then looked at Aman.

Aman started with an embarrassed laughter, 'Mohit sir! *bhenchod* I don't have one rupee extra with me. I just have enough for the rent.'

'hmm..ok so let's use your rent money now and I will pay it back to you tomorrow,' Mohit said.

Aman and Mohit both knew that that could never happen.

Mohit was called the Kaali Mori. As in, the black hole. Once anything went into his radius it would never come back, no sir. Books, pen drives, pens, CDs, t shirts, glasses and money, of course. He would borrow stuff for a day or two but later he would always lose it magically or somebody else would borrow it from him or my favourite, the denial: You never gave it to me!

'That would get a little difficult Mohit Sir, what will I tell my parents if I have to ask them for money?' Aman said feigning emotions for sympathy.

Aman used to call Mohit 'Sir' because even I called him that. Mohit was my trainer in the office when we had worked together once.

'No worries *Chutiyon*, one more round on me,' Mohit said and he called the wine shop for home delivery.

As soon as Mohit said this he knew he would regret it in the morning.

This is how it went. He would spend lavishly in the night declaring *God has given me more than I need* but in the morning he would wake up before everyone else and we would see him with a pen and a notepad counting how much he had spent in his drunken state. Then he would crib about it till evening. He would sulk in a corner as if the angels had told him he would die the next morning. That sight was always very depressing.

'Okay, Anthony, how's work man? Any new girlfriends?' Mohit asked to tease him. He knew he could never get a chick.

But Anthony totally lacked the ability to differentiate between sarcasm and a serious question.

'Yeah bro there is one, no wait, there are a couple of them actually.' Anthony would never say no this question. He would always say he had a new girlfriend. We knew where she was. In his head.

'Oh! What happened?'

'*Arre nai re*, we had our training, okay. And everyone left for the break but these two girls stayed on. So I also stayed back. So they said hi and asked me where do I live and all and I obviously said Bandra coz that's where I live. So they are like it's cool and all..'

'So?'

'So what? Nothing. They complimented me so they were interested in me ,right? I will ask them both out; let's see, once the salary comes.'

'But dude they said the *area* you live in is cool. That's not a compliment for you.' said Aman. He loved to cut off people and argue. 'The compliment is for the area, for Bandra, man.'

Anthony looked down and smirked. The smirks turned into loud laughter. He was desperately trying to control his laughter. He would never laugh when everyone was laughing. He would always laugh alone and loud.

'What happened man?' asked Aman getting a little self-conscious.

'Nothing re, you are just jealous.' and started laughing more loudly. It made Aman and Mohit a little jittery. But thankfully he suddenly went quiet.

'Dude you okay? What happened? You went quiet suddenly?' Mohit asked, a little out of concern and more out of fear.

'Shit man. Fuel! Life sucks man!'

'Why bro what's wrong?' Mohit asked

'No man, I actually realized now that how will I survive with sixty rupees for six days? I mean, I forgot the fuel part, man! I think I can survive only for one day. And even on that day I can either put fuel in my babay (sports bike) once, or eat 1 meal or smoke cigarettes'

Almost immediately Mohit and Aman both started revealing how badly broke they were. Just to be safe from Anthony asking them for money.

'But dude Mohit, how come if you are so broke you always buy so much alcohol man?'

Mohit was dumbfounded by Anthony's question. He never expected such a clever question from Anthony.

'No brother actually I am buying it on *udhaar*, credit, *bhai*.' Mohit was relieved that he could come up with a perfect explanation. But Anthony didn't look satisfied with the answer. He started staring at him. That's what Anthony would do when angry or when he knew someone was lying to him. He would stare and gather all the anger inside his head. Mohit shifted uncomfortably in his chair. After ten seconds or so when he looked at Anthony again from the corner of his eye to check, he was still staring at him. Mohit never admitted but he was a little scared of Anthony and his talks about demons and black magic. Anthony was about to declare Mohit the son of

Satan when the doorbell rang and Mohit heaved a sigh of relief. The alcohol had been delivered .Mohit went to collect the beer from the door.

'Oye Aman get my wallet, no?' Mohit shouted from the door.

'Anthony you go and give him the wallet, please!' Aman transferred the job to Anthony.

Mohit paid for the beer in cash and Anthony was standing next to him. All the thousand rupees notes were visible from his Wallet. Anthony could see the pile of cash in the wallet.

Oh shit!! Mohit thought *this is gonna be very uncomfortable.*

'Cool man, so many notes!' said Anthony with a twinkle in his eyes.

Apparently, he had forgotten the conversation he had just had with Mohit.

'It's very cool no? Come, let's have some more beer.' Mohit was relieved.

'*Tu mera bhai hai* ..'said Anthony and hugged Mohit.

Two beers down and 'See, when I was in Delhi….' started Mohit. The downfall of having to drink beer with his money was to listen to his never ending stories of Delhi and his break up. Sometimes it seemed that he bought an audience with beer. We all knew the story by heart. He would narrate it every alternate Saturday as if for the first time. I assume we had all broken beer bottles on his head in our minds whilst his narration carried on. Anthony was spared I guess, by default. By the looks of it he would be listening attentively but in his mind he would be somewhere else. Lucky bastard!

'…. So, I was on the terrace and talking to her on the phone. I had a cigarette in one hand and in the other a drink.'

'What, whiskey?' Asked Aman faking an interest.

'No no..I was beering and I didn't tell her that I was. So she asked me, what are you doing…'

'One minute Mohit sir? What were you *doing*?'

'..er.. what?..okay! I was beering, why?'

'What's that?'

'What's what?'

'What is beering?'

'I was having a beer, why?'

Mohit's English was his own. He spoke in his own personalised version.

'There is no such word. Ask Anthony, he is a catholic, his English is the best amongst us.' Aman said.

Anthony was looking at them and smiling. Pretending that he knew what was going on.

'What do you say Anthony?' asked Aman.

'No man, I am cool and all man. Just a little tipsy. I was wondering if someone can read your mind through Bluetooth in your mobile. I must say the beering has got straight through me and I am pretty high.'

'Damn! There *is* such a word !' Aman banged his fist on the table making the beer bottle in his other hand slip out and break on the floor. It was his ritual. Aman had to drop and break one beer bottle, or his whiskey glass, whatever he had. Then Mr Greasy hands would expect the others to share. But the rest had adapted to this by now. As soon as his bottle would fall down and break, the rest would gulp down their beer like mad men. Even Anthony would wake up magically from his slumber and become as alert as a deer and pour all his beer down his throat in one movement. He had paid the price many times for his slow reactions by having to share his beer in the past with Aman.

'*Bhenchod, my destiny is fucked up,*' Aman said, '*Naa daaru tikte hai haath main,naa paisa tikta hai aur naa hi ladki!*' (*Neither alcohol, money or even a girl sticks around with me!*)

'But guys tell me, who's the life is more screwed up? Be honest!' Mohit would ask us as if there was a prize on offer for the winner. I had never told my friends about my situation. That would have broken Mohit's heart considering that he would have surely lost the competition to me. But that wasn't to say he had had it easy.

Mohit Joseph was in a relationship with a girl for 3 years with a girl called Pari Gupta. They loved each other to death. She was a trainee in his batch and Mohit had immediately liked her sweet nature on the first day when she joined office. This was a first relationship for both of them and they were in a very happy space in life. But Mohit knew that their different religions would be a hindrance in the way of their marriage. Yet, they would sit for hours in a nearby park outside their office in Kalkaji talking about life post marriage. They had even planned exactly how the interior of their house would look like. Mohit wanted to give every luxury to his love. And she just wanted to sleep in his arms.

She would come to Mohit's place and sometimes she would cook for him and his mother. 'You don't have to do this beta,' Mohit's mom would tell her. 'Why? What's the harm *Mummyji*, eventually I have to do this one day, why not now!' Pari would say and Mohit would feel blessed and thanked God for a perfect life. He knew that it would all work-out eventually. Her parents would oppose and then approve sooner or later, as it happened with most inter-caste marriages in Indian cities.

'Why do you love me so much?' Mohit had asked her. They lay down next to each other in a bed on his terrace, hand in hand, gazing at the stars. Although, Mohit knew she would never object if he made an advance, he wanted to save it for post marriage. She was a goddess for him and he wanted to keep her chaste. 'I don't know Mohit! All I know is I will die without you', she had replied with tears in her eyes. Mohit looked at her and even though she hadn't put any make up on, she looked striking to him. She had very sharp features on a little roundish dusky face. Her eyes were captivating and it seemed to Mohit that they were made just to look at him. Her eyes were his. Her nose, her hair, her full curvaceous body was his. She was his.

Two years into the relationship and everything seemed to be perfect. Mohit had received another promotion and a healthy increment. They were supposed to meet at a mall in Greater Kailash and Mohit would treat her in her favourite Thai restaurant. When she arrived she was late by an hour. But the celebrations had to begin. Mohit knew that higher the salary of the guy, the less important his religion became to the girl's parents in inter caste marriages. He ordered whiskey for himself and for Pari, her favourite Vodka. During Dinner, she had seemed aloof to him.

'Pari, everything okay? You seem a bit occupied. What's the matter?' Mohit asked holding her hands.

'No, nothing. It's just that there was a guy to see me for *rishta* today. That's why I got a little late. I didn't want to tell you this over the phone and upset you for no reason.'

'Oh! Okay! How did it go?' Mohit asked without a trace of worry. He trusted her, he trusted the relationship.

'As usual! I have told mom and dad I need some time to think over it and after couple of days I will say a no', she said and smiled sheepishly.

'Everything will be an okay, once I talk to your parents.' Mohit said and looked for a waiter, 'Excuse me! Please come here,' Mohit shouted and ordered for Pari's favourite dessert. During the rest of the dinner she spoke very little. Mohit kept on looking at her while she looked at the table cloth.

After that day Mohit started seeing a lot of changes in Pari's behaviour. She always found reasons not to meet after work and seemed eager to hang up. Mohit didn't give it much thought until the night when he had called her at 1.am post drinks and dinner with office friends. Her phone was busy. When he asked the next day, she said it was her cousin from America. Gradually she seemed to drift away from him. One day on a pure hunch, he checked Arjun Gupta's Facebook profile. He was the guy, who had come to Pari's home for *rishta*. When he opened his profile Mohit saw that he was a tall and handsome guy. He looked like those male models for expensive suits in newspapers. He was the Regional head in one of the biggest MNCs in Hyderabad. Unintentionally he compared himself with Arjun. Mohit on the other hand was around 5'8' tall. He was a very regular looking guy. The only striking feature on his face was his two front teeth which protruded a little and a beer belly. Mohit checked Arjun's relationship status and was relieved that the guy's relationship status showed engaged. Obviously his mind had over-imagined, he thought. He casually checked out his profile pictures and then saw some more of his pictures on his wall. In one of the photos Arjun was in a swimming pool and revealed his washboard abs and a muscular physique. He stood with his friends who were tagged and on checking out their profiles Mohit realised that Arjun kept company with the rich. One was owner of a sports club, one son of an MLA and the other was an NRI businessman. Mohit felt very small compared to the guy Pari had rejected him for. But it also showed her unconditional love for him which made him want to hug her at that very moment. Immediately he decided to go and meet her directly behind her house. He wanted to tell how much he loved her and that they should sort out all their differences and be happy like before. He went to the counter to pay for his half an hour in the cyber café but the owner wasn't there. The owner had gone away to the bathroom. Nothing to do for the next ten minutes or so, Mohit opened Facebook yet again. Arjun Gupta's profile opened directly on his screen again. Mohit had forgotten to logout from Facebook. He saw a Photo-album titled Engagement. He clicked on it. He wanted to see who this rich good looking man was going to marry. The first was a solo photograph of Arjun. He wore a black *bandhgala* and Aman thought it looked perfect. He made a mental note of it so that he could buy a similar one for his engagement with Pari. The next photograph had Arjun's fiancée standing with him. In the pic she stood with her head down which meant her face wasn't visible. Yet Mohit somehow felt that he knew she looked too familiar. His heart skipped a beat. When he saw the third photograph, his body went cold. It was Arjun's fiancée's solo photograph. It was Pari. She was smiling and waving at someone in the photograph. Mohit started to breathe heavily and his hands began to tremble. His world had just collapsed. Everything was now making sense to him. Her phone being busy at late hours, she finding faults in him about the way he dressed, his career and everything about him. He was being compared to that perfect creature.

When he called and confronted her she said she was weak and helpless and cut the call saying that now that he knew, he shouldn't call her. She moved to Hyderabad to stay with a cousin. Mohit risked his job and followed her there. He still believed that one conversation with her and she would change her mind. When he arrived at Hyderabad airport he had called her up.

'Pari guess, where I am? In Hyderabad! Meet me in the evening.'

'Oh man! WHAT'S WRONG WITH YOU?' Pari barked, 'Don't you see I am engaged. Why don't you just leave me alone? Why can't you just see me happy? Why are you so selfish?'

Mohit didn't say a word and disconnected the phone. *Why are you so selfish?* He knew he had no replies to her question. Because her questions were a lie. She was a lie. She had turned out heartless, cold and plain opportunistic. He had developed a strong negative opinion about women at large and how they should only be used and thrown. He went back to Delhi by the next flight but couldn't live in a city for long where every place haunted him with his past. He fled Delhi and came to Mumbai. He didn't trust that city; the people in it.

Wherever this staircase is taking me to surely is going to be a small, dingy, filthy, stinky place, I thought.

He walked in front of me comfortably as if it was his daily thing. As we reached the bottom end of the stairs I could only see a brick wall right in front of us. But when I turned to look back over my shoulder what I saw left me transfixed. There was a huge glass door which looked like it belonged to an office as white bright light shone through the clean and spotless space. It had a reception counter where a man sat dressed in a crisp black suit. I followed the mystery man in the office as he swiped a card from his pocket which made the door open. The man at the reception stood up in respect.

People stand up in respect for him? Who is this guy? I literally screamed in my head.

We passed through another door which led us to a huge hall lit with bright white lights. It was all painted in unblemished white; the ceiling, the walls; the floor. I was just amazed at what I saw. I kept on following him as I saw that on one side of the hall there were six huge rooms with glass walls. In at least two rooms it seemed there was some sort of training going on with five -six guys sitting in each room with guys who seemed trainers. All the rooms were illuminated with blue neon light. The air-conditioning was strong and I wished I had carried a jacket with me. I could smell a distinct pleasant fragrance in the place. In the extreme corner of the place I saw a very small room with a board on it which read SMOKING ZONE and two guys occupied it smoking away and chatting animatedly with each other. *Oh boy! This is one school I should have studied in a long time ago*, I chuckled. As I passed them they didn't bother to give me a second look. Another small division read GARMENTS AND ACCESSIORIES. On looking in closely I found that it had the most bizarre stuff inside. The long top hats, boots with feathers and as long as your knees, loud jackets and louder pants. However intriguingly, the guys around were impeccably dressed and groomed. Gelled hair, beards of all possible styles and neat and clean shoes. Fragrances of different perfumes lingered in the air. But eerily there were far too few people for such a big place. The staircase had indeed taken me to a school in the basement, as I was told before. That, it didn't look like a conventional school at all, was a different thing all together. And probably that was the reason there was a board there which read TST: THE SCHOOL OF THOUGHTS. Without the board one couldn't guess what it was. I knew I liked the name.

He told me to wait outside while he entered a room through a wooden door. This was the only room which didn't have glass walls. If I had fear about any kind of danger to my life, it had subsided. The place looked like a well-run organisation and seemed pretty professional too. I mean, after all, the trainers and the trainees all were dressed in formal clothes. *Killers, goons and thugs don't wear formals.* And that was a relief. Then I looked at the board again . *The School of Thoughts. What could it all be about?* I wondered. *Was it some sort of personality development program?* I had definitely displayed a total lack of personality back in the pub and he must have thought I definitely needed it. But whatever it was, it was definitely something extreme. I mean why would someone have their training in an underground location, where it was kept a huge secret from the general public. Directions for this place were almost cryptic in nature. This wasn't an everyday school. I was getting more keyed up with every minute of waiting, wondering what was in store for me. This was *some* night. My thoughts drifted to the dark memory of my encounter with Richa and her huge friend. Immediately I felt very dejected again. And thirsty. Damn, I was very thirsty. The alcohol, nervousness of talking to Richa, she insulting me, the anxiety her friend put in me, and then feeling scared going with a complete stranger in the slums of Dharavi had made me very very thirsty. I was pretty hungry too. I wanted it to end soon and go to the comfort of my room at home

'Hey come in,' a young man opened the door just a little bit to peep outside and call me in.

It was a lavish room. It had a huge desk with lot, of files, CDs and notebooks kept in a neat order. The mystery man was sitting behind the desk with two other men sitting opposite him. He was definitely their boss.

'Please sit down.' he said in a very assuring way. I sat in the third unoccupied chair next to the two men.

'Welcome to the school of Thoughts. My name is Guru.' He said looking straight at me.

Oh yeah? Thank you so much for an early introduction, I thought.

'Hi I am Anuj Kukreja and umm.. That's about it.' I introduced myself as my dry vocal chords refused to throw out any more sound.

It was noticed immediately and I was offered a glass of water. I tried to drink the water in as normal a way as possible. But my terrible craving for water meant that I could only gulp it down. My throat made a strangely loud guzzling noise in that quiet room. It was awkward.

'Let me be very upfront with you, this a school where we teach you to manage your dating life.'

What! Are you serious!

'Guys, give Anuj and me a moment here,' he said looking at me all the time, long and hard. For a moment I felt he could see through me. The two guys left the room and I shifted uncomfortably in my chair. It was one of those nights where you would be foolish to predict the next thing.

'I saw what happened back there in the pub. It can change. If planned well, in a couple of months that girl could cut herself in pieces to get you. And any girl, for that matter,' he said and looked at me expecting that I would blush with joy. He was wrong, my expressions didn't change much.

'Sir, I know that in your dating school you must have made guys achieve incredible results. But I am different. You can't change much with me. Even the doctors couldn't. And so far nothing has helped me much' I said and immediately decided to add something cool about myself, 'I am otherwise very confident, intelligent and sharp.' I said. I noticed that my lips were trembling a little.

'What you are saying is easy. Life is easy. The problem is not how you look at women; it's how they look at you. You start seeing them with your eyes instead of looking at yourself with theirs.' he said casually, 'Most guys feel this at some time of their lives. What you feel is an exaggerated version. That's all.'

I just nodded. It was profound.

'Well Anuj, we will cross that bridge when it comes. For now I would just say, Welcome aboard and be ready for change. Some serious positive change. Come here tomorrow at 6.pm sharp. The training lasts for 2 months.'

'How much is the fee?' I asked realizing it was the next logical question.

'It's free for you, kid.'

'Why?' it came out immediately.

'I will tell that to you later.'

'Actually sir, I have three friends who are at similar place in dating life. So I was wondering if I can get them with me.'

'hmm..okay but they will be charged Rs 50,000 each for their training.'

What? 50 grand? I knew maybe Mohit could still somehow arrange it but the other two could be fighting and killing each other for 1 bottle of beer right now.

'Sir, I hate to say this but they can't afford it. B—but they are great guys and deserve it as much as I do. If the fee can be discounted, you know, it will do a world of good.. I know you have made a wonderful offer to me and I am pushing my luck a bit but it somehow would feel unfair. Please?.' I said.

'Okay, Anuj.' said Guru, 'I am not really bothered about money right now. I make that from lot of other sons of bitches. They will be trained for free as well, happy now?' Guru said and paused for a moment, 'But there is one condition. And you will not say no, when the time comes. Now go home and rest .My boy will drop you on the highway, get a rickshaw from there and go home. You will crave for rest in the next two months. Your life is about to change. Sleep well.' he said and winked at me.

I couldn't understand why he displayed so much concern for me. He was being too generous to me. *What could be the catch? The condition? Wait, could he be gay?*, before my mind could go that way again, I decided to go home. *Maybe he saw a lot of promise in me! But when?* I wondered.

'Thank you so much sir. I will see you tomorrow.'

Reaching home I lay on my bed, I replayed everything which happened that night, in my mind. And how it ended with me and my friends getting free training in a dating school. No, *The School of Thoughts* to be exact. I smirked a little at the thought of getting a free deal and how my friends would thank me so much for it. And to put my mind at rest I convinced myself that the condition he spoke about couldn't be that bad. *Guru seemed nice, he wouldn't...*

And then...*most guys feel this at one time of their lives. What you feel is an exaggerated version. That's all.* He had said it with so much ease and thinking about it I felt a deep feeling of calm inside me that I hadn't felt in a long time.

Then suddenly it hit me. It gave me goose bumps. The thought made me jump from the bed and stand on the floor. How could I be so absent minded? How could I not know?? Oh my god!! I should have realized the moment I saw the board.

I had just met him. Most of the guys weren't sure whether he really existed. Some had only heard about him but very few had seen him. People who had met him, talked about him as someone with magical powers. Who could make you a star in matter of days!

Yes! I had met him an hour ago.

His words resounded in my mind.

'You are the lucky one'

I had met THE ARTIST.

❦

'Let me *be* man! I just don't wanna talk right now.'

Mohit said while he smoked sitting in the dining table's chair in his hall. The place was a mess with beer bottles and cigarette butts lying all around. There was a note pad with some calculations scribbled on it and a pen lying on the table .I should have guessed. It was Mohit's sulking time. He was the only one up. Aman and Anthony were fast asleep in the bedroom at his place as it happened on most Saturday nights. It was 8.am and I was already there to meet my friends. I just couldn't control my excitement and wanted to share everything with them as soon as possible.

'Ok bro. Take your time. Where are the other two?'

No reply. I tried again.

'Bro, can I expect an answer, like, today?'

'They are lying dead inside. See how have they a fucked the room!'

I was about to laugh but decided otherwise. I just ignored him. He would bring up random things that he was angry about but we knew it was the money spent the last night that was haunting him. I went inside and kicked Anthony and Aman's butt hard. Anthony woke up hurriedly and saw me and smiled, 'good morning broths.' He was pleased that it was me and not some demon, I guess. Aman looked at me, swore under his breath and went back to sleep. He was the eternally frustrated types. As always he was sleeping only in his undies. 'What the fuck man Aman? You were sleeping next to me almost naked man.' Anthony was scared. He slid his hand in the back of his pants to check if everything was alright and dry. That was the most peculiar thing about Aman. He would get down only to his underwear whenever he found himself in the confines of a house, if there were no women around. We found it strange initially but got used to it later. Actually, initially everyone had their balls in their mouth when they first met him alone in his flat. Or when he came to visit you at your house. He would look straight into your eyes, although unintentionally, and start to undress slowly. First the shirt would go and then the pants. At this moment one hoped that the pants would get replaced by shorts or something. But no. he would hang around in his briefs. Then he would come and sit uncomfortably close to you and start talking about mundane things. And you would just nod not even listening to what he would say worrying that he might pounce on you at any moment now. Of course that never happened. He was straight. His reason was heat. Yeah right, you animal!

The maid came and cleared all the mess, muttering non-understandables under her breath. Anthony threw a cushion at Aman to cover him. The bai hated Aman. There was a very strong case for her to hate him. One night he had got so sloshed that in his sleep he had got rid of his underwear as well. He had slept stark naked on the floor. No mat, no pillow. Just a drunk naked hairy animal on the floor with legs spread and stretched as far as possible. She had come at the usual time in the morning and unfortunately for her she always kept one house key with her. It took her at least 30 seconds to understand what she was seeing. First she smiled and then when the reality struck she started panting heavily. Then she felt the world spinning around her and felt dizzy. What had made the matter worse was Aman was having an erection and a wet dream when the *bai* saw him .The young *bai* had rushed to the kitchen and wept inconsolably for 30 minutes. She was cursing her father for not giving her enough education so that she did not have to do this dirty job. She was certain she was going to hell because of the drunken shameless bastard. It was only when Mohit falsely convinced her that if she fasted every Wednesday for 4 weeks she could definitely get rid of this sin. Anyways now she made tea for all of us, which was to say the least, horrible. Maybe she was trying to tell us that she was not happy with Aman's almost nude presence and also with so much mess lying around. But I was happy. And wanted to share it.

'Bro, how did it go last night?' asked Aman, his grogginess wearing down a little with the terrible tea.

'Aman, that's a very good question. From where should I start.......'

I narrated everything to them. From Richa, her mammoth friend to Dharavi's secret basement school and Guru, The Artist.

All my friends looked at each other in disbelief.

'A secret, basement dating school in slums? The Artist? Anuj, you sure your drink wasn't spiked at the pub? Do you hear what are you saying?' Aman asked almost out of sheer concern for my mental health. They didn't believe what I had told them.

'Guys, c'mon! No I wasn't on drugs yesterday or now. This shit is for real. Imagine what we can achieve with that. Any girl, any time!' I said. Mohit walked over to the bedroom and with him got a small framed photo of Jesus Christ.

'Anuj keep your hand on this photo and swear that you are telling the truth!' Mohit said. I smirked but he looked very serious.

I kept my hand on it, 'I swear guys. It's all true.' All of them thought about it for a second or two.

'He is telling the truth.' Aman declared and smiled. And suddenly out of nowhere they all leaped at me to hug me. They were laughing loudly in sheer joy.

'Guess what we can do now. Nobody can stop me!' Aman shouted.

'It's the best thing I have the heard in Mumbai and it's for free!' cried Mohit.

Anthony was beaming too.

'Anuj dude, you are the best, man! Awesome man!'

'Yeah Anthony Thanks. But there is a problem. I don't think you can attend it.' I informed him with a heavy heart.

'But why?' the veins in his forehead began to swell.

'Dude, c'mon man, you forgot? You are doing an evening shift and the training starts at 6 pm.'

'Yeah dude I almost forgot that.' said Anthony. We all went quiet. Then, which looked like a lot of mental calculation Anthony declared that he would leave his job.

'Dude, how will you survive? Your family also doesn't support you?.' I asked.

Then what Anthony said stunned us.

'I will sell my babay!'

'What? No Anthony we know you can't live without it. No don't do that. I am sure we can think of something else.' I retorted.

'What else can we do *bhai*' said Anthony with a weary smile, 'I wanna come with you guys man. And what's the point of owning a bike if I don't have a girlfriend to sit on it.'

'But how will we sell your bike, I mean we don't have much time and by the looks of it we won't have much in the next two months also. Do you know someone who is interested?'

'Actually no man, no one. I will have to talk to some people.' he said.

Suddenly something struck me and I looked at Mohit. Aman understood what I had in mind and even he started looking at him.

'Hey guys no, don't look at the me? What will I do with the bloody bike? My office is so nearby. I can't buy something so expensive which I even don't need.' said Mohit.

I want to do sports biking one time in my lifes; it's a list in my bucket! A drunk Mohit had once confided in.

'Who is asking you to buy it? Just use it for two months and pay Anthony whatever amount you think is right. That way Anthony also won't lose his bike forever, plus your desire of riding a sports bike would be fulfilled too.' said Aman and looked at me if I agreed. I nodded.

'Hey wait Mohit; I will make it easy for you. Just let me stay at your place, provide me with food, cigarettes and beer every weekend and I am cool. You don't have to pay me and all re.' By saying this, we knew Anthony had sealed the deal. He had minimal needs. Mohit was the winner in the deal.

Mohit smiled devilishly 'okay it's on!'

'Alright then, guys!' I said, 'We are all set. Meet me at 4pm at Bandra station and I will take you to Guru'

We all said cheers with our empty tea cups.

We were excited about the fact that we were approaching change. Our lives would become the way we always wanted it to be. I hoped that it could cure me, that I would be able to live normally again. Aman and Mohit were hoping that the pain the women had given them would die out with it. Anthony, I knew would be happy with that one girl.

But in our hearts we wanted the women to look at us as their gods. We wanted to feel wanted by women. We felt super excited.

We were pumped!! Guru here we come!

❈

A man had come to receive us at Bandra station.

Although they were made aware beforehand that the venue was in a ghetto, my friends were a little fearful when we actually reached Dharavi. Their nerves settled a bit, much like mine had, on reaching the underground venue. We were offered water and then guided into the training room. It was lit with blue neon lights. The white light from outside the training room managed to enter a little bit in the corners of the training room. The blend of the white and blue lights at the borders of the training room gave it a pleasant hue. There were around twenty folding chairs and desks inside but all unoccupied. There was no one there except us. I guessed we were the only trainees in the batch. On realizing this we all gave each other high fives. It meant no embarrassment in front of new people. We waited for some time. All of them were very excited at the prospect of seeing The Artist, aka, Guru.

'He must be huge and all *naa* Anuj, muscular and shit? asked Anthony.

'No champ, you will know when you see him?' I replied. Guru was anything but the typical out of gym stud who walked as if his chest was running away from him and he was trying to catch up. He was a pretty regular guy to look at. *But regular he is not*, I thought.

After waiting for about 10 minutes someone entered the room.

'Hello guys! A very good evening to all four of you! My name is Ankit Jain. I am your trainer for the next 7 days.'

We were a little taken aback. This guy was about 4' 11" tall. He had a receding hairline. He had the most unattractive features you could ever see. His nose was wide, eyes too close to each other and had black patches on his forehead. The only positive thing about his appearance was that he looked lean and fit. But still presentation is a huge part of training. We knew we felt let down.

He took a brief introduction from all of us. We just said whatever came to our minds first. We were hoping to see Guru and assumed that he would train us but here was a guy, who seemed, well to put it mildly, incapable of teaching us anything about women.

'Okay now let me admit that I can sense you feel a little let down by seeing a guy like me to teach you how to get women. Well, let me break the news to you. I am not here to teach you that. I am here to put in you an ingredient which will get you closer to your goal. And let me say that what I teach is one of the more important things that will help you get there, if not the most important thing. The biggest hindrance faced by any man to get what he wants is hesitation. Some examples of such thoughts in the mind:

Will I be able to do that? The others will be judging me! Ohh I feel so shy in front of others. I feel I am not good enough. I want to talk to her but I just cant I feel too scared of the outcome!'

I think we all agreed mentally that we had those negative beliefs and I thought that he had missed out on gynophobia.

He continued, 'This is the way most of us think. Now the reasons behind such behaviour can be multiple. The way you were brought up, an incident in the past...', he said and I was clued in immediately. He continued, '.....the way you look and hordes of such reasons. Now what I believe is, that instead of changing the psychology of a person, it's better if we change his behaviour. *The body follows what the mind does*, is the general belief. But we will focus more on *The mind follows what the body does!!'*

We started to feel that we were so wrong about this guy. He was talking about things we did not understand. It meant that he was very smart!

'Okay let me ask you a question? Have you ever danced as if you didn't care whether people were watching? Straight From your heart? If you have, do you remember even one instance when you were dancing with gusto but still being sad? Or depressed? Ok now some of you would ask that it was first our mind which decided to have fun and then we went in to dance. So the body followed the mind! Think about it. When you took the decision of dancing you didn't feel as liberated as when you actually started to dance. Hmm, let me simplify it for you. What would you prefer, that I hypnotize you and take you to Switzerland in your mind or if I actually take you there?'

'We would like to actually go there.' all of us said together. Anthony's tone wasn't so convincing though.

'See? Get what I am saying? Most of the people try and change their attitude, their thought process and believe it will change things for them. Well, most of them waste half their lives just thinking. It's pretty ironical, isn't it? This is what I am saying and the school's name is 'The School of Thoughts.' Well, let's put it this way, we have given this theory a lot of *thought*. We believe in action here. Do it and keep on doing it until your body and nervous system becomes comfortable with it. It's like, keep on driving until it becomes second nature to you. Keep on making those cold sale calls until it sits in your system. Similarly and more importantly, keep on behaving without inhibitions until you lose them.'

Damn! This is good.. I like it here. It's wonderful man! A life without inhibitions! Half my problems would disappear with that. I looked at my pals to see how they were doing. They all looked so attentive, it was scary. I could see focus in their eyes, determination to grasp every word coming out of his mouth. I was half expecting Anthony to have that dumb smile on his face when he is day dreaming but he was actually taking notes. I leaned over expecting drawings of demons or some doodling but he was actually making pointers and writing down stuff he was listening to. *What's wrong with my friends?*

Suddenly I felt a little uncomfortable with all that killer instinct. *Focus Anuj, focus! Or you will be left behind!*

'Have you ever played a video game? Do you recall an instance when you started playing directly at the highest difficulty level. And when you got pretty comfortable with the highest level, you tried the less difficulty level just to see how the game is at this level, and you found that the game was lame at initial levels. It was too easy. You felt like a pro and actually too good for the game and eventually became disinterested. Have you ever felt like that?'

'This is what we do here. This is what I am gonna do with you guys. You see, life seems as difficult no matter at which level you are at. As a matter of fact, Life is a game which has only one level: The beginner's level. We don't do anything extreme. We don't do *beyond*. Hence life starts seeming difficult and challenging. But here, we change that. We will give you the opportunity to live life at a higher difficulty level. It will seem like too much in the beginning but you will get used to it. We all do. Humans are made that way; we adapt, acclimatize, survive and then win. And then when you go back to the real life which is played at a beginner's level, you will feel like a pro. Everything will be very easy and you will score, pun-intended, a lot more and easily than others.'

'So the first step is to get rid of the hesitancy. To lose all inhibitions. Now for me to start with it I need to know one by one, what your inhibitions are. Tell me, what really holds you back? What are your fears? What is that thought which makes you pull back your feet when you were about to walk ahead. I just need that one word or maximum one statement. There may be lots of reasons but tell me the main one. Think. I give you 2 Minutes.'

'Yes Mohit we will start with you.' Ankit said.

'That they will find out that my an English is not that great.'

That, they have just found out, I thought.

'Fair enough, yeah you Aman? '

'I am not smart and intelligent.'

Then Anthony said 'I think if I say something people will laugh at me.'

As if on cue, we all started laughing at that.

'Quiet Guys!' ordered Ankit.

'See what I mean, Ankit? It sucks!' said Anthony.

I spoke at the end. 'Err..i don't know..maybe I think people will just find me out, I don't know what!.' I said phrasing the sentence in a way that I didn't have to mention women. It could get too embarrassing to be honest in front of my friends and a stranger.

Ankit thought for a while and then said, 'Anuj, you hit the nail on the head. If you look closely that is what all of you are saying. That people will find me out! That, whatever good Impression I have created will be lost if I do something new, say something new or try something new. If they think I am pretty good I might prove them wrong. If they think I am very bad at something I might just confirm their doubts. See, this feeling is like a trap. It's like the proverbial housefly banging again and again on the glass window. It can't break it. It doesn't take us anywhere. So have to break this glass window now and free ourselves. Right now'.

A staff guy led us into a changing room. Then another guy entered. With him entered an unbearable stink. He was carrying the dirtiest clothes I have ever seen. The clothes, he informed us were purchased from real beggars on the streets.

'C'mon guys get into them.' ordered one guy.

We completely froze at the thought of wearing those rag pickers' suits.

'Look, I think there has been some mistake, we were actually invited by Guru here for training..hehe' said Mohit laughing nervously.

'Hey, brother, when I say get into them, get into them.' he said very assertively. Ankit entered and he nodded shutting his eyes indicating that it was okay.

So, we got into the clothes convincing ourselves there must be a logical reason behind it.

Mohit wore dirty stinking khaki shorts with a black net *Ganji*. He was also given a *taaveez* to finish the look. He had very old torn canvass shoes on. Since the shoes had no front part, toes of both the feet were visible.

Aman was given very old baggy trousers which were very loose on him. So he was given a yellow plastic rope to use as a belt. The pants also had a big hole on the buttocks and Aman's underwear was visible from behind.

'Hey Aman's underwear looks too rich and all man, for a beggar.' observed Anthony. So they got rid of the underwear as well. Now Aman's one naked buttock was visible. Aman was seething with anger looking at Anthony.

'Now you look perfect.' quipped Anthony nervously realizing what he had done to his friend.

But when Anthony went in the changing room to, he refused to come out.

'I can't come out man, please understand Anuj. This is no good bro.'

On convincing him for at least 15 minutes which even included some threats, he came out. What we saw killed us. I swore we could have died laughing. Aman was rolling on the floor laughing in revenge. Anthony was wearing a short skirt which just ended above his knees and an embroidered blouse. His waist was completely exposed. He looked amazingly hilarious. His expression which was a mix of anger and embarrassment did not help either, making him look all the more funny. His long hair, one day old stubble and deep voice combined with his outfit gave us a hint about what was he was supposed to look like. A eunuch.

'Bro, now who looks perfect and all that haan?' Aman mocked Anthony imitating his deep voice.

'What is this supposed to mean Anuj? You said it's gonna be training and all and I fucking left my job for it. *Aur mereko chhakka bana diya bhai.*' Anthony's voice was shaking a little. '*Mereko chhakka nai banneka hai bhai.* I don't want to be a eunuch. I don't want my enemies to win.' We all knew he had no enemies; he just liked to use the word enemies in random conversation.

When my turn came, I stopped laughing. *This bloody makes no sense, this is bizarre and what are they gonna give me to wear?* But to my surprise I got a better deal. Since I was pretty fair I could not be passed off as any regular *bhikari*, they gave a religious touch to it. They gave me a white pyjama kurta, which I should confess wasn't too dirty and a Muslim skull cap to go along with it. And then they put lens in one eye which made my eye look like it had a stone in it.

Then they added just a little make up and some finishing touches. We were given skin textures as if we hadn't had a bath in months. Mohit already had his teeth protruding out a little. So they put a black chip on one tooth which looked like a missing tooth. They also gave him black glasses to make him look blind. Aman, who was just wearing trousers with no shirt and his buttock visible in the torn pants, was given crutches. He was being trained in how to walk with crutches with one leg only. Anthony was given a fake gold necklace to wear. The Veins in his forehead began to swell again. A big round object which had a belt was tied on my upper back, inside the *kurta*. It gave the impression that I had a huge Lump on my back.

'So guys we have given all that you need.' said one guy.

'Trust me we don't need this!' I said.

'I understand guys, you must be perplexed but let me assure you this exercise will liberate you.' Ankit said.

We were taken in separate cars and dispatched at four different traffic signals of the city. Yup, we were supposed to beg. For real! The deal was that we were supposed to live a life of a beggar for the next two days. We informed our families that we had participated in a boot camp which meant we couldn't be contacted for two days. Our wallets and our mobile phones were taken away from us. We had to survive on begging. We had no option. We needed to find shelter for ourselves to spend the nights as well. Somebody would keep an eye on us throughout. We couldn't escape. We couldn't take each other's help as well because we had no clue where the others were. And if we gave up, we no longer could continue with the training.

The signal I was taken to was the *Nakka* of Chembur and Sion. I knew because I would pass that way every day to my previous job. This was the worst place they could choose for me. I prayed that I didn't bump into anyone I knew. My look was also not much of a disguise. I could easily be recognised.

Okay, now I am here and I have to survive this, I was telling myself again and again. But I got cold feet. I was nervous. I had thought that it couldn't be very difficult. But it was a task which seemed impossible from the moment I actually thought of approaching someone for money. I just could not approach anyone for the first hour at least. It seemed impossible and really pointless. But then I began to feel thirsty. I went to a nearby *Udippi* restaurant. They practically shooed me away. Even the regular chai waala wouldn't give me any water to drink. I didn't want to drink water from the public water booths because it was disgusting and dirty even to look at with one common steel glass for everyone, beggars and urchins included. I knew that the only way I could quench my thirst was to BUY water.

I then looked at the traffic signal with anger and frustration.

I need water and I will have it, the world can go to hell!

I walked with determination and as fast as I could towards the traffic signal. It had turned red and hordes of vehicles had now stopped at the signal. I stood there on the divider looking out for my first provider. Right in front of me I saw a car which had it windows down. A young boy was in the driver's seat. Slowly I walked towards him. Then I raised my hand towards him. He simply looked at my hand and without even looking at my face, dropped a 2 rupee coin in my hand. I felt strange. I could not really understand what I felt. On one hand I had that sinking feeling because there was this guy more or less of my age and he gave me money with so much disdain that it hurt my self- respect. However, on the other hand there was this sense of relief as he had given me some money at least, which would help me collect the amount to buy water. Then I noticed a lady staring at me sitting in the back seat of her car. When I looked at her she called me 'hello! Come here!' She gave me a 20 rupee note. I gently took the money from her and when I was sure that I was out of her sight I ran to buy a bottle of mineral water for myself. The shopkeeper looked a little puzzled seeing a beggar buying water.

'These guys have more money than us, haha!' a stranger smoking next to me commented. I just looked down and walked away from there. If I thought that the rest of the night would be as easy in collecting money, I was so wrong. For the next 2 hours I could collect only 15 rupees. It was getting tough every minute. I guess I had passed my beginner's luck. Nobody seemed to bother about a young healthy looking boy with just one eye and a lump for physical abnormalities. It was dark and I was hungry with very little money to eat. *What could this possible teach me about picking up women*, I wondered. *But if Guru wanted it, there should be some logic behind all this nonsense*, I consoled myself.

Suddenly I heard something. Somebody was calling out my name in a hushed tone. I looked back but there was no one. I was about to run out of there when I heard my name again and felt something moving in the bushes. With my heart in my mouth half expecting a ghost or a *chudael* to jump out at me, I went towards the bush for a closer look. I picked up a stick from close by and moved the bushes to see. The thing inside pulled out the stick from my hand with strength and I let out a loud shriek.

'Shh…Anuj quiet, it's me'. The thing was a half naked human. It was Aman.

'Dude what are you doing here? You scared the hell outta me.' I said still breathing heavily.

'Just come over to this side.' Aman said in a low voice.

'But Aman, you can't be here, you have to go or else..'

'Trust me no one can see us on this side of the bush, were you able to see me?'

'Actually, no.'

'Then jump over.' I did. I could use some company now to distract myself from the hunger and darkness.

'I saw your location when they were taking me to my signal and I made a mental note of how to reach you if need be. By the way how is it going, Anuj?' asked Aman.

'Nothing *yaar*. I just have like 10 rupees on me.' I said feeling bad for myself.

'You are one sorry piece of sucker.' said Aman.

'Bro don't flatter yourself so much. Look at your appearance. You are one pathetic, smelly, nude beggar on crutches. Obviously people will give you more money. By the way, how much do you have? Have you eaten anything? I am starving man.'

'That is why I am here, my brother.' And then from a polythene bag, he took out a cardboard box. When I realized what it was, I wanted to shout at the top of my voice. Aman had brought a pizza with him. And not just any pizza, the large size and the veggie- delite one! My favourite!

'Oh Aman, I love you man' and I hugged him tight. 'You are the best brother, I just wanna have sex with you man.' then suddenly Aman's picture of sitting very close to me in his underwear in his apartment appeared in my mind .

'Hey just joking bro.' I said with a fake laughter. 'By the way who gave you this?'

'Nobody. Actually one rich man traveling in his BMW gave me a thousand rupee note. I then bought a pizza with it. How I managed to buy from that restaurant, only I know. They just wouldn't entertain me, but somehow I managed. And then I thought it would be unfair if i ate this all alone and hence I am here.'

I just looked at him and smiled. 'Thanks a lot man.'

We must have finished the pizza in record time. We were full. He also had brought water with him. He seemed like an angel sent by God.

'Aman, how did you manage to do so well man! I mean, directly a thousand rupee note!' I asked.

'Hmm. Even I found it difficult in the beginning but then I found a technique that works the best. See all you need to do is this: Just cry as if your butt is on fire but make no sound.' Then he demonstrated it for me. Yup he was right. The facial expressions he showed made your heart go out to him.

'Dude, you know what it means? You are gonna get more chicks than me', I said and we both laughed as the night passed by slowly. The shop keepers and hawkers were winding up their business. The number of people walking by on the indiscreet footpath got fewer and the noise of the city had reduced. But we had a very important business to take care of. A roof to sleep under. Aman couldn't hang around more and he had to leave for his location. I was all alone, again. I had no idea what Mohit and Anthony were up to. I just hoped that even they had managed something to eat. I called it a day and decided to sleep on a bench close by. The moment I lay my head on the bench I immediately fell asleep. It was a long and very strange day in my life. The stress and tiredness of begging combined with a full stomach made me retire to a blissful sleep.

On concrete, under the stars.

Mohit was struggling to reach in his pocket to give some money to a beggar at a traffic signal. We liked the Kaali- moori's gesture. We all, in fact, had found a whole new perspective on beggars and their lives. Mohit gave the beggar a 10 rupee note and looked at us smiling. I patted him on his back.

'I just did it you know. See, when I was a young and one day……..', Mohit started and we got scared. Luckily Anthony rescued us.

'Mohit look at that.' Anthony said pointing outside the car.

'What?' Mohit asked hurriedly.

'Look, it's the world! Trees, kids and all. Look up…its sky.'

Anthony managed as he had to come up with some shit to distract Mohit and break his chain of thoughts.

'So? Are you mad?' Mohit looked at us expecting us to join in his laughter. We didn't.

This day seemed a lot different. It was one of the first rains in Mumbai. The city was being washed by the heavens, the trees had become greener and the city looked cleaner, at least until it rained. The monsoon in Mumbai has a personality, of its own. First it makes everyone wait endlessly for it and then when it arrives finally, it does so with a bang. Later when all are tired of it, it refuses to go away. Today, however, it was only drizzling. The fragrance of the freshly wet soil enhanced the fresh mood of everyone. The weather was pleasant and cool. We had rolled the car windows down to let the breeze come in. The cool wind sprinkled harmless rain drops on us every now and then. Everyone around seemed relieved that the scorching heat of summer had ended. I was amazed at how gleeful and happy I was feeling. As we moved towards our school in my car, I was so glad we had survived the two day ordeal we were put to.

As we entered the training room we saw Ankit was already there before us waiting for us.

'So guys, how was the experience?' asked Ankit.

'Let's just say that we are glad it got over!' said Aman.

'Oh yeah? Was it so bad?' Ankit asked us, 'C'mon guys share your experience with me, one by one. Mohit we will start with you first.'

'I was peeing in my underwear with the thought of doing this. I mean I am doing a very good job and I had to become beggar. When I reached there I thoughted of quitting after five minutes. But I held on because I could not let you guys down I mean any guy would cut his wrist for Guru's training and we are getting it for free. So running away was no option. Anyways I realized one thing that what a good life we have. Now I realize the value of money and my loved ones around me who take care of me. Lot of people shooed me away as if I was an animal. Even though I started making enough money to survive from the first day, to use that money was bloody difficult. You couldn't buy stuff easily because no one want beggars as customers because that made the other customers to run away. I had to come up with different ideas to beg more efficiently and then to buy things with that money. I realized that if you act like a zombie, people will give you more. The less you pester people for money and just stand there like a walking dead the more money they give'.

'Oh I disagree Mohit Sir, I think being animated with your begging helps more.' Aman interrupted craving for an argument.

'Aman do you realize you are not in *how to beg efficiently* training room?' asked Ankit.

'No I was just saying..'

'You continue Mohit' Ankit cut off Aman.

' Yeah, after trying almost 6-7 eateries one restaurant owner gave me some food but I had to sit outside in the stairs of the restaurant to eat. A gutter was flowing next to me. But I had to eat there. People were passing by all seemingly agitated with my presence. I was feeling pretty ashamed of myself first but later I started looking passer-by's in the eye. See I was a man who slept on the footpath. How much worser could it get.' Mohit said grinding his teeth, 'That was pretty much how two longest days of my life days passed.' All the time Ankit took notes. After Mohit, Aman and I narrated our stories. We obviously cut out our meeting and then eating pizza part. Last it was Anthony's turn.

'What to say re! You guys know how was I dressed and all. Apart from that it was all the same only.' After thinking for a while he continued. 'I made good money. You know naa, people give *chhakkas* money easily in India. If someone refuses you just begin to give *badduas* and they get scared and give you good money. In fact to be honest I have like 700-800 rupees still left with me. Maybe it will come in use for later. Anyways, unlike these guys I had good food, smoked cigarettes and had beer on both the days. Sometimes just to irritate people I would smoke while asking for money. It's just that at night men start to ask you out. That was the disgusting part. I told them also that I am a *chhakka* but they wouldn't care. I never knew guys did *chhakkas* also. Somehow I saved my ass every night. I made good money but I didn't like being approached by guys.' He then went quiet and then suddenly asked Ankit 'I mean, instead of learning to approach girls, I have learnt more about how to evade guys! Bro Ankit if you don't mind can you tell us what is the point in all this begging?

'You know it yourselves.' replied Ankit.

'We do? I didn't realize that we do?' Anthony then looked at us. 'Do you guys know?'. We looked at each other and shook our heads hinting we had no clue.

'Okay let me explain it to you duds. Take your seat Anthony'

'This exercise was to get rid of your inhibitions. Let me explain to you what inhibition is exactly. The dictionary defines it as: The act of inhibiting or the state of being inhibited. Something that restrains, blocks, or suppresses.

It stems from the worry that people will judge you. I know so many brilliant talented persons who don't achieve their full potential because they are afraid that people will say so and so and blah blah and then spend so much energy just being disturbed about it. Now for you sweet normal kids to become the kinda guy who would approach a group of people with your target lady in it and keep humouring them all, you needed a huge dose of the approach *'I don't care what people think about me'*. All of you had those moments when you were nervous and hesitant about approaching people for money and for being looked at as beggars. But all of you overcame that fear. The incentive was hunger and eventually your survival. The desperation that you feel when your survival is in question is incomparable. It pushes you to your limits and you will perform things which you wouldn't in normal circumstances. It widened your horizons. Now your nervous system is ready for more challenges and you will feel more comfortable in other challenges than you would have, had you not gone through this exercise. If you scrutinize carefully, this is what you have achieved after this seemingly incongruous exercise:

1: Your comfort levels have expanded. You will feel more comfortable in tough situations than others.

2: You have seen yourself perform in this exercise. So now you know, when approaching someone for your own gain, what your weaknesses and strengths are.

3: You have beaten and killed your shyness for good. Because you no longer worry about others judging you. Your attitude is: *this is what I want and this is how I am going to get it. I am okay with people laughing at me, shooing me away.*

4: You have used your brain and innovated with how to get the best approach in different situations.

5: You were on your own and you knew if something had to done, you had to do it yourself.

6: You now understand the reality, the basics of survival. You now know the extreme realities of life and wouldn't take the life you have now for granted. It will set your priorities right. You value money more than you ever did.

6: Lastly, you can now approach anyone without inhibitions.

So guys, was it really that pointless?' Ankit asked with a smile.

Aman had tears in his eyes. *Oh you melodramatic son of a bitch!* I thought.

'Ankit this is amazing. All this is true. We were all wondering why we were feeling so different today while coming here and credited that to the end of the begging task. To *relief!* But come to think of it, the things that you just spoke about are in fact the actual reasons. I am actually feeling lighter and not carrying the baggage of unnecessary worries today. I feel so liberated..' now Aman had actually shut his tearful eyes and spread his arms wide much like a Bollywood hero singing somewhere in the Alps. His volume was increasing gradually too, 'I now know what a big a fool I was earlier. I used to worry so much about these things that it had almost paralysed me. I was incapable of strong positive decisive action. Maybe that's how I was brought up. Beta do this, don't do that! What will people say! Our reputation is at stake! What the hell, I was a stinking beggar for two days! Half my butt was visible and I was asking people for money because I was hungry. Some were scared of me; some treated me like I was a disease. They have judged me all they could in those three days. I felt naked all the time but I became comfortable being naked. How can you ever put fear in a man who doesn't even care if you strip him naked? I feel light as a feather.'

To be honest, that impromptu speech straight from Aman's heart had left all three of us with a lump in our throats. We had seen him being so uncomfortable about what people would say about him. And now he had faced his demons and maybe killed them too.

I wondered whether it had helped me with my problem with women. I had no certain answer. Although I felt the same things as Aman, my issues were different. The solution for my problem was different. And I knew I had to seek help from Guru whenever I could gather enough courage to ask him. He was my final hope.

✤

'I am gonna so nail that Vinita man. I will teach her a lesson after I become a Casanova.' announced a drunk Aman.

'Who the fuck does she think she is? You know what she is. A slut. Just that she doesn't take money for it. And she was spreading love to everyone but she never let me touch her even once, that bitch!' then he imitated her in a squeaky voice, '*Don't deflower me before marriage* she used to say. Bitch, by kissing I am not gonna crush your fucking flower. And what about the bouquet of your flowers you gifted to that bastard and I don't know to how many more. Anthony pass the smoke.'

'I am gonna go to Hyderabad, once I have all the *powers* and show that bitch Pari who she really missed out on. I am going to hit and run like Delhi bus drivers.' declared Mohit.

We were all now drunk after our third beer. We generally would stop at two beers each but tonight at Mohit's apartment we thought that we deserved a little merry making after those two days, where even getting water to drink seemed like a marvel.

'What power? They are not making a superman outa you man!' I quipped, equally tipsy.

'No, Anuj, we may not become superheroes but we will have superpowers. The power to attract girls anywhere and every-where! Who has it? Tell me? It's a rare and hence it is super.' Mohit said and his voice seemed full of hope.

'Mohit Sir.' interrupted Aman, 'Tell me this one thing. Don't mind but this question has been lingering in my head for a long. You work in such a reputed organisation; you are now a training-head. How do you manage to train people with your not so perfect English?'

Anthony and I almost froze at the question. *What the fuck is wrong with you Aman,* I thought. Although, secretly even I was eager to listen to the answer.

'Look....' Mohit started and then coughed a little. Our eyes were on him, waiting to know what he would say. 'Oh, so you guys noticed!'

'Yes.' we all said together inadvertently and regretted it immediately.

' hmm…. See Guys, I will tell you something I haven't told anyone in Mumbai. I did my schooling in a vernacular medium. But whatever little I know now is much more than before. Trust me on that. My office knows I maybe average at grammar but I am unbeatable in training. See, I do get my point across and it's not as if I am un-understandable.'

'Mohit sir, I can vouch for your amazing training skills.' I said interrupting him to change the topic, 'Bro Anthony Sing a song for us man, I have heard you have such a great voice!'

Anthony blushed a little. He didn't bother to ask where I had heard that from.

'I wouldn't say that it's entirely untrue. I think it's time that I express my singing talent. Which song, man?'

'Any of your favourite.' the rest of us said.

'ok..hmmmm..ok….haan that's a good one , so it goes something like this…………………………………………….shit forgot the lyrics! Ok wait I have another one……….yeah…..(coughing to clear his throat) *baakuda tumhi ho har jagah tumhi ho*……………yeah that's it.'

'What was that Anthony?' asked Aman.

' *Arre* I can't remember more than one line ever and plus I am a terrible singer. I don't know who keeps on spreading these rumours about me being a good singer.'

'Ok then I will sing.' said Aman.

Then Aman sang and sang well. Then we all sang, put on the music, danced, imitated each other, cracked dumb jokes, ordered food, ate it and went to sleep. I woke up at 5.30 am to go the loo and Mohit was up already calculating with his pen and paper.

'*Acha* Anuj, tell me one thing, I can't calculate properly, tell me who paid for the rickshaw yesterday, was it me or you?'

'God knows man! Go to sleep bro, God has given you more than enough, remember?' and I crashed back with Anthony sleeping next to me. Aman was sleeping alone in the bedroom. We were drunk and didn't want something to happen which we would regret in the morning.

At around 10.am we woke up, showered and ate our breakfast. Mohit and Aman left for their office. They came back early at around 4pm. They had taken permission from work to leave early from office for two months citing personal reasons. At around 5 pm we left for our training. We knew today's topic would be 'improving the physical appearance'.

'So guys we have a new area to cover today. It's very important too and I guess you are already aware of it. But somehow we just chose to ignore it out of laziness or the importance of it just doesn't occur to us. It's called Grooming.' announced Ankit, 'If you don't respect yourself or aren't interested in yourself, nobody else will be. The most important message grooming sends is that you take care of yourself. That you think you are important enough person for you. That you have your bearings in the higher level of society. That, you have class. A woman is not as attracted by good features as much as by grooming.'

We were all given haircuts which would suit our face by a specialist hair dresser. However, Anthony was clear that if anyone came near his long tresses, he would not like it and the consequences might be dire.

Before this we had realized the importance of grooming but not so much. We would thrust our hands in the wardrobe and get the first shirt our hands would take out for us. It was only when we were sure that there was going to be female presence at an event would we give grooming a little thought.

After we came back to the class room, we were given the following tips:

1: Get a haircut once every 20 days and from a good salon.

2: Invest in good clothes. This investment will give good returns.

3: Collect shoes. Have at least 3 Pairs of formals, 3 pairs of casuals and couple of cool sandals. Never wear dirty shoes.

4: Invest in at least 3-4 classy collection of neatly fitted suits.

5: Have 4-5 cool watches with formal and casuals thrown in equally.

6: Perfume. Have at least 2-3 high quality ones.

5: Keep your hands clean and cut your nails short.

6: In summers take shower twice.

7: At home don't wear your old clothes. There are clothes made specially to wear at home.

8: Floss your mouth.

9: Don't get fat.

10: And make good money for all of the above.

Ankit continued, 'See guys it's very important that I tell you to focus on the bigger picture. The reason you are here is to acquire a skill. It's like learning to play a guitar or getting yourself trained in singing. Do not make this the centre point of your life. The biggest thing to care for is your career. If you don't make good money there is no point in acquiring this skill because you won't be able to enjoy it or maybe even execute it. What game will you play when your mind is churning with stress of pending bills and rents? However, that is your lookout. Our job is to give you that skill' he ended with a wink.

'Nice disclaimer.' I said.

'You will know Sweetie.'

Sweetie? I hate that word. *Dude I am twice your size, I can take you down now in a moment,* I thought but decided to plaster a smile on my face.

After a lot of grooming tips and discussions on such things Ankit wrote down something on the board at the end of the day. He told us to take note of it:

Botch, Off Veera Desai Road, Andheri.

'You will reach this address at 5 pm tomorrow. You will meet Vinod there. He will take over from there. Come in your best.' Ankit said and begin to walk out of the room.

'But, what is this place Botch?' Mohit asked.

'It's a new discotheque. You are going live from tomorrow.'

'What for? I guess it's a party to let our hair down?' I said.

'You will know, see you guys later. All the best.' and Ankit left the training room.

What is it with this guy and his 'you will knows' I wondered.

All of us started giving high fives to each other. But Mohit was quiet.

'What's wrong, why quiet?' asked Aman

Mohit then said 'Guys, you are idiots! Ankit just used the word live. I am a trainer I know what Live means! C'mon guys, you forgot? In here the approach is *Mind follows the body!* Tomorrow they will make us approach women even with us having no clue about what to say and what to do. We are gonna be a laughing stock for everyone. We will be royally screwed.'

'Oh Ankit! You son of a bitch!' I shouted.

There was a knock on the door and Aman walked in. Anthony and I, who were already at Mohit's place, were having a discussion on whether tall girls are more attractive than short girls.

'Bro I disagree with you. I think tall girls suck.' Anthony said.

'Exactly, that's my point.' I replied.

'Okay.' said Anthony. Whenever he got bored of a topic and wanted to end it, he would use the work 'okay'.

Mohit and Aman had taken half a day off from work.

'Mohit sir, I have nothing cool to wear, I was wondering if I could borrow your leather jacket for tonight?' Aman asked without any tentativeness. He was a pro now.

'No bro I am wearing that.' Mohit snapped.

'Shit man, I have nothing to wear, my life sucks.' Then I saw him make that crying face without sound that he had shown me in the begging task. Although the expression on his face was pretty toned down from that day, it worked.

'*Abe o*, just wait I will get it for you' and Mohit walked off in the bedroom to get the jacket for him. Aman winked at me. I smiled and thought *whether he gets girls or not is dicey, but he definitely has learnt the art of begging.*

I wore cool torn jeans with a nice dark coloured full sleeves shirt. Mohit wore a simple but pretty decent t-shirt with jeans. Anthony wore a dark red shiny shirt with black trousers and formal shoes. He looked like a trumpet player in poor weddings. We did not comment anything for fear that we would have to lend him some clothes or buy new clothes for him.

'Dude it really feels good when you are dressed up and all, I think I am going to get at least 3 chicks tonight.' said Anthony. We said yes and decided to look at the floor.

When Aman had changed into clothes he had brought with him we realized that he was the most nattily dressed amongst us. He wore a cool V-neck t-shirt along with Mohit's beige colour leather Jacket and rugged blue jeans. He had this cool chain with a cross pendant in his neck. He had a nice pair of pointed boots to go along with the look.

'And you had nothing cool to wear?' asked Mohit.

'No, I don't, all this is borrowed from friends.'

With our nice haircuts and some cool tips we looked pretty neat, with the exception of Anthony, of course. But we knew that only grooming wasn't enough. We needed more information on how to survive the evening without being kicked out or laughed at. We decided to Google the info that we required but the results were too outlandish for us beginners to execute. But *'Go up to a woman and tease her'* was the most prominent in every website or blog and looked more like something we could at least think of doing rather than approach a group of people and trick the girls in it to sleep with us. So we decided to stick with the teasing part. We were just going to find out something uncool about a girl and then tease her about it. We left in my Zen and on the way we were pretty quiet thinking about stuff we would say there. On our way we stopped the car to have tea and some cigarettes. That we were nervous was an understatement. We hoped that smokes and tea would ease our nerves. It was getting a little murky with thick clouds gradually filling up the sky. The signs of an impending storm were prominent. Maybe the weather was a metaphor for our situation. We ourselves could sense a storm coming into our lives. Or rather we were going into a storm ourselves and committing a potential *harakiri*. Anthony coughed anxiously and said 'guys we are all feeling nervous. I don't understand. The previous exercise was supposed to get rid of our nerves.'

I got back behind the wheels and started the engine '*que sara sara*', I said loudly. 'Guys let's do this and have fun with it. How bad can it get? Surely no body is gonna kill us.' I hoped it made everyone feel better. I knew it didn't make me feel any better. The fear of public humiliation had developed into a ball in my stomach and its size was growing all the time. I knew I didn't have the courage to absorb another such incident.

We asked for Vinod at a makeshift reception made outside the main entrance of Botch. We were told to wait. When we looked around, we realized that there were too many people for a Friday evening and they were the coolest looking people we had ever seen. They all looked rich. And the best part was that there were lot of girls around. Hot girls. I personally hadn't seen so many beautiful girls together at one place ever. Most of them were dressed in a way which revealed more than it concealed. Strangely the guys with them in the group never eyed them or checked them out. Maybe it was an everyday affair for them. Besides the guys looked like they all owned a Merc, at least. Gelled hair, expensive clothing and bad ass attitudes. We felt happy and cheerful looking at the stunning chicks but at the same time we felt fearful too because we were supposed to talk to these chicks in front of their rich guy friends who could have connections in society we couldn't even begin to imagine.

'Hi guys.' we heard a voice and looked around to put a face on that voice. Vinod was 6 feet 3 inches tall. He was exceptionally well built and drop dead handsome. *There goes whatever little chance we had of scoring, all the girls are gonna hit on this handsome son of a gun,* I thought. We weren't asked to pay anything as we had expected and plus we were given 5 coupons each which we could use to buy alcohol with. On a normal day we would have jumped with joy with such an offer but today we felt like we were approaching our worst nightmare. We felt as if everyone was waiting for us to come. As if we were the centre of the universe for all the people around us.

The interior of the place was the classiest I had seen. There were pool and billiard tables in the centre. On both the sides of the tables were small areas designated for groups to lounge around. They were like small dens with mattress and cushions and hookahs. At the end of all this was a swimming pool which looked like it was not open for public as yet. And when we took the entrance to the main pub, it didn't disappoint either. It was a huge place with different themes for every corner of the place. A staircase led to an elevated floor made entirely out of wood. The music was loud and good. With so many hot women around we were all stunned to silence. On other nights we would have been crazily happy and would have retired to a corner of the place and enjoyed the view from there. But tonight we had to take the stage and stir things up.

'Vinod, so what do we do now?' I asked.

'Oh that ass hole Ankit didn't brief you about this, did he? Ha ha! Yeah that's the way he rolls!' he laughed and then immediately got serious, 'Anyways guys all you got to do is approach at least 15 women tonight. How you do it, is your take. And remember you are being watched and judged all the time, so don't try anything funny. Look, it will just reveal where all of you stand'

'Oh okay.' said Aman, 'but, can you offer some tips, you know just to get us started, I mean we are all blank here'

Vinod thought for a while and said 'Yup, don't get your ass kicked'.

'What's that supposed to mean?' I asked.

'You know what it meant, now you are on your own guys, all the best' and he disappeared into the crowd.

We all started with 1 round of beers to relax a bit.

'Guys let's do it.' Aman said, his Dutch-confidence taking over.

'Yeah right let's do it, said Mohit, 'and let's start with you Aman'.

'It's okay I have no problem guys.' and then he looked around and next to us he saw a huge muscular guy talking to couple of pretty chicks who were laughing and enjoying his company.

'Guys it's only fair if we draw straws.' Aman had chickened out. We all agreed with that. But still, it turned out to be Aman's turn. I quickly took the beer pint from his hand in case it slipped in shock. This time he had no option. We saw a girl sitting alone at the bar. She was in jeans and a regular t-shirt, more of a sweet girl than sexy, a 6, at best. She was apt for Aman's first approach.

Aman went over and took the unoccupied seat next to her. The rest of us stood a little away from him. We had decided that the other three would always be around the person who made an approach, to hear what was going on. He was fidgeting and trying to lip-sync the song being played when it was obvious he didn't know the lyrics. He had his back towards the bar and rested his arms on the bar behind him, to look confident. He didn't look confident. He looked as if he was going to die.

Then he looked at the sweet girl and asked hesitantly, 'Hey, you. Er..er.. are priya, right? From Mithibai College?' She looked at him, smiled and said a polite no.

'Okay. No problem,' Aman said and came back to us.

'Voohooo! It feels great. I got the first approach out of my way. And trust me it aint so bad, although I know what I spoke was pretty lame'. I hoped he didn't start crying again. We could see Vinod at a distance writing down something on a notepad. I was sure there were more guys from the school who had kept an ear on what we were saying, lingering around in the pub, spying on us.

Now it was my turn. I had decided that I wouldn't spend time selecting a target. I knew that would make me more nervous. I had learnt this about myself from the begging task. By now, to ease my anxiety I had gulped down four pints of beer. Alcohol always had eased my nerves in the past and I found myself dependent on it again. I had to do this as I realized that if I saw through these two months I could have a serious shot at a free life.

I strode slowly into a section the pub which looked the most crowded. I saw two girls passing by me, both around 6.

'Hey, can I buy you a drink,' I asked trying to think nothing.

They both looked at me, 'Why?' one of them blurted out.

' err..err I don't know maybe just like that you know, hehe..', I said and I felt as if there were two of me. 'One me' which was inside fighting the pain and anxiety the mind gave and the 'other me' which was visible to everyone who looked as if he was just chilling out.

They both looked at each other and then said 'okay'. I didn't know whether to be happy or sad with their affirmative answer. I decided to be blank and think of them as guys, maybe that could help me but their voluptuous bosoms screamed WOMEN! I bought drinks of their choice for both of them. It had cost me my 4 coupons, because their drinks, bloody Mary and vesper martini were quite expensive. We began talking.

It was a personal progress.

The conversation went something like this:

1st girl: Hey so what's your name?

Me: Anuj , and you are..?

1st girl: I am Samantha and she is my friend Niki.

Me: And Niki, you are…?

2nd girl: What?

Me: Oh I mean..you are..you are..g-g-lad to meet me?

2nd girl: (silence)

1st girl: (confused)

Me: I am between jobs and you?

2nd girl: (silence)

1st girl: We work in a call centre, both of us.

Me: Oh that's great and you Niki?

2nd girl: (confused)

1st girl: (silence)

Me: Okay.

Dead silence for about 30 seconds.

Me: this place is very good.

1st girl: It is

2nd girl: Yeah yeah, it is.

Me: I am sure it is. It's very good.

1st girl: Yup, can't agree more.

Me: Same here.

2nd girl: (silence)

1st girl: (angry and breathing heavily)

2nd girl: We gotta go, our friends are here.

Me: Okay, bye.

They both walked off in a hurry keeping their empty glasses on the table. I slowly took my handkerchief out and wiped the sweat off my forehead. *Damn you, you lame son of a bitch.* Yet I was relieved that I spoke and the 'conversation', for the lack of a better word, lasted till their drinks did. So what if they started to gulp it down to shorten their stay at the table with me, realizing how boring and dumb I was. I was in a way glad they fled because I was honestly reaching a dead end in terms of topics, I had only one left about how good the music was. But whatever! I had opened my account. I had spoken to girls and even though I had behaved like a dummy, I had survived it without an attack. I thought maybe it had to do with the begging task, maybe I it had reduced my anxiety of judgement by others. Then I realized that a guy was standing at a hearing distance from me all the while when I was with the girls. On looking closely I recalled that he was around Aman too when he had made his approach. *Yup I am right, listening to every word we utter, you assholes!*

Mohit was next. 'Dude, how did you feel?' he asked me.

'I won't say I was completely at ease, I was nervous but maybe the begging task has improved things a little. I mean, like before, I didn't feel I was having a heart attack.' It was true, although we were all nervous but it was manageable.

Mohit picked a woman who looked like in her early forties. The man who sat with her and looked like her husband left to go to the loo. Mohit knew it was the right time to strike.

'Hello! How are you doing Aunty..err..Madam?' he had made a start at the wrong foot.

'I am okay. Tell me?'

'Is this the right time to speak with you ma'am?'

shit!, I thought, *he has started with the sales pitch he trains people in his office.*

'Oh no no, I don't wanna buy anything. I am here to relax and have a good time with my husband my dear,' she said as politely as she could get. Mohit's face dropped and quite visibly too.

'No no, I am not selling you anything ma'am, I was just asking the how you are.'

'What's the matter Mary?' Her husband had come back.

'No, I was just asking aunty how she is.' Mohit said trying to save his ass.

'She's good thank you and so am I young man, now if you may excuse us.' her husband said calmly.

'Thank you it was nice talking to you and sir, I will put you in do not call list, don't worry.' Mohit said and immediately realized his folly and began laughing as if he cracked this joke intentionally.

Mohit came in and shouted 'Bloody fuck man, I chose the wrong girl'. *Yeah right, GIRL,* I thought. It was Anthony's turn now.

He zeroed down on a girl and stood next to her. A minute passed, no move from Anthony. Two minutes passed, nothing. He just stood there with a pint in his hand and behaved as if enjoying the music. Almost five minutes passed away and then the girl moved to the other corner of the pub with her group. Anthony followed her there. He stood there again for ten minutes but no move from Anthony. We were getting really frustrated and foul words had started to pour out from Aman's mouth.

He came back to us, 'It's time that I go for a smoke and think of a new strategy and come back.'

NEW strategy?? I thought.

He came back after 5 minutes. This time he marched towards another group with conviction. There was suddenly this air of sureness about him. He then halted behind a pretty big group of 10-12 people. Anthony then looked around like a lion choosing its prey. He then went over and stood behind the most stunning looking girl in the group, an almost 9, and tapped her shoulder from behind.

'Hey! Excuse me!' Anthony said as if he meant business.

'Oh fuck man, this guy is cool, he is going to pick her up man!' Aman cried. We gave each other high fives.

'Yes?' the sexy babe asked.

'Can you give me some space to walk ahead?' The girl courteously stepped aside and Anthony walked slightly ahead and then found himself right in the centre of the huddle of the group with everyone staring at him. Anthony froze. He kept looking at the floor and grinning like a child who was forced to dance at a birthday party by his mom and who could just smile shyly and do nothing.

'Damn it! Say something man, do something.' I said in a whisper.

'Hey excuse me, what's up man? What do you want?' one of the girls asked. Anthony looked up and his head turned in a circular motion to look at everyone who were staring at him and he immediately looked down again.

'What's the matter dude? What the fuck do you want.,?' someone from the group blurted.

'No, I have a very important question for her', Anthony replied still looking down and pointed one finger at the hot girl who had made way for him to come in.

'Who me?' she asked, 'Yeah tell me what is it?' she asked with a worried expression.

'AA...umm...nothing re..Hope to meet you soon....and..I really l----like the..the... music and all here, man. What about you?' he asked looking at her for a second and again went back at looking down.

'Yeah it's cool, why? Is that all you wanted to know', she said with a confused look

'No no..there is a more important question.' Anthony said and paused again.

'Yeah, what is it?', she asked.

'Oh yeah...the question is..is....err...wait....hmm..yeah.....the important question is ......err.......Whatsup?'

'What? What whatsup?', she asked in a shock.

'I mean, hey whatsup and how are you doing and all.' Anthony said slowly.

There was a long pause, no one reacted for a while and then suddenly they burst into a loud laughter. Before everyone in the pub came to know, Anthony got the fuck outta there, and came to us.

'Dude you okay?' I asked.

'No man, Anuj, will you come to the loo with me?' Anthony said panting heavily. I noticed sweat dripping off his eyebrows.

'Err..No. just sit here, for a while and you will be fine', I said

'You sure? I will be?'.

'Yup'.

'Just cover me so that nobody can see me for a while, I think somebody just hypnotised me there. I had rehearsed the lines outside but they all came out in reverse order man!'

'Bro, should I take you to the loo?' asked Aman with genuine concern.

Anthony then looked at Aman's crotch and thought of something 'no bro, I will be fine. I know of a chant. Give me some time.'

We had already spent 45 minutes in the pub and we made negligible progress. Vinod informed that only Aman and my approaches were counted. Mohit's and Anthony's approaches were dismissed. We were out of coupons too and whatever alcohol we bought from there onwards what would be from our own money. Now we decided that we should start with the teasing routine. It was round two. We decided that we would keep the same order. Aman saw a group of 5 *firang* ladies sitting at the bar. All of them were taller than Aman by at least half a foot, gorgeous and between 8-10 by Indian standards. 'Brave boy.' said Mohit.

'Hi girls,' said Aman.

'Hello.' they said quite warmly.

'How are you ladies doing tonight?'

'Very good thank you.' they said.

'You are dressed pretty smart, I like your jacket.' One hot girl said, actually flirting with him. My jaw dropped but the real owner of the jacket, Mohit, was fuming.

Aman said, 'Thank you, but why are you dressed like this? Such short clothes, it seems you have been stealing clothes from your niece.'

She was taken aback. 'You are so bad.' the girl said and punched Aman's shoulder playfully. *Its working* I thought.

'Hehe, I mean, girls with such short clothes are considered characterless in India and potential rape victims in Delhi, its funny right?' She just stared at Aman for a while to process the words in her head and then she stood up in anger from her seat. Aman's height didn't even reach her shoulders.

'Just fuck off. How dare you talk to me like that? You bastard!'

'No I wasn't talking about you, trust me no one will rape you.' The girl started crying and the rest of them shooed Aman away.

'Dude not bad until you screwed up talking about rape.' I said to Aman. 'You know Anuj, *gaaon ki bahut yaad aa rahi hai be.*(I miss my village man) Sometimes I think the slow life of the village with fresh air and peaceful lakes and rivers is the best. What's your take on arranged marriages?' I decided not get into a discussion with him and focus on my approach.

'Hello baby!' It was my turn now and I approached a very pretty, super sexy slim Manipuri girl, dancing alone next to the bar. She looked sloshed and hence unassuming to me which gave me the confidence to go and talk to her. She was there with a couple of friends who sat on the adjoining chairs and looked completely absolved in each other.

'Hello... who are you?' she asked without stopping. *Wake me up before you go go*, was the song being played.

'Hi I am Anuj, I was wondering why are you performing Manipuri folk dance in a pub?' I had to be very loud as a speaker was blaring loudly just close to us.

'Hey this is no Manipuri folk dance, hahahaaaa, you are so funny.' and she put an arm around my neck and started to dance pretty close to me. *Wow this teasing bit really works and now I just need to know when to stop or I will end up like Aman*, I thought, controlling an erection. Since she was drunk I strangely felt that I was with a doll that could talk and amazingly felt no fear at all.

'Can you dance? What kind?' she asked.

I did a couple of pelvic thrusts and said 'I am more into the Mumbai fuck dance.' She laughed out loudly. I was enjoying my interaction with a girl after ages. I don't know how but my confidence was soaring sky high every minute.

'Oh you are so naughty, I like the you.' she said. *Damn, with her English she would have been perfect for Mohit*, I thought.

'Hey do you like me?' she asked. The song in the background went, *You take the grey skies out of my way, You make the sun shine brighter than Doris Day, Turned a bright spark into a flame, My beats per minute never been the same.*

I felt as if I had achieved nirvana. *The relationship stages do go at a fast forward speed in pubs,* I thought. *Is she the one? Who could take me out of my inane problems?*

I shook myself out of my idle reverie, 'Of course I do, you are so pretty and any guy would feel lucky to be with you.'

'Oh you are sweet.' and she pushed her slim magical body against mine. My eyes shut automatically.

A woman against my body, hugging me, is it real god? Have you stopped hating me? Oh hug me tight, your kind has given me enough problems, make it up for that baby!

Everything was going perfect. And then suddenly, 'Hello, can I dance with you.' a mountain of a stud asked her standing next to us.

'Oh please, just go.' she said refusing to be detached from me.

'Actually, see my girlfriend over there, she is a little depressed and I want some tips to cheer her up.' he seemed persistent and when I looked where he was pointing at, there was no one.

'Oh that's so bad, but I don't know what to tell her. hmm but actually what you can do is....', she said breaking my arm lock around her waist.

'Why don't you come there and explain to me, it's too loud in here.' and he grabbed her by her hand and took her away.

The song went *'Cause you're my lady, I'm your fool, It makes me*

crazy when you act so cruel, Come on, baby, let's not fight, we'll go
dancing, everything will be all right...'

'Hey.' I called the bartender.

'Yes Sir, tell me.'

'No just checking. I thought I was invisible.'

She turned around to look at me, 'I will come back' I read her
lips saying to me.

But she did not.

I went back to my friends after about 10 minutes of waiting.

'Dude that went okay, don't feel bad.' Mohit consoled me.

'In a way it did. Yeah it did. But that fucker took her away and she
didn't come back. She need not have gone, if she wanted to. Hey Aman,
you were saying something about your village. Please tell me more.'

Mohit approached a pretty young girl this time and as usual the
rest of us were around at a hearing distance. Maybe he wanted to
compensate for his mistake earlier. The girl looked barely 18 and was
with a girlfriend. She was slim and attractive, a 6, we decided.

'Hello there, can I see your ID?' Mohit asked assertively.

'I am sorry, who are you?' she snapped back.

'Well, I am the owner of this place and I don't want underage
kids to come in here.' He had rehearsed the first two lines with us
and we had helped him iron out the grammatical flaws.

'But, I am not underage, there is some mistake....' , she fumbled
nervously.

'Ha-ha, just kidding, I thought you looked pretty sweet and I
should tell you that.'

'Ooohh, how mean of you haan!' both the girls started laughing
and it seemed they had enjoyed Mohit's innovative approach.

'Honestly we don't come here too often, it's just that she had a break up and I wanted to show her a good time tonight. I am glad you came and spoke. We were getting really bored. By the way I am Bhavna and she is Sheetal.'

'Oh hi, I am Mohit. It's okay Sheetal I know breakoffs can be a bad for you.' the loud music was covering up any grammatical errors Mohit made.

'So you have gone through that too Mohit. Was it very bad?' Bhavna asked him sympathetically.

'Oh don't get me started girls.' he replied.

'Darn right, don't get him started.' Aman muttered.

'No tell us what happened.' Sheetal asked. Girls always dig a *relationship gone kaput* story. And Mohit always for some vague reason thought that he was a damn good story teller. If you asked him how his day in office was, he would start right from breakfast at home, how he travelled, what he was thinking while traveling, whom he saw first when he entered the office and so on. And if you interrupted him and said something like you got the point, he would tell you to wait as the interesting point of the story was yet to arrive. Of course that point never came because it never existed in the first place.

Mohit started, 'Okay, it goes something like this. While growing up I was always a shy and a dumb kid……..'

Aman said, 'Good, he didn't say: I felt I was coming out from the dark place, something was pushing me out and when I came out I saw lot of people dressed in white with gloves on..'

'They have dug their own graves.' I remarked.

Anthony said, 'Let's go and have a smoke man, by the time we are back he would have at least grown up enough to join office.'

'Yup, you are right.' I said.

When we came back after 10 minutes Mohit was saying, 'After that when I was going out after the interview, I saw a her. I thought for a while. I took 2 steps ahead and then stopped and then…' the girls had begun to yawn now, 'and then I thought again', Aman was echoing Mohit, word to word, 'I looked back and saw her but she had gone. I had to see her. I then started to search…' we laughed at the correctness with which Aman was matching words with Mohit.

'Mohit please tell us how you guys broke off no.' Bhavna pleaded.

'You will not understand and get the picture properly if you don't know the background…so then I asked…'

After five more minutes of the ordeal, Sheetal, the girl who had had a breakoff, suddenly grabbed her drink from the table in a jiffy and threw it at Mohit's face.

'Oh shit! What the bloody fuck.' shouted Mohit struggling to open his eyes. We wanted to go over and hug the girl, Sheetal. We saw her as one of our own and could understand her agony completely.

'Oh I am so sorry.' said Sheetal, 'I don't know what happened to me, I just couldn't control myself.'

'Was my story so the worst?' Mohit asked still unable to open his eyes completely.

'No Mohit, it is pretty good it's just that she is going through a lot now.' Bhavna consoled him. Although she was equally mind-fucked, she was just being nice to him but Mohit didn't understand. The lust of narrating his fucked up story was getting the better of him.

'Okay, no problems, so where was I? Yeah I was sitting on a bench smoking cigarette. I was alone and…' Mohit continued, his face still wet with alcohol.

'We will be back, we just need to go to the loo.' Sheetal blurted. Then we saw them walking towards the loo and when they were sure

Mohit could no longer see them they took a sharp 180 degree turn and literally ran out of the pub as if to save their lives.

'I have never seen women with high heels run so fast.' Anthony observed. Mohit's break off story and his narrative style were so powerful that it usually brought out the survival instinct in people.

'*kya chutiya giri hai bhenchod,* all was going so well, I don't know what happened to the them? This female cast cannot be trusted.' Mohit said. *Female cast?? Oh, aurat zaat, hmmm..*I thought.

We were literally pushing Anthony to go and approach than but he refused to move.

'Arre, dude I am already in trauma. I won't be able to perform like those years. I am half the man from the days when I used to pick up women just walking in a street.'

Yeah, Right.

After a lot of convincing Anthony approached a girl who was obese, ugly and drunk. We decided she was a 2. Anthony was adamant that she was a 5.

Whatever we rated her, one thing was for sure; nothing possibly could have gone wrong here.

'Hey how are you doing?' asked Anthony, imitating Sylvester Stallone's accent in *Rocky*. He always thought it sounded sexy on him. Well, we knew, at best, he sounded retarded with that accent.

She glanced at him from head to toe and made a face, 'What's wrong with you, just go away!'

'You know what, I am a fighter because I can't sing or dance.' the asshole was mouthing off Rocky's dialogues now.

'Hey why can't a good looking chick just sit and enjoy the music by herself.'

'What?' for a brief moment Anthony came out of his Rocky avatar.

'Whatever! *babay babay. Baby..*' she was singing along with Justin Beiber.

'I feel like a Kentucky fried idiot' Another dialogue from the movie. No response. She was ignoring him completely. Then, Anthony stood there next to her adamantly for around 2 minutes.

She gave up and asked, 'yeah what is it? What do you want?

'Nothing just wanna be friends and all', he had come back to his own voice, realizing Stallone was going down.

She smiled and said, 'I am Honey, what's your name?'

'I am Anthony.'

Then there was dead air for about 1 minute.

'Do you want a drink Honey?' He accidentally stressed on the word Honey. She looked at him with suspicion. 'No No, I meant … honey as in honey, your name and all. I didn't, you know, call you, you know…t..tha..thhat.' he looked down, blushing.

'Hehe, its okay, you are sweet. I will have one.' People on the dance floor were going berserk and the party seemed to have peaked now.

'What do you do for a living Anthony?'

'I work in a call centre.'

At that moment two of her other girlfriends, who were dancing away forever on the floor, came back. They both looked around 6.

'Hey Girls, had a blast on the dance floor?' Honey asked the girls.

'Yeah too much man!' one of them said loudly, adrenaline still pumping in her veins.

'Hey this is my new friend Anthony, Anthony these are my buddies Pri and Shri'. Anthony shook hands without looking at them. The girls then kept on talking among themselves. We realised that Anthony had stopped talking and even moving from the time her friends had come. He was losing his confidence.

He froze, again.

'Hey what's wrong with your buddy?' Pri asked Honey.

Not a muscle in Anthony's body moved but his lips, 'Nothing.'

'What nothing? You seem like a statue to me.' Shri said and they all started laughing and went back to their girl chat.

Then we saw Anthony shut his eyes for a moment and his lips moved in haste which seemed like a recitation. Suddenly his lower lip began to bend downwards and he opened his eyes. He had turned into Rocky again like people turned into werewolves in movies.

'You know you got a big mouth, you know?' Anthony said to Shri. He imitated the accent better this time.

'What? Hey excuse me but..' Shri said in complete confusion

'I will go for your ribs, I won't let you breathe, bastard!' He obviously remembered every dialogue from the movie.

'Bastard? What the fuck, Anthony?' shouted Honey.

Anthony looked at Honey, 'I wanna kiss ya. You don't have to kiss me back if ya don't wanna. I wanna kiss you.' he was saying when I realized it was time to pull him back from there.

'Sorry ladies, he is just a little high.' I said and pulled Anthony by his wrists

'Just tell him to fuck off.' Honey was shouting and was furious. Her friends were holding her tight and not letting her go. They knew Anthony could be in for some serious hiding from their fat friend if they let her loose.

A couple of bouncers came over and asked, 'What's the matter guys? The girls say you asked her to kiss you?' and they held Anthony by the collar.

'You gonna eat lightning and you gonna crap thunder.' Anthony shouted.

'Hey relax guys!' I intervened, 'Look at her! Do you think anyone would hit on that..that..lump of meat , c'mon man? Its..its.. j..j.just a lover's tiff. He dumped her and they want revenge, it's all cool.'

They looked at the girl hard, talked in hushed tone between themselves, smiled and let go of Anthony. 'Just take it easy guys.' they said and went away. They bought my story, thankfully.

'What the fuck was that *chutiye*?' I asked Anthony, almost scolding him.

'Arre nai re, I just dint want to come back like before. You guys doing so well I didn't want to look like a fool. I knew only Stallone could help me so I prayed for his soul to come into my body and he did the rest.'

'What the fuck?? What bullshit do you keep on throwing at us man? Stallone's alive and kicking how can his soul travel into your body.' asked Aman.

We saw Vinod pacing towards us, 'It's enough guys, don't want any more trouble for tonight. We will finish this tomorrow with a new crowd. You can stay if you want to but just don't talk to any girl.' said Vinod and disappeared in the crowd.

'It's all because of you, the mad fellow.' Mohit was saying, 'Dude you should be in a mental hospital and guys c'mon! I don't know why are we even carrying this dead weight around? He is a psycho and talks about ghosts and what not. Look at him, he is never getting anything in life. No girl and no good job or money. Bloody Loser! Dumb ass even makes the us feel like dumb in front of the others.'

He seemed livid with Anthony. I had a clue earlier that Mohit wasn't particularly fond of Anthony but I had no idea he could have so much in him against him to say things like that.

'Mohit sir, relax. Let's chill. And for the record we all behaved equally dumb today.' I said

'Hey Mohit I am really sorry man, if you felt embarrassed because of me.' said Anthony, his voice trembling a little.

Aman and I took Mohit aside and convinced him to let Anthony stay with him till the training got over. He agreed reluctantly.

We then decided to leave. There was no point hanging around. We were all in a bad mood. Mohit was livid. Aman and I felt sorry for Anthony. And Anthony, well, I knew his eyes were clammy and was trying his best to hide it.

I woke up to a beautiful sound. The inimitable sound of rain. I stretched my body with my face beaming. I saw the clock and it was 10.am but it looked like the sun hadn't risen as yet. I opened my window and a gust of cool wind hit me. It was peacefully dark and quiet with only the musical rhythm of rain audible. My mom came in and gave me my bed tea. She was saying something about how I came in so late in night and when I was gonna take up my next job. But I was hypnotized by the beauty of the scenery outside. I took my tea mug and sat near the window allowing the peace and beauty to enter my anatomy. It was meditative.

Then after a while my mind drifted slowly to all the things that happened the night before. I wondered why Mohit lent everything to Anthony. Did he really think all those things about Anthony or he was just frustrated with himself for being completely inept in attracting a woman? And then Aman had displayed total inadequacy in displaying a sense of timing. *'Don't worry nobody will rape you!'* *What was he thinking?* I thought and smiled. I thought about my own conversation with a Manipuri girl and wondered whether I had taken a step ahead towards a cure to the onerous situation in my life. Then I wondered whether I needed only to reach a state of normalcy with the opposite sex or was it more to feel desirable by women? Once I achieved that, would I be happy forever? I compared what I was feeling at that point; looking out at Mother Nature at its best with the feeling I had when the Manipuri girl put her arm around me and danced as if glued to me. I wondered what between the two felt better. I had no clear answer. I continued sipping on my tea and decided to be thoughtless for a while.

At around 1 pm I received a confirmation call from Vinod reminding us to be present at the club at 5pm. They would always call everyone at the site a little early so that our nerves could settle. I replied in the affirmative. I went over to Mohit's place, which was 30 minutes' drive in my Zen. When I entered I saw Anthony there sitting on the couch smoking a cigarette.

'Hey Anthony, how are you?' I enquired.

'All good, man!'

'So what are you guys up to?' I wanted to know how things between Mohit and him were after what had happened yesterday.

'Nothing, Mohit is out somewhere on the bike and I just washed the utensils. The maid did not come today, so he told me to do that, which is okay.'

Mohit Sir, I thought, *you mean, in-human ass hole!*

'C'mon dude you could have refused?' I told Anthony.

'I know but see he is letting me stay here and also somebody had to do the utensils, just forget It.' he said dismissively.

'Wow bro!' I was stunned by Mohit's shallowness but decided to bring it up later with Mohit himself, 'Anyway what are you wearing tonight for the party?' I asked.

'I have brought some clothes from home, and', he paused for a moment, 'guess what Mohit didn't give me the bike when I told him I would need to go home to get clothes for the party, so I had to go in the bus. And the bike was just parked outside, not that he needed it then. I don't understand why he is behaving like that. I didn't do anything bad to him.'

'Don't worry I will talk to him.' I assured Anthony.

At around 3 pm Mohit came back along with Aman.

'Mohit Sir, why are you making Anthony do the maid's work?' I asked insistently

'Leave it Anuj! What you got to do? People who don't have fucking brains will do only labour work.' and let out an evil laughter. Anthony excused himself to go to the loo.

I felt sick seeing this side in a friend, 'This is not happening Mohit Sir! You can't be so rude to him. What has he done to you?'

'Look Anuj, I want to be among cool and intelligent people, okay, not like mentally retarded people like him. I want to grow in life and honestly I am totally ashamed to be with him in front of others. People have MLA's sons and NRIs as friends' man! He is an animal man, bloody fuck. And because of you guys I am a stuck with him in my own house.' Anthony came out at that moment and I decided to talk it out later with Mohit as his indiscreet comments would only hurt Anthony more.

'*Oye chutiye*, have you flushed the toilet?' Mohit barked at Anthony.

'Yeah bro relax, I have.' He answered gulping his insult down. I was aghast.

When we reached the pub at five sharp, we knew that we were feeling a little less uncomfortable than the day before. That unfortunately didn't mean that we were in any way confident of what we were supposed to do. But unlike the first day, today we at least knew what to expect. It was Saturday and the crowd was supposed to be bigger and better. We met Vinod and he took us directly to a private lounge where we were served drinks immediately. I looked at my watch and it was only 6pm. By 6.20 we all were drunk, Vinod including.

'Guys, I don't know who you are and what the fuck you are!' Vinod said and paused, 'no no, I know what you are, lucky! I mean you getting this shit for free.'

'Oh yeah? I disagree with you on that. We thought the same, but what have you guys taught us thus far? All that we have done has been without any guidance', Aman said hunting for an argument.

'You know but the free alcohol counts *bhai.*' Anthony said and then looked at Mohit and decided to be quiet.

'You are so handsome, Vinod.' Mohit said, 'give us some tips for tonight man?' He was buttering Vinod.

'Tips? For what? You guys are doing nothing tonight. You will just sit and watch.' Vinod paused to take a deep breath, 'because Guru will be here tonight, performing.'

Our faces lit up hearing that. It was a set of two good news for us. First we didn't need to approach and second we would be one of the fortunate few who would watch The Artist perform. Perform, here meant approaching a woman, getting her interested and then deciding any course of action you wanted. And Guru had stopped performing for an audience long back. There were only a handful of videos of him on YouTube which were recorded by his over eager students against his wish.

'Why is he performing tonight?' I asked Vinod.

'Guys there is a duel tonight. A duel between the Masters! I am so fucking excited! I never thought I will witness a duel of masters in my lifetime. Not at least in India! Hence the treat for you guys from a very happy man.' Vinod said, as his nostrils flared. I swear there was a lump in his throat. I was drunk yet I found that a little weird. I mean, c'mon! You are talking about pick up artists picking up women and not someone dying for his country. You can't get emotional about that!

Vinod continued 'What you will witness tonight will be hard to forget. The two masters making their moves like battle hardened warriors. Throwing in tricks and routines our minds cannot even begin to fathom. One school versus the other! We five are Guru's only cheer leaders because he didn't want a lot of attention. As a matter of fact he didn't want to be a part of this duel'.

'Why?' I asked.

'Because Guru is an Indian and we don't compete with our teachers.'

'What?? Wait, are you saying….' I couldn't finish my sentence.

'Yes, Guru is gonna have a duel with his own teacher, Mark David, better known to the world as The Artist.'

We jumped from our seats.

'What? You mean Guru is not The Artist!'

'There is no choice now, you do this or it will be too late.'

'What? Things have gone way out of hand. Nobody can change this.'

'What's wrong with you? I know you. It's not right. You can't live without her.'

'Whatever. But this guy who calls himself The Artist, what is he? Does he have a magic wand that he will use and get her back to me from the hands of that rich bastard? You know it's hopeless.'

I could not understand what my two colleagues were talking about. This was more than a year ago when we were sitting in a bar having a few drinks post work. This was also where I had first heard the name, or rather the term, The Artist. I tried asking them more but they wouldn't tell me anything. All I know that the friend had got his girl back two months later from whoever 'the rich bastard' was. When I asked him whether it was that Artist guy who helped him to get her back, he had laughed it off. 'What's wrong with you Anuj? How can you even think that such a guy exists? It was just a matter of time that she got back with me. After all, we loved each other.' I was asking foolish questions, I had thought. Then after couple of weeks I started hearing that name more often from a lot of other guy friends. Some spoke of him as a genius, others just ridiculed the mere mention of his existence. I understood why the reactions were so extreme. Although Love Gurus were not unheard of, the tales about what this guy could help you achieve were too good to be true. The stories going around were sensational: An out of shape geek who had never had even one proper communication with a girl before, getting a super-hot manager in his company to be his girlfriend and later marrying her. A small town average looking guy who had major self-confidence issues picked up several foreigners online who came to India just to have casual flings with him. Recently divorced man living in the suburbs of Mumbai who was dumped because 'he was ugly', came out in dating life again and meeting 8-10 hot chicks in a week, and so on. The stories were nothing like one had heard in India before and every guy wanted to meet him. There were a couple of articles about an incredible love-Guru in a Newspaper but the writer only dismissed it in the end as a rumour and wrote that even if he was out there who would really care about a loser claiming to be a love Guru! But there was no real information on him and how to get in touch with him. When you googled the name, the Artist, you only got some white men in America or Europe and a movie with the same name. And nothing at all with 'Guru' except for a bad footage of a guy picking up women from a bar. You couldn't understand a word what was being spoken in the video and what that guy looked like. And when I had met Guru and realised that he was The Artist, I was pleased beyond imagination. It felt like God had sent for us a guy who would change our lives forever. And now Vinod was telling us that Guru was not him. I felt that we were back to square one.

'I hope you are not taking a mickey out of us, Vinod. I mean so many of them even in TST refer to him as The Artist!' I said although I fathomed he wasn't lying because of the passion in his voice.

'Oh, does it really matter to me Anuj what you believe in or not? Do you have any idea how much I know and you don't?' Vinod said flippantly and continued after a pause, 'You know what, it's not a name. It's a title you earn in the community. It means that you are the official number one Pick-up Artist of the world. Mark David is currently TA, The Artist, for the last 4 years . The duel or the match happens in the presence of 2 former TAs. See, the whole community keeps a track of all the prominent and talked about PUAs of the world and then decides on a contender who will challenge the existent TA every year. They have a website where they declare the contender's name based upon votes. Guru's name has been up as the contender for the last 3 years but he refused to participate each time. Because every year his opponent was David, his teacher. The second best challengers then had a duel with David. Beating each one of them for the last 4 years has been a cake walk for David. The only one who can challenge him and maybe even beat him is Guru. Guru is so good that nearly 50 percent of the community believes that he is the best and already calls him The Artist',

'Oh that explains why everyone in TST calls him that too.. hmm', Aman said.

Vinod continued 'David wants to prove Guru's followers wrong and has tried everything to push Guru to a duel this year challenging him and even insulting him by saying that he is fearful of him. But it didn't matter to Guru; he does not crave for the fame or attention of anyone. He has reluctantly given in only after hordes of e-mails and requests from his fans across the globe.'

That explanation from Vinod put my doubts about Guru to rest. But what was most fascinating for us was the fact that there was a secret community out there of men from around the world who were like us. Trying to decode what a woman wants from a man and how we could gratify our desires of lust, craving, romance, satisfy our male-egos and maybe even getting an ideal life partner. We were unknowingly part of the PUA community which thrived on the Internet. Vinod told us that the place where the duels were to be held had camera's installed at strategic places to record the events as they unfold live on the Internet. There were huge sponsors for the event on the website because the hits a duel get were unmatched even by the more popular events in the world. Guru was always against it because he believed that the only way in which this community could survive and expand was if it remained discreet and a secret society. But on the other hand was his objective to introduce to everyone his new concept of ethical gaming.

'So, was Guru like us before?' asked Anthony.

'Oh yeah! Very much. He was a pretty regular guy and says he was terribly shy too. While he was in college in Mumbai he had a steady girlfriend, Natasha who had fallen for his simplicity. They continued their relationship post college too until she dumped him for a guy with a 'bad boy' image who was also known to be abusive towards women. Guru could not understand that. He was everything a girl would want. Or they say they want. Educated, humble, a good job, a car and never wandered towards other women. She said the relationship had lost its spark and it had turned out to be dull. And then subconsciously he had developed a mindset that girls like only bad boys. And as fate would have it he went to London for work and there he was introduced to the PUA community by a friend and his belief that women find bad boys irresistible was only confirmed by the Co- PUAs. Then what followed was a storm. Suddenly there were talks everywhere about a new PUA from India in the community. His method of going overboard with bad-boy image bordering on insanity made him an instant hit. His methods were dangerous, risky and cave-man like. He had an unapologetic madness about him. He soon was touted as one of the best in London with his edgy, fearless, in your face arrogance. That's when David heard about him and took him under his wings. He then shifted to America with David and hordes of workshops and picking up women later, he had only fine-tuned his method. Every night he would post the videos of whatever happened in the field on the forum. David, whose method was largely NLP, was proud of his protégée. He knew by adding NLP in Gurus method only made him lethal. And lethal he had become. He helped Guru give method to his madness. He would pick up anything remotely female. From hospital nurses to super-models, from college students to strippers! But his weakness was a woman in a committed relationship. Everyone in the community agrees that such women are the most hard to game. Even if he as much as smelled a young woman who seemed dedicated and devoted to her partner he would try and pick her up using every skill or information that he had acquired. After he won over her, he would make sure that he posted her photograph on the PUA forums. It gave him a high to pick up women from the most difficult category. But actually more than the high it was a sort of getting back at the world, his sweet revenge. If the world could take away the person who had been his life, why couldn't he do the same with others? But it changed when he went to his recently married sister's house in India for a vacation. He had company in the form of Nick, his wingman. They had decided that they could spend time with family in the day and go out gaming women in evenings. India was a virgin territory for the community, so it was a different kind of challenge for them. And then one evening Guru and his brother-in-law went out to pick up some booze from the neighbourhood. Guru forgot his wallet and they had to come back to the house midway. They came back only to see Nick making out with Guru's newly married sister. Her husband and her brother were stunned at what they saw. It turned out real bad and she was divorced by her husband. Guru was devastated because everything that Nick used on his married sister were routines taught by him. She confessed later that she was aware that it was wrong but Nick had created something so strong in the moment that she just couldn't stop herself. She'd had a love marriage and they were only into the second year. Post-divorce she had become so depressed that she became a recluse and hardly interacts with anyone till date. Guru wanted to kick Nick's ass but he blamed himself and just told Nick to go away. That incident changed Guru so much that he declared to David that they should introduce and encourage some ethics in the game. David laughed it off. So much so that he started spreading rumours about Guru that he had some mental issues and had gone nuts. Guru parted ways with him and came back to India and took a year off. He did massive research at that time and came up with an approach which suggested that this game could be played considering that no one was hurt or conned and still maintain a high success rate. Ironically his new approach's success has bettered even his own performance in the past.'

'So, so you mean there is no room for a revenge?' Mohit asked nervously.

'No sweetheart, yeah you can bring an off-track gal on the right track, but you gotta make sure that you don't cause any damage to her life or image. See we are aware that there are women too, out there who take love-struck guys for a ride, use them and dump them. You can change their perspective, as long as it's not in a bad taste', Vinod replied and Mohit smiled displaying his teeth which looked like they came out to shake hands with him.

'So all in all guys, tonight is the match between the two biggest Pick-Up Artistes of our times. Once friends and now rivals. So brace yourself coz you got the best seats in the house.'

'Anuj man, I don't know why am I feeling so happy…come here I wanna hug you', Aman said. It was 7.30 pm and we still were in the lounge waiting for the duel to start in the next one and a half hours. 'All this is because of you. You made this possible Anuj. We are going to watch this Duel of Masters guys, fuck! This is the end for me! If I die tomorrow, no issues.', Aman had entered the emotional room in his brain, escorted by Teacher's whiskey. I thought it was better if we stopped drinking and be in our senses when the duel began. We went out for some fresh air.

At around 8.15 pm a BMW arrived and stopped right in front of the main entrance. Close behind it a Hummer came to a screeching halt. We had seen a Hummer before but this one looked Mammoth. They had put huge tyres in place of the originals and it had increased the truck's height by at least a foot and a half. The graphics were loud and eye catching. 2 bodyguards from the BMW ran out to open the door of the Hummer. From the Hummer came out a tall, white pale thin man, about 6'5" tall with long hair going down to his waist. He looked around 40-42 years old. He had a long roller coaster nose with small sharp eyes. He wore a long black coat and a top hat. The hat made him look taller by a foot. Something about him looked evil and strong. With him came three young white guys.

'Here comes the great Mark David with his three students all the way from America.' Vinod informed us.

Anthony kept staring at him 'Dude he is awesome man…o fuck what a personality as if some Star has arrived.'

'Guys this is what he does and not only during duels. He always makes sure that his entry is strong at the location. It helps him inside with girls already thinking of him as belonging to a superior class. He generates a feeling in a girl that she would feel for a famous celebrity. That's one of his tricks.'

'Isn't it unfair I mean you give Aman here a Hummer and he would pick up chicks too, where's the talent in that?' I asked and looked at Aman who didn't know whether to agree or disagree with that.

'You are right but if you have it, why not display it, right? Money is *talent* in this game.' Vinod said. David went to the pub with his entourage.

'Guys doesn't Anthony look like his son? Haha, Vinod, did David ever game women in Bandra 27 years ago?' Mohit said and laughed aloud by himself. Nobody found it in good taste and Anthony just smiled timidly at the stupid joke.

After around 15 minutes more, Guru arrived in his car, alone. No show-off, no drama. He wore a cool shirt with jeans. He could have been anyone in the pub. We all went up to him and shook hands. My friends were baffled that he knew all of them by their names.

'Heard a lot about you sir, I feel so lucky to be around the you and I am from Delhi..', Mohit started with his corporate buttering when Vinod interrupted him,

'Guru, he is here.'

'Is he? No surprise, he is always before time! I will meet you guys in a minute. Let me go and meet him. It's been long.' Guru said and walked into the pub.

We saw the crew who had secretly put cameras in the pub come out, their job was finished. They would go into their van, which halted in the area behind the pub so that nobody could notice its presence, which would throw the event LIVE on their website. The pub owners would be royally screwed if anyone found out about it but they were also getting the kind of money in one night alone that it took around a whole month otherwise, plus the international publicity. Beside even if someone saw a camera it wouldn't be a big deal as every public place is anyways monitored these days for security reasons. So their asses were covered.

We had two VIP lounges reserved, one for the Guru gang and one for the David gang. Only a thin wooden wall separated the two. Guru was in his opponent's lounge and we could hear the conversation.

'David it's good to see you again, how have you been?' Guru asked.

'I am good. How are you, you poor man's TA', David's tone was filled with hate, 'And how are you planning to compete with me? Hope your rope trick is in place.' David said and everyone in there burst out laughing.

'You know I am not into tricks anymore. Anyways, David it's nice to see you and hope you know all this is meaningless.'

'Oh Gurjeet' he uttered the name in a mock Indian accent, 'so you concede defeat already, you spineless Indian!'

'I didn't say that David, trust me. What I meant was, don't take it personally if you lose, it's meaningless.' Guru said. His voice too was now peppered with rage.

'Wait, who is this Gurjeet? Is there another person in there?' I asked Vinod.

'It's Guru's real name, Gurjeet Singh Gill. He is a Jat Sikh and I know Guru well, he is angry now. David shouldn't have made a comment on India.' Vinod said.

'Dude how many names does he have? I mean does he have a name for every place he goes to. That Guru sir is also weird, man! Who has so many names these days? I think you should tell us all his names at once so that we don't get confused.' Aman was laughing loudly and Guru entered at the same moment.

'Whose names do you want to know Aman?' Guru asked making strong eye contact with him.

'No, no I was talking about….er…..umm…haha… Lord Ram and his-his multiple names and I that's why was..' .

'So do you want me to tell you Lord Ram's names?' Guru was already angry and Aman smelled danger.

'No, No, I am cool, I will find out later…I mean I have lots of er err history books at..'

'What kind of history books do you have?'.

' err.. some other books like Mahabharat, yeah those Mahabharat type books.' At that moment a couple of guys entered to wire Guru for the sound.

'Anthony, will you come to the loo with me?.. hey! Anthony, Oye, Anthony, listen man?' Aman was asking Anthony because if he went alone it would look rude and he wanted to get out of that situation but Anthony wasn't listening. He was in one of his day dreaming sessions.

'Why do you want Anthony to come to the loo with you?' Guru asked.

'Hehehe, just to....hehe. You want me to go alone? or with anyone else? Coz that's okay with me too'.

'No kid, its okay, relax! Anthony go with Aman to the loo.' Guru said and hearing Guru's projected voice Anthony came back to the present moment.

'Yeah what's that?' Anthony asked very politely as we all got frustrated with this meaningless and awkward conversation.

'Oye, Guru Sir wants you to go to the loo with Aman.' Mohit said.

'Why?' Anthony looked a little scared.

'Shit! Just like that..you just go, no?', Mohit said in wild frustration

'I am not going to loo with anyone and least of all with him, if there are no girls it doesn't mean that....', Anthony said defensively

'What the hell man! Aman, I will come with you, c'mon let's go.' Mohit said trying to end the nonsense.

'Let it be Mohit sir, forget it, I will go later.' Aman said.

'Now what happened to you?' Mohit asked.

'Actually now strangely I don't feel the pressure and I ....'.

'You assholes', Guru thundered, 'all four of you just go out, now.' and we hurriedly walked out.

'Dude what was that? Why did everyone want me to go to the loo with Aman, what's going on, is there something I should know?' Anthony asked once we were out.

'I will take off my shoe and hit you, bloody fuck.' Mohit said.

At around 8.50 Vinod called us in, the clash was minutes away. Every PUA or a wannabe PUA around the globe would be watching it. We took the first VIP lounge and the opposition camp, so to speak, took the one next to us. The judges arrived and they took the last lounge where they would watch it live on a giant LCD screen and judge it. Vinod gave us sheets which had details and the rules mentioned on them.

Both the participants had to take the maximum number of phone numbers from the women. They couldn't ask for numbers for business or claiming to be just friends. They would get 1 point each for a phone number depending on how the judges would rate a girl. If the judges rated a target 6 and the player got her number he would get 6 points for that and so on. They would score 5 points extra for a kiss; however, if they go beyond kissing they would still be given 5 points. So if a player got a phone number of a girl rated 6 and he kissed her as well, he scored 6 + 5=11 points. Only the activity that happened within the premises of the club would be counted. The approaches would be made on alternate basis and one player couldn't game a girl already approached by the other or make comments or even mention the other player to a girl or a group. The rules were strict, the cameras were everywhere and we had legends fighting for the title. They had 3 hours. From 9 pm-12 pm.

It was game on.

Guru and David introduced themselves looking in the camera installed in the lounge with the judge's presence. Then they shook hands and came out of the lounge into the pub area. The place was full. David warmed off with a drink and we could see Guru sitting on the bar ordering a mocktail. We were surprised to see that he wasn't having alcohol.

'He does drink but not while gaming.' Vinod informed us, 'He says it's an advantage that you have over everyone in the pub. You are quick at your feet and your mind works faster.'

One of the crew members, Mite, was posing as a bouncer who would play the middleman between the players and the judges. He gave thumbs up to David. It meant he was the first one to go. We all watched it on a laptop in the lounge so that we could even hear what the players would say. We couldn't control our excitement and were giggling like school girls.

David moved towards two women standing with a guy sitting on a bar stool. They were both facing the sitting man. Both were hot. Around 8s we guessed but didn't know how much the judges would rate them until he stopped gaming them.

'Hello there guys!' David said in a strong American accent. All three of them were taken aback by the enormous guy approaching them.

'Hello.' they said nervously.

'This is David's technique; shock and awe.' Vinod explained to us, 'He intimidates people with his size and the hat makes him look even bigger. Plus he is now in India where he is almost a foot taller than an average Indian male.'

Then David said, looking only at one of the girls, 'I am sorry to interrupt you lovely people, but you know my friend out there (he pointed to one of his students) thinks that I can't make friends in India because I am very rich and look very big. What do you guys think? Isn't that a pretty lame thing to say?'

'Hehe, of course you can make friends here. Anybody can.' the girl said.

'Yeah your friends are lame I guess!' the second girl said.

'awww, that's so sweet of you ladies, so kind. But what do you think, boy?' he asked the guy in the group.

'Well, no, they are..', the boy was saying when David interrupted him

'You know what! I would love to have *you* as my friend (he looked at the first girl he had spoken to), and maybe (then looked at the second girl) you too. I mean, you are okay too!' Both the girls started to laugh loudly at this.

'You don't want me as your friend?' the guy teased David but he ignored him again.

'You know I have really heard a lot about Indian women; how they are very beautiful and exotic. But I have also heard that most of them are slow up here (pointing to his head) and pretty conservative in their approach. Do you think Indian women are very different from women from the west, haan?'

'Oh no, not anymore.' the first girl said.

'Liar, I don't believe you haha..you sweet little naughty thing.'

'Oh no seriously these days Indian women are pretty broadminded and independent.'

'Oh yeah how would you feel if later in the evening you saw me passionately kissing a girl, standing next to you and the girl looked as if she was enjoying it too? Would you judge the girl?'

'No, not at all.' both the girls said but the guy was quiet now because he was being ignored not only by David but also by his girlfriends.

'hmm…we will see, would you be comfortable, really, seeing a girl enjoying a kiss and being careless and adventurous?' and he pulled the second girl whom he had given a little less attention than the other, pretty close to him.

'No.' her eyes were closing on their own as if she had lost control of herself. When David came very close to her and kissed her on her lips, she did not object. Sitting in the lounge we just looked at each other with our mouths wide open. Aman started jumping around clapping in disbelief. The kiss then turned into a full-fledged smooch and the girl was letting out moans of passion while kissing. She had left her body loose and could stand only because David had held her back with his huge skinny hands. The guy friend shook his head in disbelief and left. Then David let go off her and looked at the other girl 'Oh there you are.' and then pulled her towards himself.

'Oh don't feel bad sweetie', and hugged her, 'She isn't as good as I expected, you smell wonderful', he murmured in her ear and came close to her and then suddenly she too started kissing him. The bartender and some people around were as shocked as we were, in the lounge.

'Hey you know I have to go to my friends as they are waiting for me. Why don't you lovely ladies meet me later, give me your numbers for now.' The girls gave him their numbers and David found it a little hard to leave as they wouldn't let him go easily.

The website updated the scores. 7+5=12, 7+5=12. Total: 24.

'He is too good guys, isn't he? He has got himself a twin start, pretty rare for a duel.' Vinod said.

'Vinod we are nothing in front of him no?' Mohit said who was as excited as a frog on a rainy day.

'Obviously! How can you even say such a thing, you retard!' Vinod shut him up. 'If you looked closely whenever he used words like comfortable, adventurous, careless, enjoying, he twitched his eyes and made his head tilt a little to the left. Every time. So they associated these feelings with the gesture. So when the girls came close to him, he repeated the gesture and all those strong feelings overpowered the girls who now associated the feelings with him, his face and they reached a state of high arousal.' We were left speechless and I thought about how we had approached. The Stallone, the Aunty and the rape routines. And I could only laugh at our inability.

It was Guru's turn now.

What could he do? We thought.

Guru approached a girl gang of five.

He went up to the group 'Excuse me.'

'Yes', a girl from the group turned around and replied, she looked like a 7.

Then what Guru did, we couldn't understand. He just looked back at her with a very faint smile without blinking. He didn't say a word. He held this position for at least five seconds and then maintaining the eye contact he said 'Nothing' and left. The girl put her hands up as if to say *what was that?* More than anything else there was something about his body –language. He looked so self-assured and calm that even such a gesture didn't scare-off the girl. Guru walked and stood at a distance from the group facing them. The girl kept looking out at him regularly and he made eye contact all the time. It was obvious that she wasn't looking at him out of attraction but out of curiosity. Then after five minutes she herself went up to him.

'Excuse me! You were saying something and then stopped. I mean I didn't understand.'

Guru waited another ten seconds to reply, 'actually I wanted to ask you a question but then I realised you are single, so I backed off.'

'But what's the problem if I am single and what was your question in the first place?'

'Why are you so interested? As I said it's only for a committed girl. Anyways, my question was, are you single?'

'What?..wait..hahahaa' the girl bent forward and put her hand on the mouth to control her laughter, 'So you just want to know whether the girl is single or not and then do nothing about it and by the way how did you come to know that I was single?'

'It's simple, first when I said 'excuse me' to the group you turned around before anyone else and second, I didn't see a ring in your hand',

'Oh is that so? That would surely tell anyone that I am single, right, hehe',

'And the fact that when I was quiet you looked twice at my mouth and kept on fidgeting with your watch.'

'So what does that mean, Sherlock?'

'See when a person is devoid of any intimacy for a period of time his or her eyes will automatically go to the erogenous parts of an eligible person of the opposite sex. Fidgeting with watch meant that built up tension needs an outlet. So these observations are generally true and there are lot of others'.

'Oh that's nice, very interesting, what's your name?' she asked touching her hair.

'I am Guru'

'I am Tanisha, you look like you have come here alone.'

'In a way, yes.'

Then Guru playfully looked at her from head to toe and the girl stiffened. He let out a laugh. 'Hey you look too tight now, relax I am not observing you anymore..haha, you are so cute, come here' and he hugged her and five minutes later kissed her. We were dumfounded at the ease with which he closed it. We all clapped including Vinod.

'Hey Tanisha lemme tell you that I am not looking out for a relationship at all but give me your number if things go right we could date!' and took her number as well.

Score on the website: 7 +5 =12.

'Guys did you notice that he didn't lie to her even once and didn't con her. But still he got result similar to David's. And the most important thing was that the girl wouldn't feel bad about it later. The girls David approaches bathe every hour the next day when they go home, I guess', Vinod said and we all laughed.

David then selected a tall stunning girl sitting alone at the bar.

'You know what life is full of confusion and everything we do is to distract ourselves from the confusion.'

'That's actually true.' the girl said and looked down getting a little intimidated by David.

'Hi I am David.'

'I am Shona.'

'So what is your distraction these days?'

'Umm..it's my fiancée I guess, he keeps me distracted', she said running one hand through her hair

'I mean what do you do when he is away, what distracts you then, look he is not around now?'

'I guess, as for now, it's you, hehe.'

'Interesting, you have immediately put me up with your fiancée! A very strong statement, indeed!' David said with half a smile.

'Stop flirting with me, I told you I am engaged!' she said laughing and showed him his ring.

'Have you ever let yourself go, Shona..do you know how it feels to break the rules and to go just with the flow..it's amazing and makes you feel alive.' David said slowly and his pauses were perfect.

'Hey but why are you asking me all this?......I might have broken rules here and there but I am generally well behaved!'

'I like it when people use the word generally…they give you a subtle hint ..anyway are you in your general mood or not so general?'

'What do you mean?' she said in a flirtatious tone.

'Why don't we go over there and quietly break a rule and smoke inside the pub..Let's see what happens?

'Oh my god! You are such a child'

'I am! Come my new best friend' David said in a mock child voice, 'let's do something naughty there.' and he pointed to a corner of the place.

'No sweetheart I can't my fiancée is out for a smoke he will come any..'

David interrupted her, 'It's okay, you can introduce him later to me.' and he grabbed her hand and took her to the corner. He lit a cigarette and immediately a bouncer told him to put it out.

'Oh you are such a spoil sport, Mr Bouncer. You sure, I can't smoke in here?'

'No sir!' said the bouncer and the girl kept on giggling all the while.

'Hey is this allowed?' and he hugged the girl. She kept on laughing as the bouncer went away.

'You are funny…'the girl said. She looked wide-eyed.

'I am?' and he gave her a peck on the lips and then she gave him a peck and then they begin kissing. After half a minute, she came back to the reality of her world and broke the passionate lip lock with the tall American who had given her thrills in a matter of minutes. While leaving she gave away her number.

8+5=13. Total: 37.

David's gang gave each other high fives. 'The muthafuckin Indian is a dead chap man..haha, The Artist..haha..' , they scorned.

'Vinod how many girls are single these days? Isn't Guru playing against himself here by only approaching single girls?' Aman asked and I immediately agreed with his question.

'I know, but there is a difference. I know there are very few single girls out there but trust me if questioned, most of them will tell you that they are single, if they haven't come with their boyfriends. And that's a green signal for Guru; I mean you can't hire detectives to check their real status.'

Guru approached a group of friends of around 6 guys and 8 girls. He went over to one girl and said 'You are sweet, I had to tell you this', and she ignored him 'Does your boyfriend think the same?'

'No, I don't have one and it's none of your business.' she snapped

'Green signal!' we all said together.

'What's the matter man, why are you bothering her?' , one of her girlfriends asked Guru

'No I liked her and wanted to know if she was single, because I date only single girls.' Guru said as if it was a very natural thing to say.

'Excuse me?? No she isn't interested.' the friend said.

We heard a huge cheer from the neighbouring lounge, 'haha... She just told the Artist to fuck off.' one of them said.

'Okay I accept that but why are you telling me this? Shouldn't she speak for herself? I had to compliment her. She was staring at me for long and I thought it would be wrong if I don't say something nice.' The rest of the group was dancing and having a good time 10 feet away from them.

'grrrr..Let me put this straight to her, for you dude...', and she looked at her friend, 'do you like him?'

'Wait, why are you asking her this?' Guru interrupted, 'Why do you want the road to get clear for you. If *you* like me just tell us both and trust me she will sacrifice her love for you'.

'You are such a nonsense guy..I can't believe you,' the friend said and both the girls smiled and eased up.

'Guess what! You can dance with me, I can at least do that much for you', Guru said this to the friend and she looked only glad to oblige. So they both danced. Then they jived and Guru took her breath away with his mean moves. Even I was a little taken aback with his fast paced dance moves because before this I had only seen him moving around pretty leisurely and he took time even to look at his watch. After the Jive, they slow danced on a number. She kept her head on his shoulders and it seemed they knew each other for a long time. Then they both looked at each other and he asked her whether she was single, she said yes and they kissed. Guru took her number and explained to her as usual that they could date on and off. Then he went away giving a signal to the bouncer in disguise that he was done.

Guru's score: 8+5=13 total=25.

'That was so simple', I said. 'But couldn't he have at least taken the other girl's phone number?'

'Ha, smart you noticed....' Vinod said.

Mohit feeling left out interrupted, 'actually he could have taken the other girl's number as well, I was thinking.'

Vinod ignored Mohit and said 'See, Anuj I told you earlier it's against his ethics. The friend Guru kissed would have felt bad and used if he had approached the first girl. At least she now thinks that a guy was genuinely interested in her and they spent good time together. That she wasn't used by a womanizer.' I was impressed by Guru's integrity

'But Vinod I don't think many woman care so much about such things these days. I mean why Guru decides what the girls would like or dislike. He could have outscored David in *this* approach itself. I don't understand the ethics he keeps on displaying. If he is so morally conscious then he should be in some social service and not in this game.' Aman said, his system was dying for a disagreement but he didn't realize that Guru again stood behind him all this while.

'What's that?' Guru asked standing at Aman's back.

'What's what, man?' Aman turned around and saw Guru standing directly behind him. We thought Aman was going to faint, 'No, no I was talking about a friend who is..is is.. in ...s.s...social service' .

'Yeah what about him?',

'No, it's it's a gg..ood thing to do. Everyone should be ha..happy and my country should p...prosper and..'

'How will the country prosper?', Guru asked sternly.

'It will no? If we get our children educated and females educated and take care of the poor, one day India can compete with any country and..' Aman muffled

'Whatever! Vinod I just need to sit here for a while; the music is too loud outside, I need a break!' Guru said and retired on a sofa. Then we all watched David perform. Then Guru went out and he performed. To say that they were excellent every time would be an understatement. Every time they used a new technique and routine. Guru stuck to his 'ethical game' and Aman had sworn he won't utter a word for the rest of the night. It was 11.15 and the David had a massive lead over Guru .

The score read: David 145. Guru 110.

It was pretty obvious now that David would defeat Guru by a huge margin. It was just a matter of 45 minutes with time only for one approach each. Our group was pretty quiet now.

'I feel bad; not so much for the fact that Guru will lose.', Vinod said in a pensive tone, 'but for the hard work and years he put to come up with ethical gaming and now it will be dismissed by the PUAs and aspiring PUAs. Guru's ethical gaming slowly will die down in the coming months.'

The time had come for the final approaches. We were aware that a group of six super models had entered the pub some minutes ago. They were very popular and well known models in India. There were all either 9s or 10s. It seemed that the entire pub was aware of their presence. It was David's turn and he wanted to finish with a bang and decide to approach one of the models, a 10, we thought. She was 5'9" inches tall with a broad bone structure with minimal fat. She had the prettiest features and an inviting pout. On her thin body she had full breasts. She wore a red dress which ended way above her knees. Her hair was straight and open. All in all it looked like she was made by computer software and not by God. She was that perfect.

'Hello senorita.' David said putting his hand forward for a handshake. 'Hello', she said shaking hands with him.

'My apologies for my limited knowledge but my Indian friend tells me that you are a huge celebrity here?'

'Hi I am Sandy, and I think your friend isn't wrong', she said confidently.

'I am David, pleased to meet you', he then spoke about models in India and in America and that he knew at least ten of the world's top fashion designers. She was intrigued and interested that he knew so much about the international fashion scene and was so well connected.

Then he changed the topic 'Sandy It must get very uncomfortable for you sometimes to let your hair down because it seems everyone is watching you all the time, judging you, I am sure you just can't be yourself. My model friend in London only attends house parties among close friends, it's sad, in a way.'

'Yeah that's so true. That's why alcohol and Mary Jane become good friends!' Vinod told us Mary Jane was slang for marijuana.

David nodded indicating he understood her plight. She took a sip from her glass, 'Hey I am so sorry. I can be such a narcissist! What do you do, you look like a magician to me? hehe..'

'No, no I am a business man. What you are looking at, is my evening wear. But you know coming back to what we were talking about, at this place, I am better off than you are. I mean if I go and talk to a lady I want to, nobody will give me a second look. But you can't do that. Tell me, what if you were to suddenly look at a guy and felt the bolt from the sky and be tremendously aroused for that man? Would you feel comfortable with being sexually aroused to the point that you would just want him.' David was saying and he was moving his hand up and down his chest area when he said words like *tremendously sexually aroused* and *comfortable*. Obviously David was going to use the gesture later to attract her towards him sexually. With those words David took her to a place in her mind where the feelings of arousal were and in effect she would associate the feelings with him.

'What would I do? Umm..generally that never happens with me'.

'Oh really? Haha, I don't buy that. You know what I just need to go the John. Can you keep my drink with you until I come back?

Don't worry, I will be back and think of this glass as me until I come back' he chuckled and again made those hand gestures in a very subtle manner.

'Hmm..Guys, you know what, David, I think, not only wants to score her for the Duel but I think he kinda really likes her too and wants to take it with her outside. See, he is trying hard now. What he did by telling her to keep his glass and simultaneously making that gesture was Condiment Anchoring. Even when he is away those feelings would stay with her because the object, the glass, is with her. Whenever she would look at the glass she would think of him and feel aroused because of the gesture.' We just heard Vinod in awe. We were learning so much new about this game that we were amazed beyond belief.

After five Minutes David came back, 'Oh there, you are a nice lady, my drink seems as it is.'

'Hehe, I thought you aren't coming back. So you were asking me some questions?' it seemed she was eager for their conversation to continue.

'Yeah what do you feel when you are intimate with a guy, what's in your mind space then? I mean when a guy is slowly touching you gently at all the right places and then he climbs on top of you.' Sandy's eyes widened and she started to breathe a little heavily. David wanted to take it a notch higher all the time making the hand gesture and continued 'and when you have animal sex and both the bodies melt into one and the thrusting begins. And then your eyes shut and you feel him coming in and going out and you digging your fingernails in his back. Then he goes down on a very wet you and ..'

'Wait wait, stop right there, eeewwww...that was gross... what got into you suddenly? You know what, I need to spend some time with my friends as well, I guess I will see you later!' She said despondently. Clearly David had gone over the top with his graphic choice of words. He looked blank for a moment, he couldn't understand how it hadn't worked, 'oh sure.' he said coughing a little realizing that everyone could be laughing at him right now.

'Oh so this is your wall of defence indicating that this conversation is not an everyday thing for you but imagine how life can be so much easier if we just go with the..'

'I got to go. Thanks for the advice',

'Hey whatever! But let's exchange numbers and we can talk later.' David voice was creaking a little and he was clearly breaking under pressure. Vinod said that he would have handled it better had there been no cameras to record the insult.

'I am sorry but I don't give my numbers to strangers.' and she turned around to her friends. David looked straight into the camera above instinctively and a funny embarrassed smile appeared on his face. We burst out laughing together. Maybe we were a little louder than otherwise. 'Awesome Anchoring.' Vinod shouted loudly and gave high fives to all of us. After a while we stopped but strangely Anthony wouldn't stop. We tried to make him stop but he couldn't stop himself. Unknowingly we joined him too and it wasn't long before we were all rolling on the floor . 'Yeah losers keep laughing you monkeys. Even after this you still lose, you are that bad.' a voice came from the neighbouring lounge. 'I will take revenge of Guru, one day', Anthony shouted back.

'*Oye* Stallone, chill.' Vinod said.

'What dumbness man, what bloody dumbness, Anthony!' Mohit said.

'Dude why you are behind my life all the time', Anthony said.

Mohit stood up aggressively 'Should I tell you, crack.' and rolled up his sleeve as if to attack Anthony.

'Guys calm down! Both of you!' Vinod said. Mohit abused Anthony under his breath and leaned over and whispered to me 'We have to get rid of him, or no one will take us seriously.' I just ignored him for the time being. I had to watch Guru's final approach even though he had already lost it.

We saw Guru walk up to the same group. He could do that as long as he wasn't approaching the same girl David had.

'Anuj, Anuj, Guru needs you.' a voice came from the laptop. It was the voice of Mite, the fake bouncer, 'He need you to wing him'

'What???? No no no no..I cant go. Why me? Vinod, do something man. You go Vinod, I will screw up everything for Guru as well. No I can't, not with so many cameras.' they didn't know how I could actually fuck it up.

'Anuj, come now..I repeat, Anuj come now and stand next to me.' Mite repeated.

Vinod held me by my hand, 'Think of the begging task, Anuj. Nobody will judge you, and even if they do it's..its.. none of your business..now go!' and pushed me out. I went and stood next to Mite. My heart was beating so loudly that it seemed to be breaking my ribs to pop out! Everyone was going to watch and judge me and laugh at me. Clearly it was too much for me. What if the community tagged me with a name like 'dumbkid' 'Indiananjoker' or whatever.

'Hello Rebekah, I am Guru.'

'Yes tell me.' Rebekah was the most popular one among the girls. She had also acted in couple of movies but she was generally popular because of the music videos she had featured in where she had been more than bold. She was around 5'9" inches tall and only a little less attractive then Sandy.

'See I am so sorry to interrupt you.' Guru said with the kind of smoothness and confidence unique only to him, 'but I have a young friend of mine here and I have brought him over with me because he is a little uncomfortable around hot women and I want him to get a little used to it. So I am going to call him over and just be a little nice and polite to him for a minute or so. But don't tell him what I said, okay.'

' Awwww, that's so sweet, please call him, where is he?' she asked and Guru waved at me and I waved back at him, making some cool gesture I had seen a rapper do on VH1. I could easily have cried there. I knew I looked foolish. Begging was difficult but it wasn't being aired to the world. Guru gestured at me to come to him. My worst nightmare was about to come true. Just to stand next to the hot women would have made my head spin. Now I had to go there interact with them. The introductions went okay. Then Rebekah asked 'Hey you are a handsome chap, where is your girlfriend.'

'Oh she is, she is, there somewhere..' and my hand pointed somewhere I had no clue about.

'Aww sweetie! You don't have a girlfriend?'

'No, actually I don't. Haha.' I laughed in embarrassment and put my hands in my pockets just in case they trembled. I had predicted right. I was making a fool of myself in front of the world.

'You will get one soon, don't worry......' she said and paused to listen to the song being played, 'nice track this one..what kinda music do you listen to?'

'Anything good to the ears, Pink-Floyd, Beatles, eagles, Bruce Springsteen..', I immediately hoped she wouldn't ask me about any particular track. I had never listened properly even to one song of theirs and was repeating the names of bands Anthony would talk and rave about.

'Oh you have a taste for the classics! You got some taste there handsome...wait....Hey guys', she called her other hot friends, 'This is my new cool friend Anuj.' They all introduced themselves to me. I felt surreal with all the assortment of the fragrances. I had never felt so much beauty around me ever. I was trying my best not to look wide eyed, literally. I looked at Guru; he was standing back and gave me a warm smile. The smile of an elder brother, I thought. Then he took Rebekah by the arm to one side and said 'Thank you so much baby. But I gotta go. I now need to give him lessons in a very important topic. You enjoy your evening and I thank you, again, so much'

'Anytime! Look at him he is so cute.' she kept gushing. Anyone else in my place would have believed the super model had fallen for him but not me, I guess my low self- esteem kept me grounded.

'What are you going to teach him, Naughty man?' she now sounded a little too high.

'Nothing, just the rare art of kissing; after which every woman would want to kiss him again and again.'

'Oh, is it, what are you, a love -Guru?' she scoffed.

'Maybe, Maybe not.'

'So how will you teach him, by kissing him yourself? Surely you can't just teach just by 'telling'. You gotta show it too, right?'

Guru leaned over and said to her 'Hey why beat around the bush so much. You like me, its obvious, so stop pretending. I will kiss you and teach you too, but on one condition. It will be in front of all your friends. I won't like you taking advantage of my teaching ability in private. Just ask all your friends to come to the VIP lounge with me.'

'Hmm, you are one confident guy, very rare! VIP lounge, hmmm I wonder who you are, really!' she said biting her lips, 'You know what, just wait here for a moment'. And then Rebekah went over to her friends and said something in their ears. I would find out later that Guru was using a technique called Urbcave, developed by him. The better the girl the more you dominate and show more of leadership qualities. Caveman of the modern age technique.

Then Guru took us all in the Lounge where my friends and Vinod were. But now there was nobody there and the computer was switched off. Obviously Mite would have conveyed the message and they had left the room. Now Guru and I were there with six hot supermodels in the confines of a pretty small lounge.

'Okay, so all are here. Let's get this started. Hmm.. Anuj go over and hold Rebekah's by her shoulders.'

I just laughed at that.

'Oh come on here, Anuj.' a sloshed Rebekah said. I went over reluctantly and held her by her shoulders.

'Now lean over and give a peck on her lips' Guru said and I looked at him, expecting a smile as I thought they were all pulling a fast one on me but he was serious and so was everyone else. *What the hell!* I thought and pecked her. Suddenly my nervousness disappeared.

'Now Rebekah I want you to pout for me. And Anuj kiss her on the outer lips and then go a little inside in the sensitive part. But remember, no tongue as of now.' *Oh my fucking god, Guru have you hypnotised this hottie here. Why is she agreeing to this in the first place?* I thought but now I wanted to make full use of this god sent opportunity. I kissed her and she shut her eyes while I went into a trance and began smooching her, forgetting Gurus instructions.

That was the first kiss of my life. And I was kissing a supermodel.

But it could last only for 10 seconds as her friend Sandy interrupted, 'Hey what's this?' she said, luckily with a smirk. By now they looked high with the alcohol and maybe Mary Jane.

'Rebekah stop this, you weirdo! Let's go.' sandy said.

'Wait a minute. Anuj please step aside' Guru said, 'See what I meant was...if you don't mind, Rebekah?' and Guru came close to her to kiss 'Umm..no I don't mind..you are a hot teacher and it's a very useful skill', she said winking at him. Then Guru kissed her and I had never seen a woman respond like that to a kiss. She was letting out moans I hadn't heard even in a porn movie. He was exploring her mouth and going soft sometimes and a little hard sometimes. He stopped for a moment and said 'see Rebekah what I want to you to do is...' But she didn't let him finish his sentence and held him by his hair and continued with the kiss. I looked at other girls and I could make out that they were getting pretty aroused themselves. I felt that I should do something too because such an opportunity would never come my way again.

I looked at Sandy and gathering enough courage I asked 'Hey you..you.. want to practise this too? With with me..er?' She looked high and aroused yet she looked away.

I tried again 'What's the harm in practising, you get only comfortable with this.' and while saying this suddenly something struck me and I moved my hand up and down like David had done to her. Her expressions changed suddenly and she walked slowly towards me, hugged me and kissed the shit out of me.

That was my second kiss in life. After five minutes of my first. With a hotter super model.

There is justice in life, after all!

For half a second I looked at the camera and winked and murmured 'Sorry David'. Suddenly I heard a loud cheer from nearby; I could recognise the voices of my friends and Vinod. I was on cloud 9. I was kissing a girl who had rejected a master, minutes ago.

Then when Rebekah finished, one of the other hot girl asked, 'Don't mind, but can you teach that to me, hehe, I have a movie coming up with some kissing scenes and maybe it could help.' Then Guru kissed her. Same response. Sandy and I meanwhile couldn't let go off each other. We started making out a bit. Oh boy! I was floating! *What a night*, a thought crossed my mind while kissing her,

If I die tomorrow no issues, I remembered Aman's words.

When my hand for a moment brushed her voluptuous soft breasts, she let out a smile while kissing. I was falling in love, I thought.

And then I looked out of the corner of my eye and what I saw transfixed me. All the other five girls were glued to Guru. He was kissing and making out with them in no particular order. This was turning into a fucking orgy. Then I saw one of the models struggling to get a piece of Guru. After all it was one guy and five tall girls on him and she wasn't getting any space to do anything with him. She then swiftly went down on her knees and was trying desperately, almost out of anger, to unzip Guru.

It was hilarious and I couldn't stop laughing but then suddenly, as if on a cue, my eyes fell on the camera on the ceiling and suddenly my mind shot back into reality. I saw the time, it was 11.55 pm. I forgot all about the supermodel making out with me .The girl on the floor was about to show Guru's dick to the whole world when I bellowed ' Gurrrruuuuu! Look down!' and leaped to push the girl away. Guru didn't pay heed to what was happening on the floor below him. He looked in a state of trance. I literally had to pull away the other women as well, using all my strength. I whispered in his ears 'Guru, I don't know how may points exactly you need but you have scored only *some* points with the kisses and I guess you need quite more points to win, We are in a duel, remember', I almost shook his whole body to bring him back to his senses. 'Oh fucking yeah…..wait girls…girls..!' Guru said and stepped into action right away. 'girls, me and my friend need need to go now but you give me your numbers now, all of you now, I really need to rush now', Guru said it so fast that nobody understood a word and he had to repeat himself. I had never seen him panic before. The clock in the room showed 11.59. We had a minute to take the numbers from the aroused women who were clearly put off with the sudden change in the atmosphere and were painfully slow. We could manage only two phone numbers and the girls began to leave, all a little dejected with the anti-climax. 'We will see you girls later.' I said once we were all out of the VIP lounge and I went over and hurriedly gave a peck on Sandy's lips. I saw two guys staring at me from a distance. They didn't look at me all that happily. But I had no time to find out who they were. *Probably some jealous guys*, I thought and dismissed it. We looked around for our friends and noticed everyone had gathered in the judge's lounge. Guru and I ran in there and saw the final scores appearing slowly on the Giant screen in the room.

David :145 +0

Final score: 145

Guru : 110+ 15

+15

+5

+5

+5

Final score: 155

We, the Guru gang, let out a huge victorious scream. David's gang immediately hurried out swearing under their breath. David shook hands with Guru, 'Well played sir, you are a better player and more importantly a better human being. I had no shame to having lost to you. Thank you for the match. It was a pleasure.'

'Thanks David.', Guru said and touched his feet, 'As I had said, it's all meaningless.'

'But I really hated what your wingman did there. However I guess this is not the time to talk about. He looked at me sternly and left. I could just look down and scratch my head.

Guru was given a winner's check of 20 lakh rupees. Vinod hugged Guru. Guru said something in Vinod's ear.

'Guys! These are four checks of Rs 10,000 each for you, from Guru!' Vinod said and handed over the checks. We were really dumfounded. *I know what you guys are, lucky!* I remembered what Vinod had told us and right now I couldn't agree more. I saw my check and immediately realised there was a mistake. The amount showed Rs. 50,000 instead of 10,000 in my check. I looked at Guru and before I could say something, he came over to me and hugged me. 'Thank you kid, you saved my ass there. You deserve this.' he whispered in my ears and then stood back, 'The way you scored with Sandy…well I wouldn't say it was completely ethical but it shows you have in it you for the big moments.' For the first time in my life, I felt important, I set that I was not completely useless.

'Thank *you* for everything! I mean me kissing a supermodel…' I could just come up with that.

'Don't thank me, you made her like you.' he said winking at me, 'I just got them in.'

'Yeah bro.' Aman said, 'along with Guru you are a big star too tonight, look at the comments in the website.' Aman said. I read the comments made by people who had watched and my eyes went moist. *is he the next TA?, a super-hot model fell for the newbie;, Anuj, you stole David's girl! Respect to the new kid on the block; best wingman in the world; and* so on. I was thrilled. There were no comments like 'loser' or anything of that sort. From a nobody I had become known in the community all over the world in a span of 45 minutes.

That night, I felt I was not low- life after all.

How I wish Richa could have seen this.

We were walking out of the pub and I saw my friends all in high spirits shouting and enjoying. They couldn't stop hugging me. It felt nice. A lot of Guru's students and fans had gathered outside the pub in large numbers shouting and cheering. People who didn't know, didn't understand. Although Guru maintained it was meaningless, we felt his victory as ours. He had won. An Indian was now the number one pick-up artist in the world.

Guru was now, officially, The Artist.

'Let's sit down, nothing will happen to the clothes man.' said Anthony.

We were in the open ground which the pub used as a parking lot. My friends insisted that I give them every detail about how I felt during the whole thing. Although they had watched it, they wanted it from the horse's mouth. Everyone else in the pub had left. Vinod had left with Guru but we wanted to stay on and talk. It was around 1 am. They had switched off the halogen lights in the parking lot and it was pitch dark except for the street lights in the lane opposite. But ee had enough light to see each other and talk.

'So Anuj, how was she? Was her body soft or a little muscular?' Aman asked excitedly.

'Why? Do you prefer muscles, Aman? What sort of a question is that?' Anthony interrupted him.

'Just relax bro, okay? Yes, Anuj tell us, how she was.' Aman asked taking a puff.

'Oh to be honest she was something.' I said going back an hour and a half in my memory. 'I could feel so much heat in her body, as if her skin was made up of pieces of coal. And while hugging, the way her boobs pressed against me, oh man! She got some hooters! And her thighs..oh god, since she had a tiny dress on, my hands had a gala time feeling up the skin on her thighs. It was so soft and I slipped my hand up a little once or twice.'

'Oh that was sensational man! You are giving me a hard on in my softie' Mohit said, 'No, honestly Anuj, bloody fuck. We were like ki Anuj will screw it up but it was awesome.'

'Yeah man. Let's celebrate it.' Anthony said, 'Look, Anuj you can't drive your car and I can't ride my bike, we are both drunk.'

Mohit interrupted him, 'Oye potty head it's my bike, not yours!'

'Yeah bro whatever. Because it's Saturday and the cops will be checking on drivers. But the *naka* is there only till 3 am. So why don't we sit here, celebrate and leave at 3 from here. What say? I will go and get some alcohol. There is a bar like 15 minutes from here.' Anthony said. We all agreed to that.

'But it would be better if you go with someone, it's very late. Aman go with him.' I said and they both left.

I asked Mohit' 'I have this question. Why didn't Guru ask the five models whether they were single before gaming them? Did Vinod say anything about it?'

'Yeah he did. He said that Guru and Vinod had seen the group in a lot of parties earlier and they were known to have casual flings with a lot of others.'

'Hmm, hence he must have assumed that it's no point asking them, fair enough. But you know I feel funny about everything tonight. It's very surreal. Do you think it's really happening to us? And don't you think Guru has the best job on the planet? He must have kissed 18-20 chicks tonight and he gets paid lakhs for it!'

'How much do you want us to pay you?' we heard a deep heavy voice asking us. We looked around and saw a couple of guys standing six feet away behind us.

'Gotiya, are you sure this is that boy?' One of them asked the other and they walked a little closer towards us. When their faces were visible I realized I had seen them before somewhere but couldn't recall where.

'Hey guys what's up....what happened? Tell us no, brothers?' Mohit said. I could smell fear in his voice.

'You know who I am? I am Shiva. Bhau's son! *Saang yaala Gotiya, mee kon aahes*'(tell him Gotiya, who I am!)

'Oh I know you, I know you sir. I have read a lot about you in the newspaper. I am Mohit and am from the Delhi, how are you sir? What's the matter?'

'No problem kids. I just want to see your phones. Just that we think you might know someone you should not. Let me check your phones.' Gotiya said. We handed over our phones to them; obviously we didn't know anyone who could be their enemy. He took the phones from us and began checking them. Then suddenly he bent down to squat. He picked up a big rock from the ground and right in front of our eyes banged it on our phones, one by one. Our phones were shattered to pieces.

'*Arre* sir! What are you doing,' I was shouting. I was very angry.

But I realised Mohit whispering, 'It's some shitty shit Anuj. Let's run. Now! I have heard it's no big deal for him to bloody kill, he can kill us too and get away with it.' I got scared for my life and decided to pay heed to Mohit's advice. We ran away from there but two more guys who stood at the exit caught hold of us.

Shit Mohit is right! This is some big trouble, I thought.

'How long has it been going on?' Shiva asked me and then slapped me so hard that I felt like my cheek was on fire.

'What are you talking about?' I asked barely able to talk.

'Since when do you know my Sandy? Were you in Goa too with her? Tell me now?' Shiva was shouting at the top of his voice. And then I realized I had seen them both staring at me in the pub while I kissed Sandy goodbye. It gave me shivers. It seemed like a case of a jilted lover and not any jilted lover but a powerful politician's son. Anything was possible now, even death.

'Look there has been a mistake I met her only today for the f—f-first time, ask my friend.' but then he slapped my around 5-6 times continuously. I couldn't feel one side of my face not even my ear. My mouth began to bleed.

'You have no idea what I could do. I have been looking for you for 2 months now.' he said and at that moment an SUV arrived. Around five more guys came up in, all dressed in white with a tilak on their foreheads. Shiva hugged one of them, who looked like their leader.

'Vishnu, *haech aahe toh*!(he is the one!)' Shiva told him.

'Oh these…Oh you have called me here for these two *lukhas*? Chi! What Shiva? Why can't you deal with such things on your own, haan? Why can't you just fucking shoot such assholes, haan? *O Patil gun de re maazi* (Patil, give me my gun)'.

'Sir, sir what are you doing we are like your sons. There has been some mistake. Trust me we don't know her at all. We saw her only today. Trust me I am a manager with a bank, we are from good families.' Mohit said while he was held by his arms by two guys behind him.

'Okay okay..you seem nice but what you did wasn't nice. But, I will let you go..*ae zau de re yaana* (let them go).'

'Thank you so much sir.' we both said and felt relieved.

'Just one thing, You come here.' he pointed towards me, 'This guy Shiva here. He is like my kid, more than a son. I don't like it when he is in pain.'

Then what he did was unbelievable. In one motion he removed a pistol from his pocket in the kurta and pointed it towards my leg. I felt a surge of panic in every cell of my body but yet something told me that he wouldn't shoot. *This isn't a movie; people don't go shooting around others over trivial matters.* Then I heard a small click and in a split of a second I felt a sharp object exploding into my thigh.

The bastard had shot me.

The bullet hit the bone in my thigh. A second later when the pain registered it was so unbearable that I thought I was dying and I started screaming my lungs out. One guy held my mouth tightly. Mohit too started screaming and in a moment of panic he let loose and started to run away as fast as possible. But he was chased down and overpowered by two of them.

I was on the ground now, my vision blurred and last thing I remembered before passing out was that they were kicking Mohit in his stomach. He had given up and was motionless. He didn't make any sound and was bearing the kicks in silence, his face covered in mud and blood.

When I regained consciousness, I was on the backseat of a car and Mohit was bundled next to me. Our hands, feet were tied and mouths were gagged. When Mohit saw me conscious he let out a sigh of relief. Maybe he had thought that I had died. I could see tears rolling down his cheeks in fear. The pain I felt was unbearable. I knew that another hour like this and I would die with either the pain or an infection.

'Now what to do Gaikwad sahib? *Zaala tar zaala aata kaay karaycha te saanga?*(what has happened has happened, now tell me what to do?)' Vishnu was asking someone from the police on his phone. 'Oh! I guess we have to do that. There seems to be no other option. I don't want Bhau to know about this! What to do! You know how my rage is uncontrollable. But you have to give me your word that you will take care of it…hhmm…haan haan..okay..okay I will do it and call you.' he said and then looked at the guy driving, 'Take the car to Marve creek, fast.' Mohit began to cry uncontrollably and my heart beat began to beat faster. We knew they had planned to kill us and throw our bodies into a creek. I could only think of my parents.

What a way to die. They will never come to know how it all happened.

Now I could never give the fifty thousand rupee check to my mom! We both began to frantically move our bodies to untie ourselves but to no avail. After a while, we gave up. I felt terrible for Mohit because he was in this situation because of me and was going to die, all because of me. And I had thought *if I die tomorrow no issues* while kissing Sandy a couple of hours back.

Well, God you do hear me, don't you? I thought, *although at your own convenience! And if you hear me, please save me and my friend tonight, we don't wanna die like this, not now, please god, please …* tears were now rolling down my cheeks too. And as soon I finished praying, our car came to a screeching halt.

Guess we have reached our final destination, I thought.

But nobody moved an inch in the car. We heard no doors open.

'*He kon aahes* (who is he)?' someone said nervously in the car. I used all my energy to lift my head up to see. But I couldn't see as all the tears had blurred my vision. After 3-4 seconds when my eyesight adjusted I couldn't believe what my eyes were showing me.

I blinked twice to reassure myself thinking I could be hallucinating. But I wasn't.

There in front of the car, in the middle of the road was Anthony D'cunha. Standing alone.

I saw his bike fallen on the road behind him and those veins swelling on his forehead. A small sense of hopefulness rose in me but I knew that what he would try to pull off was impossible. Mohit lifted his head to see him and I guess said 'bloody fuck' in a muffled voice. Anthony then put his hands behind him and took out a bamboo stick and threw it on the car's windshield so hard that it broke the glass into pieces. The guys from the car all ran out to tackle him. *'Gooli maar re madarchodla* (shoot the mutherfucker)'. Anthony, screamed loudly and got hold of the bamboo stick again and hit two of them on their heads so hard that they bundled on the road bleeding. Once they fell on the road they didn't move.

'C'mon man! Anthony c'mon', I tried to shout even with my mouth gagged. My chances of coming out alive had increased, albeit marginally.

Vishnu hurriedly put his hand in his pocket to remove his gun. But before he could get to his weapon Anthony roared loudly and leaped at him with force. Immediately, he took him down and began punching on his face. The other guys, Shiva and Gotya grabbed hold of Anthony from behind to pull him away. They pulled him so hard that Anthony fell some feet away and landed on his forehead which began to bleed immensely.

'Oh fuck! That's it! Now even Anthony will die with us!

All three of them stood close to Anthony who was lying face down at their feet.

*'bhadwe madarchod…*You think you are a hero! I am going to kill you first here before your friends.' Vishnu said and he put his

hand in his pocket to get out the gun. Instead, he started fumbling and trying to search his other pockets.

Anthony lying below gave out a laugh. He got one hand out from under his chest. In his hand was the gun. He slowly stood up and pointed the gun at them.

'Mereko maarega?…mere doston ko maarega….?' And he fired a shot which zipped past the Vishnu's ear. He looked as if he had peed in his pants.

'*Ae* look..look..we don't know you..we we can talk about this.. you d---don't know who I am?' Shiva said, 'You can get in big trouble for this…just hand over the gun to me and leave. No one will do anything to you..I give you my word'.

'*Tu koi bhi ho*…Do you know who *I* am?' Anthony said and I realized even I didn't have an answer for that, 'and If you know you will run away from here.' Then Anthony came towards us all the time pointing the gun at them. Anthony opened the boot of the car and came towards us. He untied Mohit with one hand and the other still pointed the gun at them. 'Mohit untie Anuj.'

'S..ssure Anthony. You Just get their mobiles here.' Mohit said.

'Mohit use my phone, I have balance, I had recharged in …'

'No bro, just get their phones so that they don't ask for any backup..that's what they did'.

'Oh! Okay'. Anthony collected their phones and Mohit untied me.

'I will take the bike and you drive the car.' Anthony told Mohit.

'Let's first go to a hospital' Mohit said and kicked the splintered windshield and the rest of the cracked glass fell down to give a clear view. Anthony rode straight ahead, in front of us. Suddenly his bike move towards the left of the road. Anthony turned his head and looked back from the moving bike. I saw rage in his eyes. He looked like a man about to do something drastic, just on an impulse. He took out the gun and I heard that familiar sound of a tick again. I spun my head around in a flash to look behind. Vishnu held his leg tightly and was screaming aloud as blood poured out of his thigh.

'Oh fuck, no Anthony, why man!' I cried

'Bloody fuck! Let's leave..fast Anthony..fast' Mohit screamed. Anthony and he took shortcuts to reach a hospital. On reaching Mohit said 'I don't think it's a good idea..It will be a police case and they have the police in their pockets…..wait, I know where to go.' We dumped the car at the hospital and went on Anthony's bike to Mohit's cousin's house who was a nurse. It took us another 15 minutes to reach her place.

His cousin who lived alone opened the door 'Oh Jesus, Mohit what happened to you.' she said looking at Mohit's face which looked he had played Holi with mud and red colour

'Don't worry about the me Sherly; I first need you to take care of my friend here. He has been shot in the thigh. I will explain everything to you later.' She then made a shallow cut in my thigh to get the bullet out. She put antiseptic on my deep wound. And I felt hundred times more pain than when bullet had hit me. But I was glad that for the moment we were safe in Sherly's house who was really being a sister to us. She then stitched my wound and took care of Mohit's cuts and wounds. Anthony only needed a dressing on his forehead. We explained everything to Sherly and Anthony.

'I have informed Aman, he is on his way here.' Anthony told us.

Anthony then told us that on the way back after buying beers they had seen us in the car going in their opposite direction. Seeing the way we were tied and Mohit crying, Aman had decided to note the car's number the car and go to the police station while Anthony decided to keep a track of where the vehicle was taking us by chasing the car. 'Then I don't know what happened I thought it could get too late and I had to do something myself and overtook the car. I couldn't see my friends die like this and the thought that I didn't try would have haunted me forever. Then after tackling them I saw these fuckers had shot Anuj in the leg. I knew I had to give it back'.

'Anthony come here', I said and I hugged him tight and didn't let go of him for some time. I was choked with emotion. What this man had done, even a real brother couldn't have. The stud had taken five men down alone. Five goons who were happy to shoot and had guns. He used to say that he was very strong but we always took it lightly. That night he showed that not only did he have the power of a lion but its heart too.

'Bro, Anthony if it's possible', said Mohit who went down on his knees and joined his hands in front of him. His voice was quivering, 'Please forgive me if you can for the whatever a nonsense I spoke to you. You are not a mad but a brave loving boy who is more than brother to me. My life is indebted to you henceforth.' Anthony smiled, his eyes misty too, 'It's okay re..forget about it'

Mohit went over to him and embraced him tightly and said what seemed like the most appropriate thing at that time,

' Anthony, *Tu mera bhai hai*............'

'The Police suck man! As soon as they knew whose car it was, they started coming up with weird excuses and told me to go home or else they would lock me up too.' Aman said. He had arrived at Sherly's place half an hour after us. All that while he had tried to contact people for help but no one came except for Guru and Vinod.

'The only problem is', Guru said, 'that Anthony made a mistake by shooting Vishnu. Or the matter could have died down. This guy Vishnu is the man Bhau goes to eliminate people. He is untouchable for the Police and he would want revenge. He will surely come after you guys.' then Guru paused for a moment and continued, 'But you guys are in luck. I know Bhau very well. A common friend had told me that he wanted to meet me to resolve an embarrassing sore issue in his life. He had told me that his second wife who was very young and pretty wasn't really showing much interest in him. I had guided him and she, as things would have it, fell for him big time. He was ecstatic and thanked me a lot showering me with expensive gifts and more importantly had told me that whenever i needed a favour I could call him. I guess the time has come'. Guru then went over to the farthest corner of the room where he would be inaudible to us and dialled Bhau's number. After about half a minute, it seemed somebody answered the call and Guru began talking on the phone. I looked at the time and it was 4.30 am. Surely, he really liked Guru. We were all glued to Guru's facial expressions to get any hint we could about how the conversation went. When Guru was done he looked at us and smiled, 'Bhau was cursing his own son and Vishnu. He said to get you guys in hospital right now and he would even pay the bills! Come on, let's go!'

We heaved a sigh of relief and thanked Guru. But before we left I had another very important person to thank, Sherly.

'You are like a sister to me, I will always be grateful to you for saving my life.'

She only smiled in acceptance of my gratitude.

We went back to the same hospital where Mohit and I were admitted without any police enquiry. We didn't have to think too hard about the reason for that.

I was put on the drip as I had lost a lot of blood and was very weak. Mohit's nose was fractured and even he needed to be admitted. Anthony and Aman slept next to us in the hospital.

In the Morning, Guru came over and visited us.

'Hey guys look who I have with me.' he said and behind him I saw a huge man who wore a white pyjama and kurta. He had a thick moustache and his skin was dark with even darker patches on his forehead. I saw a familiar tilak on his forehead. He looked dangerous and intimidating but the moment he smiled it seemed that you would never meet a more charming man.

'Hello Anuj. Hello Mohit. Guru told me what my son and Vishnu did to both of you yesterday.' Bhau said, sitting between our beds, holding our hands. His hands felt coarse. 'I am really sorry sons. Guru is one of the nicest guys I have met and he said you are like his brothers. Guru's brothers, my brothers! haha! But it's very good, haha...I like it! These things should not happen in this age haha' He gifted Mohit and me top notch Phones.

'Thank you Bhau..what has happened has happened. Even though it seemed your son was hurt by a girl.' Mohit said.

'I know! How many times have I told him to leave that girl alone! But he is mad and does whatever he wants because he knows Vishnu will save his ass....anyways where is that guy, what's his name...Anthony?' When Anthony walked into the room Bhau went over and hugged him, 'Oh my son! I am proud of you. People like you are rare. You didn't care for your own life and what you did was the bravest thing I have heard of. Look, if you want, you can work with me whenever you want. I need men like you with me.'

'Oh I will tell you sir, give me some time. The thing is, I haven't cleared my final year and all, so the documents could be a problem.'

said Anthony. Bhau looked puzzled at the answer. He left after another 10-15 minutes of chit chat.

I knew one thing for sure. That I had best people in the world as my friends. Our friendship was strong but Anthony had just made us come closer. It was one of the weirdest 12 hours of my life where I felt so many extreme emotions. It all began with the excitement of making out with one of the hottest woman in India , helping Guru win, becoming famous world over for that and then the feeling of staring at your death. The thought that, *this is it! Now, I die.* And then seeing your friend fight it out for you, putting his own life at risk! Later a stranger putting you back together without questions, Guru bailing us out and then Bhau showing so much affection towards us.

Then I thought about my mom. I knew she wouldn't believe that all this really happened and ask me when I was taking up my next job. I knew my check could be the answer to her questions.

'I think it's time.' Aman said as we were sitting in the smoking zone in TST.

'Time for what?' I asked stubbing the cigarette under my foot. I felt only a tinge of pain in my thigh.

'Anuj, it's time I teach Vinita a thing or two about heartbreak and cheating others. Girls like her should know that it just isn't right. For them, it's a joke but guys like me live with the pain for a long time.'

'What are you going to do about it?'

'I need help. And I will take it from Guru….haha, she is so screwed!'

I understood what he meant completely.

It was almost two weeks and this was the first time I had stepped out of my house. We were waiting for Guru to arrive. This was also the first time we were going to interact with him in TST.

'Anuj, can you walk properly?' Guru asked.

'I am okay just a little limp.'

'We can get that to work for you. It will make for a great opener!'

'Oh yeah.. We can. I thought about it too.' I lied trying to create an impression.

'Guru sir, err..can I ask you a question...I mean..if, if you don't mind..it's just..', Aman fumbled for the words.

'Relax! Yeah, tell me!' Guru said

'The thing is my ex- girlfriend treated me badly and later cheated on me big time..she literally used and dumped me. I want to teach her a lesson now. I want her to fall head over heels for me and this time I will dump her.' Aman said with a killer instinct that was visible.

'I see. And what will you achieve with that?'

'Me? Oh I will be at peace. And besides she will also become a better person'.

'Did you become a better person when she cheated on you? All you have become is bitter. You just want revenge and feel good so don't hide behind that you want to do it for her. See the thing is, we all know that something isn't correct in a relationship yet we continue with it because of our own weaknesses. The world is such that if you are vulnerable and the moment people smell it they will take you for a ride and when you give them a hint that you are okay with it, they continue taking advantage of you. So it's as much as your fault as her's, you should have got out the day she treated you badly.'

'Oh come on! Guru Sir!' Aman stood up, fuming, 'What is with you and all this morality?'

'*Oye*, Aman quiet! Do you have any idea about what you are saying?' I tried to stop him.

'Anuj please let him speak.' Guru said, sternly.

'Sir, do you really know how much pain the girls are giving to guys out there, right now, as we talk? Do they care about us? Do they sit and rationalize as you are doing? They just say oh that guy is a loser and fall for the next stud without blinking an eye. Do you have any idea sir how much pain that girl gave me. I opened my heart to her and became vulnerable because I loved her and I thought that's what people in love do. But she took advantage of me so bad. Aren't people supposed to accept their partner's anger and tantrums in love? What wrong did I do by loving even her flaws?' his voice was wobbly now, 'How the fuck would I know that there are rules here too? All I wanted was her to love me for the way I am and I thought she did. Because, she told me so. Every fucking day, every night, over the phone. How would have I known that she was lying to me? Had she told me even once that she didn't feel anything for me I would have stepped away immediately, I loved her that much. But why cheat? Why fool someone like this? And the fact is that even now when I am alone all I think about is her! And now yes I want her to feel the way I did. First the feeling of love and then the feeling of being used.' I knew he wasn't entirely wrong. I never thought of people as good or bad because everyone had their side to the story but that girl had evil in her. I knew that much.

'Oh man!! Hey sit down. Have some water.' and Guru threw a water bottle at him. Aman drank a little and some over his face.

Mohit and Anthony entered.

'What's up Sir, how are you? Oh! Aman is crying again, haha! Hey Anuj, nice shirt!' Mohit said.

'Yeah after Aman is done with his crying, I have a question to ask, Guru.' said Anthony. Aman in tears was too much of a regular sight for us and nobody seemed to give a fuck anymore.

'Look Aman, I see your point. We can work something out. But if you thinking of hurting her badly or leaving a scar in her life forever, that would be uncool and I would personally kick your crying ass.' Aman lit up hearing that.

'Thank you Guru Sir, Thank you..and no I have nothing so bad in my mind!'

'Oh wow! That is really good and I also have something in mind ..hahaha, I will ask later', Mohit said.

'Guru I have a question as I may have brought that up a little while ago when Aman was crying and all as usual and then you started talking, remember? and then Mohit started to talk...' said Anthony

'Anthony, just ask man!' Guru shouted.

'Okay, here I go, from day one I was wondering what are all those accessories in that room, all those cool hats and boots...much like what David wears. When are we going to use all that?' Anthony asked.

Guru thought about it for a while and then said, 'Actually it's good you brought that up. Okay so I have to go to a Mall for some shopping and I want you guys to tag along. Anthony, you will Bling up', Guru said.

'Awesome! That will be fun.' Mohit said.

'Hey wait. What is bling up by the way?' Anthony asked.

'It's putting on interesting things that will bring all the attention towards you. I used to do a lot of that earlier. Now I haven't done that in a long time. But only one guy in a group can bling up or we all look like a bunch of faggots!' said Guru.

'No no, I thought that we could all dress like that, I am not blinging up alone and all.'

'You have to, you don't have a choice, do you?' Guru said.

Guru shopped for himself and we made a mental note about his taste. I noticed that not even once did he look at the price tags.

Anthony was made to wear a long coat which reached his boots. He had a hat on and wore dark shades. His hair was open. He wore black, from head to toe. He looked like an alien let loose in the mall. The fact that Anthony could never walk slow also added to the attention he attracted. A lot of young kids wanted to play with him. Some were hanging on to his coat and some asked him whether he could fly. Then Anthony and I went into a book store. Anthony started checking out some books on science fiction next to a beautiful girl with spectacles. She looked at him and burst out laughing while Anthony grinned and began to walk away from there.

'Hey I am sorry, didn't mean to offend you by laughing ....' she said in a sexy voice.

'Oh that's okay. So how do you mean to offend me?' Anthony asked visibly agitated at being laughed at the whole day.

'No, I didn't mean it like that! I am sorry, again!' she said and paused, 'but you will admit that it is a little strange way to dress unless you are doing some show for kids in the mall, hehe.' the girl said.

'I know. My friends wanted to me wear this and all. They think it looks cool on me. But I know it looks stupid. Hey you want to grab a coffee?'

'What? Why? You got me wrong here.' she asked a little in anger.

'Because when we can talk over a coffee and when we run out of topics, we can start having sips before we have something else to talk about again.'

'What? You know what! What the heck, let's go. I can use some coffee now and you seem pretty harmless too!'

'I may look harmless but I am very dangerous and all *re*. I shoot people when I am angry', Anthony said.

'Haha! You are funny too! Let's go, can't wait!'

While Anthony had coffee with the beautiful and sexy babe I joined Aman and Mohit who were with Guru in the same coffee shop. We sat at a distance from them. Guru wasn't analysing and judging because he wanted Anthony to be at ease. After 40 minutes or so Anthony came over to us and flashed her phone number. He had got himself a date with a girl who was clearly out of his league. The rest of us didn't want to game anyone right now because we had so much to ask Guru. Especially Aman. He asked Guru about what his approach should be with Vinita.

'You've got to show her that you have a backbone, that you are a man not only because of the thing hanging out of your crotch but in essence. It's simple. A man loves a woman, a woman loves a man.' Guru said and we all pulled our chairs closer to him because for us, it was gold dust.

He continued, 'No matter how much women harp about equality, a woman would always want her man to lead, to show her the directions. Hmm..See when a woman insults her man, let's say in an argument and the man doesn't really get upset about it, she would say things like 'Aww..you are the only one who accepts me the way I am, but actually from her insides she wants you not to accept such behaviour. See, you need to have a life too. I mean you cannot have a life around her and trust me she would be the happiest if both of you get enough space. If she misuses the space, obviously consider yourself lucky that you found out soon enough and move on. I always tell my students don't cheat in a committed relationship and don't accept it either. And yes Aman, there is a way you can get your ex back, no matter what had happened, who dumped who, nothing matters. But I seldom share this because such knowledge can be dangerous.' Mohit and Aman were clearly beaming. And I was thinking of Richa.

'Have you the used it Guru Sir? We knew that even you have a past and that..' Mohit was saying when Guru interrupted him

'I don't talk about it. Never ask me about my personal life, is it clear?' Guru retorted, his face flushed with annoyance.

'Oh no, I am a sorry.. I didn't mean to.' Mohit managed.

'Okay guys I have to go now, I will be in Bangalore for a boot camp. I will come back and we will take it from there Aman. And Anthony… what's wrong with you? Never dress like that ever, who tells you to go out like that?' Guru said, tongue in cheek and left.

When Guru left we sat in a restaurant for drinks and dinner. We could afford that now, at least for some days.

'I guess the coming days will be more exciting.' Aman said taking a sip of the chilled beer, 'There is a way you can get your ex back, Guru Sir said, hahaha'. When people are happy they smile or at best have a glow on their face, but this guy laughed. Aloud.

'You bet and fix.' Mohit, who looked equally happy, said. Whatever Mohit meant by that I knew they were right. Getting your ex back has never been a cake walk for anyone in the world and Guru said he knew how to do that. Everyday unintentionally I was making him my role model. I wanted to be like him, acquire his brain, his body-language and his calm rock-like self-confidence. And more than anything I wanted to be like him because that man was not a con artist. Among the thousands of men around the world from the community who took pride in tricking women into attraction, love or beds, Guru was someone who understood women; that they get hurt too. Yet, that guy was a genius, miles ahead of anyone. And how lucky were Aman and Mohit that now they would get a shot at something very few people get. Coming out of my thoughts I realised Mohit wasn't around at the table. I looked around for him and saw him at table with two pretty girls, talking to them. Gaming them. There was no stopping us now.

'Toast to us, we are the Best!' Anthony said raising his glass and Aman and I joined.

'I think that now we can get any girl! It's all cool but promise me guys that we would play the game only ethically as Guru says. That man has spent years on the ethical game and we should carry his torch ahead. I will personally sleep better if I know that I am not hurting anyone.' I said.

'Oh you don't wanna hurt the girls. Let's first stop them hurting us Anuj! But forget that, right now it feels awesome man! We can get any girl interested in us anywhere, anytime, so cheers to that feeling!' As soon as Aman said this we saw the manager walking towards us,

'Sir, I am sorry but you have to leave the restaurant now, your friend has been very indecent and impolite with a couple of our lady guests and the girls are uncomfortable with your presence too.'

I hurriedly looked around to see Mohit but he wasn't there anywhere. Then I saw him outside through the glass wall waving at us, giving us the stupidest smile. We had no option but to leave.

'Bloody fuck guys. I was just trying the anchoring method of David and was trying a hand gesture. But they thoughted that it was a masturbation gesture. Such women don't deserve to have a sex.' Mohit explained.

Clearly we had jumped the gun about us being players and gamers. We still had a long way to go.

❧

'You have to tell me everything', Guru told Aman in a small cabin where strangely even I was invited.

Guru had come back in the morning from Bangalore and finished with a training session with a group of foreigners who had come from the world over. Aman gave Guru every minute detail and even I was surprised about the things Aman hadn't shared with us like Vinita being nice to him only during his salary days and making him shop for her while his family's financial situation was such that they could use every penny that came their way. That girl was surely a bitch.

'Hmm, let's see. She obviously isn't high on morals or sensitivity. Anyways our job is to now make her fall for you and then make her realize how it feels to be on the other side. So hear me out, first of all we need to change you from the inside. Grab a pen and paper and write down what I say.

1: You have to pretend that you are high on self-confidence. You will slowly start believing in your own lie.

2: You have to behave in a little self-absorbed manner and in tune and present in your own reality.

3: You have to stop smiling too much. I want you to maintain a deadpan expression so that it's difficult to know about what's going on in your head.

4: You need to understand that although you love women you would never chase them. When I say chase, I don't mean pursue. There is a difference.

5: You won't accept any behaviour which you dislike even remotely. You will express your dislike at that moment.

6: When texting a girl, the sentence shouldn't be more than one line. Maximum two lines

7: Finish the call first. You are busy and have other important things in life too.

8: Always try to be happy, gleeful and energetic from inside. But show little outside.

9: Don't get angry or emotional with what girls do. Sometimes they want that from you.

10: When you want a girl, convince yourself that you don't.

Aman couldn't wipe off the smile he had while writing down all that.

'Will you stop grinning? Why do you keep on smiling for no reason at times?' Guru asked but I knew what the reason was. Revenge was on his mind and now he was sure he was going to get it.

'And now I want you to add some of her friends on the Facebook'.

'Ok, but why would any of her friends accept my friend's request?' Aman asked.

'You guys are fucking amateurs, aren't you?' Guru said and took us to his office. Aman logged into his Facebook account on Guru's Laptop. Guru took over from there and began looking out for hot girls in Vinita's friends list. He zeroed down on one Chaitali Bose and Aman confirmed that she was one of her best friends. He clicked on 'Add Friend' and typed a message along with the request.

Hi Chaitali. I want to talk to you about something you won't believe. But under an oath that you wouldn't disclose what I am going to tell you to anyone. Add me immediately so that we could chat.

'That's superb! How can a woman refuse to acknowledge a statement pregnant with gossip.' I said and gave Aman a high five.

Within minutes she accepted the friend request and replied

Hey it's nice to hear from you. Where have you been man? And what's that you want to tell me about?

Now Guru went on chat mode and continued chatting from Aman's profile.

Aman: 'It's nice to hear from you too. You are one of the sweetest girls I have known. Well, I have been working in TCS for the last year and you?' (He was building up on the excitement by not breaking the suspense soon)

Chaitali: I have finished a course in Fashion Designing. Aman, you were going to tell me something.

Aman: Yeah, but on second thoughts I wonder if I should tell you this! Since it's about someone who is a very close friend of yours and you are a girl, you know what I mean? L What if you tell her that I said so and so?'

Chaitali: No baba…just tell me now!!

Aman: See the deal is this. Vinita, your best friend isn't someone you can trust. She spoke so negatively about you when we were together. She said that you were interested in me and every other guy she liked. But forget that, the main thing I want to tell you is not this. Oops my boss is around so give me five minutes.

Chailtali: R u serious? Okay I am waiting

'But what if she asks Vinita about this? Then I am screwed right?' Aman asked Guru.

'Okay, you do it Aman! no, no you do it..you know better, isn't it?'

Aman said. 'No I didn't mean it that way..er..obviously you you h..have something more in your..in your..'

'So what did you mean?'

'No sir, I was thinking …'

'Please be clear about what you want. What were you thinking?' Guru asked.

I sat there next to them with a hand on my forehead. When Aman and Guru got into this awkward question answer mode, they took forever to come out of it. And it was always meaningless. Luckily Guru decided to continue with the chat.

Aman: 'Yeah. Where were we? Yeah, she said that she hated you but still had to be with you only out of sympathy because you didn't have a lot of friends and that you are socially challenged. That had me shaken up man. How could someone be so demeaning about her best friend? And today somehow I was thinking about what she did to me and I realized that in a way even she is doing the same with you.'

Chaitali: 'You know Aman, I am not really surprised. I have been thinking, she isn't the person she pretends she is. I have heard this from a couple of the other friends too. She is a super-bitch!

Guru explained, 'Guys relax, don't get too impressed with me. See, Aman you already told me about your ex's bitchy nature and c'mon it's any one's guess that she would do this with others as well and even bitch about them. Now you and Chaitali have one thing in common. Your enemy'

Aman: 'Oh my god, is it? I will tell you a lot more later. Anyways my intention is not to break your friendship with her it's just that I want you to keep your eyes and ears open. Wait, you know what, remember we all had gone for a movie in town once and you were wearing a little short skirt...oops boss around..gimme like 15 minutes..i will be back.

Chaitali: Aman, give me your number, you have too many distractions in your office.

Then Guru typed in Aman's phone number. She called back 30 minutes later. Aman said everything that Guru had instructed him to.

'You know what', Aman took a deep sigh, 'I always wanted to get Vinita back in my life; I was ready to forgive her. But guess what? *She* called me a week back saying that she wanted to be back too. Strangely I said no. Maybe I was just confused in the past about wanting her back.' By telling Chaitali that her enemy, Vinita, liked Aman even today, a door of revenge was shown to her. Aman and Chaitali spoke everyday over the phone talking about each other now. Guru had warned Aman not to fall for Chaitali if he wanted to get Vinita back. And Chaitali meanwhile had kept all her interactions with Vinita at a formal level.

Whenever Chaitali posted something on FB, Guru told Aman to comment. Then Chaitali would respond and Aman would reply. Chailtali's updates now had only long conversation threads between Aman and her. She was intentionally flirting online with Aman to get back at Vinita, because she knew Vinita could read her posts as she was on her friends list too. Sometimes Chaitali would say 'Hey enough for now. Call me NOW, I am waiting!' Aman would reply 'Oh yeah? Baby, give me minute'. A week passed and another of Guru's prophecy came true. Vinita called up Chaitali to ask whether she was dating Aman. Chaitali told her that they weren't now but since she was attracted to him, who knew what lay ahead. Vinita tried to dissuade Chaitali by telling her how big a loser Aman was and how he would get too lovey-dovey later. Clearly, Vinita was jealous now. Guru's theory of displaying pre-selection had worked. Women respond to men who seem attractive to other women, especially their competition. They then want to find out why and what is so special in him. Besides the ego rush of getting something much in demand makes them lose the power to think logically, as attraction takes over. It also explained why a lot of women fall for married men. He told Aman to take 'pre-selection' a notch higher. They would go to different pubs where Guru would game women and make them click pictures with Aman. Aman's profile had pictures with some of the hottest women; some with their arms around him, some pictures with a group of 6-8 women all around Aman with him in the centre. Because of these pictures, a lot of other cool women began accepting Aman's friend requests as they thought of him as a star! At least on Facebook. After a couple of weeks, when Aman opened his profile he couldn't believe his eyes. There was a friends request from Vinita with a message

'Ahem ahem..Someone is very popular these days. Actually I am kinda missing you. Just kidding! Wonder why it all happened….Call me at this number, Vinita.'

Aman just kept staring at the monitor and didn't move. Slowly he walked towards Guru, his face devoid of any emotion and bent over to touch his feet 'Guru Sir, you are great' and went back to where he was sitting.

'Whoa..whoa! What's wrong Aman? You are scaring us now?' Guru said.

'Sir, it's you who told me not to smile much or display much emotion.' Aman said and continued with a straight face, 'I am cool but in my mind I have torn my shirt , rolled on the floor and cried a bucket but I am cool.' and he continued looking at the screen with a deadpan face.

The music was easy on the ears as Kenny g's saxophone in the background made the evening very pleasant. We were having dinner on a rooftop restaurant which overlooked the sea. The beautiful sound of the waves, blending perfectly with the music, made for a relaxed ambience. But what made the evening more pleasant for Aman was that two hot women were competing for his attention. Guru had told me to accompany Aman when he would meet Vinita and Chaitali. It wasn't for Aman's moral support. It was a strategic move.

Chaitali and Aman had already met a couple of times before this for shopping and movies. They had hit off brilliantly as friends. But as a side effect of all these mind games and Aman coming close to her, yet keeping himself at a distance had created a strong attraction in Chaitali for him although she had never expressed it in words. Vinita had met Aman briefly for half an hour over coffee couple of days back and she was weighing him from head to toe. Aman had maintained a distant attitude and indicated that he had come to meet her just to kill time. When Chaitali had objected at Aman being friends with Vinita, he had simply told her that he had forgiven her and she just wanted to be friends in a platonic way.

Now, sitting in the restaurant I noticed how amazingly hot Vinita looked. From the last time I had seen her she had put on weight in the right places. She looked curvier and smoking hot. She wore dark red lipstick and a dress of similar shade with a deep neck showing ample cleavage and had left her flowing hair open. She looked like the goddess of seduction. Chailtali herself had come with the intention of outdoing Vinita. She wore a black dress which ended just below her butt revealing her voluptuous thighs. Although she wasn't as busty as Vinita, there was something about her slim waist and a perfect butt that made her look like an hour glass. Her smooth voice and deep eyes only added to her lightning sex appeal. If god were to come down and ask any man which of the two he would want, he would have told him to either give him both of them or neither. Both looked amazingly desirable and every man in the restaurant was secretly checking them out. And they were here to win Aman over. *Who can understand the nuances of life!* I thought. *Maybe Guru*, I smirked to myself.

We started off with wine.

'Aman you remember I was telling you about that movie, now I remember what its name is! *Life Stinks*. It is so hilarious! Compare it with the movie we saw last week, duh!' Chaitali said.

'Oh, you bet. Bollywood is churning flops by the week man.' Aman said looking away and kept his arm over the sofa behind me. His body language was that of an Alpha male. He had followed every minute detail that Guru had instructed him with.

Vinita feeling left out said, 'My all-time favourite movie is Titanic.' Aman spit out the drink and began laughing.

'Why? What is so funny Aman?' yapped Vinita

'Nothing, the drink is a little weird; you are alright.'

Conversations like these went on for another fifteen minutes or so. Everyone was playing mind games there. Aman and Chaitali were ignoring Vinita big-time without making it obvious. So she started talking more to me and even trying to flirt a little with me to make Aman feel jealous, as Guru had predicted. My job was to react strongly first as if to be happy by her attention. Then slowly I was supposed to pretend that she was boring me and behave as if I were not interested. Then she would have no option but to seek validation from Aman directly. Guru told us that a woman is at her vulnerable best when she thinks that she is coming across as a bore. It would be useless if you shout at her, scream her, push her for attention but if you pretend that you are ignoring her not out of anger or punishment but because she bores you, her mind gets into a frenzy and her ego would take over making her do anything to get back your attention.

Vinita spoke about how she and I were so similar in nature and that we should meet more often. I showed that I was more than glad at that suggestion. Then she insisted that we exchange numbers.

Aman made it a point that every time Vinita spoke to me he stopped his conversation with Chaitali and listened. That again was a ploy so that Vinita was misled into believing that her efforts of making Aman jealous were working. Knowing her, Guru had said, she would take jealousy part a notch higher because ultimately her goal wouldn't be to get love from Aman but his attention. If she got attention from Aman, it would be enough to satisfy her ego and answer her questions about her own self. And that's what she did. After a point when the wine had given her enough kick, she held my hand, 'Anuj, your eyes…they are so beautiful'. Aman leaned back as if angered by what she was doing and kept his glass hard on the table. Vinita then gave a sharp look at Chaitali and smiled as if to tell her that she had conquered the evening.

'Anuj darling, would you be kind enough as to escort me to the ladies room?' Vinita asked.

'Oh sure, why not.' and I walked her to the ladies room. To my utter surprise I wasn't feeling nervous at all, even with a hot girl like Vinita. Maybe I knew that irrespective of whether she liked or disliked me, she would make her moves. I knew it wasn't about me, it was all about her. Her ego, her battle and her self-esteem. There was no one outside the ladies room and sensing that the opportunity was right she literally jumped on me. She held my head tight and kissed me. Then she put her tongue inside me and I felt as if a snake had entered my mouth. My hands squeezed her gorgeous boobs and I was mesmerised. I was having a blast and wanted to throw her on the floor and fuck her guts out when I realised what I was supposed to do and with a heavy heart and a hard dick I made a sacrifice for my friend. Besides I had sworn to play the game ethically,

'Wait, wait, Vinita, something is wrong'

'Why what's wrong?'

'I don't know I am not feeling anything. I mean I don't feel aroused at all. Sorry sweetie'

'What? Are you fucking gay?' she said loudly and a woman passing us by to go to the loo, smirked. I felt the blood rush to my head and I wanted to jump as high in the air and punch her head on the way down. But instead I imagined what Guru would have done in this situation and I just smiled and walked away seeming perfectly cool. I came back to our table where the meal was served. Vinita joined in after 10 minutes or so. She had retouched her makeup and looked gorgeous and although I was still livid at that remark she had made, I couldn't control the attraction I felt towards her. I watched her eat with head down and looking a tad distracted. I realized again how stunningly attractive she was. *Had you married her Aman, our friendship would have been in trouble*, I thought. For a brief moment I considered apologizing to her and requesting her to continue with what I had stopped. But I took a heavy breath and decided to focus on the beach in front of me.

You owe me big time Aman, son of a bitch!

In the meantime Aman and Chaitali were talking, laughing, joking all the while. Vinita was rather quiet for the rest of the evening and left hurriedly after finishing the dinner. Aman and I dropped Chaitali home. While entering her building she stopped and turned around to look at Aman. Aman gave her the most honest smile and waved at her. I knew I was looking at two people in love. Aman then hugged me tight and I felt happy for him. Suddenly Vinita's statement *'Are you fucking gay?'* replayed in my head and I politely moved away from Aman.

'I think I am in love….no no, I won't, I can't…' Aman said to himself. I thought he was being foolish.

The next morning Aman saw that someone had sent him a text message at 3.am. It was Vinita.

Can't stop thinking about you. Meet me at my home in the evening, I am alone tonight.

'I am, I am in a meeting for some real estate investment', Anthony said.

Actually he was with us sitting on some bikes parked in Lokhandwala, smoking cigarettes and just being a bum. It was Saturday and Aman and Mohit had a day off. It was a day off at TST as well. Some old student of Guru was getting married. Anthony got off the parked bike and walked pass us every 15 seconds talking to his friend he had met at the Book store on the phone.

'No no, surely I will dress normally. Okay…okay..hmm..no problems Madhu, I will be there.' Anthony had a date. And Aman was visiting Vinita in the evening.

'Mohit sir.' I said, 'how good are you at dandiya?'

'I don't know what to feel Anuj!' Aman told me before leaving for home to change, 'I mean whatever I had dreamt about Vinita is coming true. But now that she is the one vying for my attention, the whole idea of getting back at her seems rash. Suddenly she doesn't seem that wicked to me!'

'Are you saying that you are backing out from the plan?' I asked him.

'No, not really. Actually I don't know.' he replied.

I knew Aman well. He had a soft heart. You be a little nice to him and he would forgive you for murder. I knew that if I told him about Vinita jumping me in the restaurant, he would definitely feel revengeful again and go ahead with the plan. But maybe I didn't have the heart to see his heart break again.

Anthony and Madhu were supposed to meet at 6.00 pm for the show at 6.30 in a multiplex in a Mall. A tense Anthony had heard that they would meet at 5.00pm. When he reached an hour early he called her up.

'Hey where are you, I can't see you?'

'I am taking a shower, you won't be able to see me.' she replied and Anthony went quiet.

'What's wrong, you there?' she asked.

'I am there but see, I haven't heard of anyone taking a shower in a Mall. It doesn't speak highly about a girl.' Anthony said.

'Excuse me I am at home. Why would I be in the Mall now? We are meeting at six right? Wait, are you already there?'

'Oh yeah...umm... I was just joking with you re, and yeah I am here, I like to be a little before time and all. Anyways come soon.' and he hung up.

To kill time he logged into Facebook from his phone. Mohit and I read his first status update,

'Life's a bitch when you have to wait'.

After 5 minutes another one

'Wonder how many cigarettes one can smoke back to back without stopping!',

Then another

'I wonder whether smoking continuously makes everyone dizzy or is it just me?'

After 15 minutes,

'To all the brovs I love: smoking non-stop may give you gas and it's not advisable before a date.'

He was just being Anthony. When she arrived at 6.30 Anthony

had smoked around 15 cigarettes and his stomach had bloated horribly.

'Oh so that long coat was to hide the baby bump!' Madhu asked.

'No re it's just an allergic reaction I have after drinking... umm... cold... water', Anthony would bullshit when in a corner. While buying popcorn Anthony suddenly realized he couldn't hold on to that gas anymore.

'Madhu just wait for a moment, I have to attend a very important call' and he went at least 20 feet away from her. Anthony would always tell us that he had mastered the art of farting without sound and that he was so in sync with his body that he knew which one would stink and which wouldn't. He thought that this one was a non-stinker and hence it was safe to let it out as there would be no sound as well. He pretended that he was talking on the phone and he decided to let the gas go. To Anthony's astonishment it made such a loud noise that everyone around was startled thinking there was a minor blast or something heavy had fallen on the floor. And the sad part was that it didn't stop quickly. So Anthony tried his best and used all his energy somehow managing to stop it mid-way .But he lost control and it came out making a louder evil sound. 'oh fuck!', he said when the smell reached his own nose and when he looked around he saw people around him had gone away in disgust. Anthony hurriedly went over to Madhu before she could notice the commotion he had caused,

'hey what happened out there, what was that noise?' she asked.

'No clue re. I think..I guess..nothing actually, I don't have an answer for that. Maybe something fell down. Something .....really heavy.'

'Wait! How come your stomach has suddenly gone in?'

'Oh has it?...yeah man, it has, finally! cool! Err..no.. I have a condition. Actually I used to work out a lot and the stomach has retained some of the muscle memory.' Another bullshit answer. They went inside to watch the movie. After a while another update,

'A man should know what he can and what he cannot do, especially in public.'

During the interval Madhu leaned over to Anthony and said 'I know what had happened!' and she shut her eyes and let out a loud fart herself. 'Oops! Something heavy fell down.' she said. Anthony smiled and they held each other's hands tightly.

'We have so much in common.' Anthony said. Their eyes were soggy.

'Do you believe in ghosts and spirits too? I mean I have had so many freak experiences but people think I am a little nutty and don't believe me.' Madhu said.

'Tell me about it! I will tell you. Once I was at home, alone …'. They hardly watched the rest of the movie as they were busy narrating incidents to each other. They had at last found an audience in each other. Anthony had finally met his match, his soul mate.

Meanwhile Aman reached Vinita's place at 6.00 pm. He had made sure that he looked his best. That meant a lot of borrowing. Mohit's Jacket, my shirt, a colleague's shoes and Anthony's bike. On the way he had stopped in a mall to go to a perfume counter where he pretended that he wanted to buy and the sales girl had sprayed all kinds of samples on him. Yet, that night strangely he felt nervous. He felt something wasn't right.

Nervously he rang the doorbell. He was expecting her to have dressed sensuously, showing a lot of skin. But when she opened the door Aman saw that she had worn a pretty regular t-shirt and jeans and immediately it hit him that he had overdressed.

'Hello, Aman, come in!' she said in a very friendly tone.

'Hey! How are you? Actually I had a business meeting and I am coming directly from there.' and he stood with his back towards her expecting her to remove his jacket but she walked away towards the kitchen.

'Oh! And I thought you had dressed up for me! Hehe so, what will you have, tea or coffee?' Aman was taken aback by all this. He had expected a romp immediately when he entered but she was asking him about tea or coffee instead of beer or vodka!

'Nothing, but water will do just fine!' he said as dejectedly.

Then she continued talking about random things but said nothing romantic or suggestive.

Meet me at my home in the evening, I am alone tonight, Aman thought about her message and wondered what it really meant.

He dialled Guru from her bathroom. Guru couldn't receive his call as he was in a wedding and the call went on voice mail. Aman got a little frustrated and was really getting confused about what to do next.

'I am going to order some beer for myself. Give me the number for home delivery.' Aman said anxiously. Although she said she would only have a sip or two, Aman ordered four bottles of beer. He knew she would guzzle down two bottles in 10 minutes. After having a beer each Aman asked Vinita to sit close to her.

'You know what Vinita,' Aman said looking deep in her eyes, 'the sad part is? That you will never know what I really felt for you then. I just wanted to spend my life looking at you. I wanted to catch your every smile, hold every teardrop. I just wanted to get old with you.' Aman said, the two beers had already hit him. Immediately Vinita seemed lost in Aman's words. She had never heard him talk with so much of depth earlier. Besides he hadn't asked her 10 times before ordering for beer. She liked the change in him and leaned forward and placed her lips on his. He noticed that her eyes were shut. They began to kiss passionately. Vinita was so aroused with the passion with which Aman kissed her that she accidently kicked the empty beer bottle and it broke into pieces. His kiss grew intense. Over and over he devoured her mouth as if he'd not had any love for a long, long time. In all her life, Vinita had not known passion this explosive. She then looked at his hands reaching for her waist. And without a warning he took off her t-shirt, shocking her but she couldn't take her eyes off his deep heavy gaze. He pushed her on the floor with glass pieces all around them. They had lost track of things around them. For all they cared they could be making love on a sheet of needles. He was looking at the only girl he had loved with so much desire and there she lay under him, in his arms, giving herself to him.

We can still be together…you are mine and I am yours baby, he thought.

She was breathing heavily, 'What are you going to do with me?' she whispered.

'You don't want to know that, trust me!' he said and a bolt of ecstasy went through her.

Aman on the other hand had fantasized this event thousands of time in his mind knowing that in reality she would never even let him touch her. He now saw the surge of her enormous and shapely breasts. She wore a red bra and Aman unclipped it from behind swiftly. Aman touched the silk softness of her upper body with the tip of his fingers. He used his tongue masterfully on every inch of the skin he could see. Her eyes were shut and her body stiffened with pleasure every time Aman touched her. Aman then put his hand on zipper of her jeans. His hand stopped there for a while before he pulled it away. He then hastily stood up. Breathing heavily he walked away to the window and lit a cigarette. Vinita opened her eyes slowly

'Aman…. what happened.' she asked softly.

Aman spoke after what seemed like an eternity to her. 'This... this is wrong Vinita. I will be honest with you. I don't think that I love you anymore and this would be wrong for you, I had come here with the intention of just...just... fucking you. Actually I had planned this all along.'

'What??' she hurriedly put on her top, 'Hey is that true, do you really mean it?' she asked. Aman didn't reply, he continued looking out of the window.

'I don't know what to feel.' Vinita said softly, 'I feel bad because of what you have said but...but you also have shown a lot of respect towards me. Today with you, I felt like a real woman.'

Aman kept a hand on her head 'I am sorry, I had become blind.' Aman said, his eyes moist, 'Whatever happened in the past has happened and I shouldn't have done this. You aren't a bad girl' and he took off from her apartment in haste leaving the glorious sight of the woman who had finally warmed up to him.

On the way back while riding the bike he heard his phone beep. He read the message and a smile appeared on his face.

'I know it's too eager of me, but will you marry me?'

Aman texted Guru.

'Sir it went exactly the way you predicted. The bitch has fallen for it. She wants to marry me. You are God!'

We had stopped going out to game completely by now. The focus had shifted from pick-up to revenge. We had improved a lot in general but the fact was that we still were pretty average in the pick-up game. And I was not comfortable with that.

'Was this your only objective, haan guys?' To take revenge on your ex-girlfriends! Is that all you want? You guys seem completely disinterested in learning the real thing from Guru!' I said and was completely pissed off.

'Anuj, I understand what are you a saying.' Mohit said, 'Have you ever seen a bucket half full of a dirty muddy water? What will the happen if you put fresh clean water in it? Even the clean water will get dirty! That's our situation right now. First we have to get rid of the dirty water of our past and only then can we start afresh. We basically want to empty our buckets!

'Hmm…I see your point. But don't take forever to empty them. In most cases people start liking the dirty water; I hope that's not the case.'

We reached TST and it was filled with a lot of people today. We saw Vinod speaking to a bunch of guys explaining something very animatedly to them. Apart from the locals there were guys from everywhere; America, Germany, Australia, Japan, Sri-Lanka, Kenya and other countries. TST buzzed with activity after Guru had won the duel. Ankit was taking a training session with a new batch and I could see the guys in the new batch smiling and looking in high spirits. They were unaware of what kind of tasks waited for them. Soon they would all be begging all over the city.

Guru asked for us inside. 'Guys it seems I should have participated in the duel a long time ago. It has really helped. Anyways Aman any update on Vinita?'

'She has called me over 40 times since yesterday, but I haven't picked any of her call. See, here, she is calling me again. I am so happy and relieved that I feel like the happiest person in the world.' Aman said with a blank face.

'Good. But what's with you and the straight face all the time?'

Guru laughed, 'You can let your guard down sometimes man, at least among friends!'

'Hmm…okay..see the real thing is this…', Aman walked over to Guru and knelt to hug Guru who was sitting on a chair.

'Haha. Hey that's okay Aman. I am happy for you, didn't know it meant so much for you!' Guru said. Suddenly we heard Aman sobbing. Then it turned into a full-fledged crying. We knew that those were tears of joy but it sounded like someone had died. *What the fuck man, not again!*

Aman controlled his tears said, 'You don't know sir, in fact none of you know what this means to me. The way she had treated me earlier I had lost any faith I had in myself. She made me believe that I was hopeless. I had decided that no girl could ever be attracted to me. I used to look at other guys who could have every woman they wanted and wonder what God forgot to give me that those guys had. And she would tell me the meanest of things to me. Sometimes she wouldn't pick my calls for days for no reason, just because she didn't feel like talking to me and I would sulk. I would get aggressive and take out all the frustration on my family. I would abuse my body smoking non-stop from morning to night. And today you, Guru Sir, have turned the tables. It's a miracle. Now she would feel the pain I felt. I feel I am born again, I feel like a computer with virus removed.' We laughed at the last line which helped us all, including Guru, to hide our tears. I sometimes envied Aman for this quality. He could express everything in his heart fearlessly and openly. He laughed freely and cried freely. And now he would live freely.

'Guru sir, err…', Mohit said and I immediately knew what he was going to say, 'You see I have a similar problem. My ex-girlfriend it seems is living in my head without rent. I have the tried to throw her out but she comes back again after, few days. I believe I need the same a cure as Aman….hehehee'.

'Cure? What do you think I am? A doctor? It's not a cure Mohit. Aman just got his self- esteem back. That's all. There is no magic happening here.' Guru said, firmly.

'No, no, I meant I also want my self-esteem back then, if it's okay with you. I mean this girl has tortured the me like…like..a lot..a lot..too lot…heheheee….I wasn't able to sleep for months it was that bad…heheheee…..I used to wake up in the middle of the nights and smoke cigarettes at 3.am..hehehee'.

'I see. But why the fuck you laughing?' Guru said, chuckling.

'I have no bloody fucking idea..why am I laughing…hehehe… and then on some bad nights I used to fall asleep while smoking…. then sometimes I used to fall asleep while training in office....and people thought that I am on charas, ganja or cough syrup. I also felt that I was shit, like Aman. If you compare me with Devdas, you will think Devdas was the happiest person ever, hahahahahaaaa, I was so screwed. The best part was that I did not have sex with her because we had planned that we would do it only after marriage. But she bloody fuck, fucked that guy before their engagement. After her marriage I tried getting a girlfriend but I was like shit zombie and no-one liked me. So I went to a prostitute and out of depression could not get it to rise to an occasion..hahahaaa..but I tried , I kept on humping with my softie until she kicked me in my crotch and two men threw me out..hahahaaa. I remember once I got drunk and bought a can of petrol, came home and poured it on myself but bloody fuck I had ..I had..hahaa..no match box at home, hahaha. So I went to my neighbour to ask for one and they realised that I was drenched in petrol and they called the police and ..hahahahaaaaaa, and then haha then one day..',

'I got the point man.' Guru interrupted hurriedly, 'You need urgent help. Oh God!' Guru said, 'Come with me to my cabin and we will see what to do. But I gotta say this man, you guys have a weird past; I mean at first glance you seem pretty normal. But whoa man, you guys got some stories to tell! Trying to burn yourself alive! The girls really fucked you up. Anthony what about you, do you have some score to settle too? Any ex-girlfriends?'

'No-no...nothing of that sort. Wait, maybe there was this girlfriend. In general she was very sweet and all. She lived like 2 hours away from me but there was this one confusing issue; whenever she wanted to buy maggi or soap and shit from below her building she used to tell me to come all the way and buy it for her. So I used to drive all the way for 2 hours, buy it and give it to her. And she wouldn't let me in also, she would open only half the door and take her stuff and shut the door on my face. Once she told me she wanted to see my handsome face, so again I rode for 2 hours to reach below her building so that she could see me from her window. But when I called she had forgotten about it and was away with friends to watch a movie. I always thought it was a little weird. And the next day when I told her that I didn't really feel like a *boyfriend* these days but more of a personal home delivery guy, she broke the windshield of the car I had then...'

'Mohit, hurry up lets go to my cabin, now!', Guru said.

Mohit told all the details to Guru and Guru drew out a plan for him on a sheet of paper. The objective was to take revenge on her but completely avoid any physical intimacy as she was married. Mohit agreed and now the plan was waiting for execution.

'Hello Pari?' Mohit said on the phone.

'Yes, who is this?' the voice on the phone asked.

'It's me, Mohit'.

'Who Mohit? Ummm...okay, yeah yeah...Mohit how are you?' Pari asked recognising the familiar voice of her once boyfriend of 3 years.

'I am good. The thing is I am in Hyderabad day after tomorrow for work and....'

'No, Mohit I can't meet you, I am hanging up now, bye.'

'No wait, I don't want to meet you, I have to go to this office in Banjara Hills and I am not able to figure out how to go there, so I wanted directions from a local, hence...'

'Oh! I thought....anyways tell me the address.'

'I will call you back after some time, I am getting a very important call on the other line..' he was saying when Pari abruptly disconnected the call.

'See, Guru Sir, the attitude? This is what I hate about her, she is a ...', Mohit said.

'Is she like this with everyone?' Guru asked.

'No no no, in front of the others she is sweet as sugar. Everyone thinks she is such a nice human being. But she is actually a nice human bitch.' Mohit said, his nostrils flared.

'Hmm.. so whose fault is this? Think about it. In a relationship everyone tries once to cross the line of respectful conversation and if at that time you behave okay with it, you are digging your own grave. Now that two years have passed by, its human tendency to expect change in a person you meet after a lot of time. It's your job to show the changes, the good changes in you. I don't want you to call back now. She will be expecting a call from you immediately but you will not. Subconsciously she is checking whether you have changed or are the same shitless Mohit she dumped years back. Not that she will come running to you if you don't call but she is a woman and is interested in knowing what sort of a person you, her ex-boyfriend, is now. Has he grown a spine? Or is he the same person with no self -respect?' Guru said.

'I am a person with loads of self-respect Guru Sir.' Mohit said pushing his chest out with pride.

'Don't tell me anything, show it to her.'

'Okay I will tell her…should I call her now..hehehe?'

'Oh my God!! No Mohit, that's what I just told you.'

'Okay, okay..I get it.'

'The thing is she will call you tomorrow.'

'Is it? That's good. Very good.'

Three hours later she messaged.

'What happened? You never called?'

Mohit didn't reply.

'See, it's the nature of women', Guru said, 'They are wired that way. When a woman dumps someone she may say that she feels bad for the guy but she would in other circumstances also boast that she was the one who rejected him. It adds a feather to her cap. You have to snatch that feather away and she will come back searching for it.'

Then another message in the evening from her,

'Whatever dude. Wonder why you can't even reply to my messages, go to hell.'

It was another message from her to scare him into calling her. But Mohit didn't reply even this time. Next day Mohit messaged,

'Sorry, was very busy. No worries, I have the address now, thanks!'
This time she didn't reply.

The next day Mohit took a flight to Hyderabad and checked in a hotel which was at least an hour's drive from Pari's home. He spent the evening by himself and called Pari up at 11pm in the night.

From her status update on Facebook account Guru had gathered that her husband was away for a month and hence this was the right time to strike.

'Hello Pari.' Mohit said on the phone. He was two beers down. As per the plan. 'Pari, I feel lonely today. Very lonely. You know all this time I have fooled myself that I am okay that I have moved-on.' Mohit said.

'I know you Mohit, very well. I have seen how emotional you are. But you have to accept the realities Mohit, I am at a stage of life where I am happy and content and you need to respect that.' said Pari, with a hint of relief in her tone. It was a confirmation that Mohit was still crazy about her. She still had the power to depress a guy. She was important after all!

'I am so happy for you Pari, but the thing is…' Mohit said and he was taking deep breaths now, 'the thing is…shit! I can't tell you, it won't be right!'

'C'mon tell me fast Mohit. I have to go to sleep now, its past 11, already.'

'The thing is, this girl, this girl Sneha won't talk to me anymore and I miss her so much now. I made a mistake!' Mohit said and Pari was left dumbfounded. Mohit was depressed because of some other girl!

How dare she? That's my right!

'What? Who is this Sneha? You are missing *her*?' she asked almost in agitation.

Oh c'mon, there are guys who will die for me, who just live for me, in my dreams she would say to her girlfriends with pride.

Then Mohit told her a scripted story of how Sneha fell for him in office and after some months he dumped her for another girl. He now realized how much she meant to him. That, she was his first true love!

They spoke for another 5 minutes and when the call was over Mohit lit a cigarette and looked at his reflection in the mirror. He could see no expressions on his face.

Guru was watching a reality show where boys had to woo girls and then then take them out on dates. He was relaxing on his couch at home. . He laughed at how foolishly the boys behaved. *If only they knew…,* he thought. But some guys managed to attract girls with some lame tactics. *Maybe the show is doctored.* Then a tall, beautiful woman walked towards Guru and put her arms around his shoulders. Guru held her hand and kissed it, 'love you baby', he said and pulled her gently towards his lap. He smelled the freshness of her inviting pout and leaned forward to kiss, *I will always love you baby, no matter what, wish I could tell you how sorry I am!* he thought, his eyes shut.

At that moment his phone beeped and when he read the message he frowned. The message was from Mohit,

'*Sir, she has told me never to call back again. I think the plan has failed.*'

Aman and Mohit were dealing with their scars. Aman's was already healing. Anthony had in all probability found 'her'.

It was time I faced my demons head on. Although I had improved in dealing with women, I still wasn't where I wanted to be. But I was sure of one thing, no amount of therapy sessions or medicines would cure me. I had got results thus far only by taking the plunge and interacting directly with women. But I had to wipe out any final traces of fear still left in me. And I knew who my go-to man for that was.

The decision to seek guidance from Guru wasn't as difficult as actually doing it. I had never shared it with anyone, not even my parents or my closest of friends. Only two people on the planet were aware of it. One was my therapist and the other was me. Now I was going to let in another person to know about it. To talk about it meant going down a very difficult and uncomfortable memory lane. A memory which was best left alone, untouched. The feelings the memory created seemed almost like a serpent. It lay there in a dark corner motionless and lifeless but the moment went even close to it, it would spring up to life and attack you sending a shiver through you.

When I asked Guru to meet me for what was a very private matter, he had been gracious enough to call me at his residence in Bandra. He lived in a 21 storey tower on the 18th floor. His flat was everything a young man dreams of owning one day. It was obviously a bachelor pad, as everyone was aware that he had no committed partner at this point in time. It was an enormous 3BHK flat and the interiors looked elegant. Somehow it had Guru's stamp on everything from a small photo frame to the mini-theatre that had been restructured from a bedroom.

We sat in his hall, on a comfortable couch.

'Yeah Anuj, tell me.' Guru asked in his usual calm manner.

'Er..the thing is.. I have a problem and it's just that I am feeling uncomfortable talking to you..', I said and realized that I was a huge ball of nerves

'Look, Anuj, life is too short for hesitation. You want a solution fast, so tell me your problem fast.'

I gathered enough courage and shared everything with him and how it had affected my life negatively. He heard every word I said with complete attention and when I finished I expected empathy from him, to console me. But he didn't, instead he seemed angry.

'Dude, what the fuck are you? Are you fucking insane? And what the fuck is gynophobia?' He seemed aghast and I was perplexed as I couldn't comprehend his bizarre reaction.

'I didn't get you, err.' I said

'You didn't get me? You ass hole, you don't get life! You have lived with the fear of women all your life, even left jobs for that? Just because when you were a brainless little scum you peed in your pants in front of some girls whose brains were not even developed properly to judge you right! What's wrong with you man! I must have peed in my pants a hundred times in school days, sometimes even on purpose. Worse shit happens with people when they are young, they are molested, tortured and what not? Sometimes by their own people, yet they deal with it and carry on with their lives. And you are fucking living with it and talking to me as if your dick was cut off. Boss, you know what you are, a chicken, and a fearful piece of shit.'

'Wait, Guru I don't need this.' I retorted. I didn't want him to lower my self-esteem further.

'You don't need this? You are a fucking girl. A softie whose only option is to fuck off as far as possible from a problem. You deserved to be laughed at then and you deserve to be laughed at even now.' Guru went on and he was making me angry now. *Is this guy fucking mad? What have I done to him? Just be quiet man!! Please for your own good!*

He continued ripping me apart 'Do you even hear what you are saying, *Guru sir, I can't talk to women as I get nervous because I did pee pee in front of them when I was a kid.* Your parents must be ashamed that they gave birth to a sissy. Wait, there could be another reason for it. You must be gay and this could be your reason to delude yourself that you don't like girls...'

'Enough!' I thundered and stood up. 'Say it once more and I will fucking kill you, here right now.' I fumbled with rage and I knew I meant it. At that point in time all it would have taken was one more offensive sentence from Guru for me to attack him. He had put me on an edge mentally.

But suddenly his face become expressionless and he let out a smirk.

'Brother sit down. I like it. I like anger. That's what I wanted to see whether you have it in you. I had to bring it out in you.'

'What? Oh...so...' I was confused.

'Now hear me out carefully. This emotion of anger that you felt inside you, I want you to take care of it, nurture it. The way you wanted to demolish me because I had offended you, in the same way I want you to destroy this irrational fear, because it's not only offensive, it makes you immobile. I bet my life that you were never extremely angered by this problem. You were only hurt and depressed by it. Had it angered you, you would have killed it by now, the way you were going to kill me.'

'Oh my god! I am so sorry Guru. You know that.. .', I was saying when he interrupted me,

'Let's go to my study. Let me break this muthafucking problem in detail for you to understand. I promise you, when you leave my house today, you will see a path which will lead to a fulfilling life.' he said.

'Oh..okay', I succeeded in saying.

I followed him to one of his bedrooms. He had converted one portion of it into a study. He took a black marker out and began scribbling on a small white board.

'See Anuj, what you experience is fear. Now let's understand what fear is. In its essence fear is very important in life. In fact we need fear. Imagine a man without fear, walking on a railway track; he will not jump away on seeing an approaching train. The fear of the dark, of strangers, of heights and so many such other fears make sure that we grow up safely. Everyone experiences fear, whoever says otherwise is lying. Now what we don't want to experience is irrational fear. Unfortunately that's what you have.'

'....I will explain it to you in layman's language. In a scientific experiment the process of fear was observed in rats. They were made to hear a sound, let's call it T (trigger) and immediately after the sound they were given an electric shock, let's call it E (Experience) and the rats froze, we will call it R (reaction). This entire process, let's call it RF (Rational Fear).

Now this entire process of RF is repeated. But this time stage E is omitted, yet the rat will have a similar R of freezing.

This means whenever the rat hears the tone it will freeze even if there is no electric shock. It associates the tone with the shock.

This is what I call IRF (Irrational fear). Pretty similar to your situation. You associate women with fear. In fact I believe everyone has at least one moment of his or her own IRF.

CAA, is another term you should know. It's for Chronic Anticipatory Anxiety. It's the fear that you are going to have a panic attack in an impending situation. People may fear a certain event in their lives and the worry of its fear begins days and sometimes weeks in advance.

I think your major problem is CAA. Which then leads to IRF.

Oh because of one bad experience your situation is as following:

Women are your T (trigger)

Embarrassment and shame are your E (Experience)

Fear is your R (reaction)

Now when you are an adult and know that you aren't going to pee in your pants in front of women, you still freeze. And when you know there is going to be an interaction with women you start worrying hours before you actually talk, that's CAA. You with me brother?' he suddenly asked me.

'Oh yeah Guru. I am. This is clearing the rut in my head. This has told me what actually happens with me…', I said. I felt I at least understood my problem better now rather than the term Gynophobia being thrust up my ass by the shrinks every time.

'Good. Now let's look at its solutions…', Guru said and my body leaned forward to hear. I was so keen that I felt as if my entire body had become one single hearing organ

'The only solution for your problem is TST, The school of thoughts', he chuckled and I thought he was joking. I was wrong. He continued, 'So in reality, without you being completely aware, you are curing yourself here. What I mean is the only way to cure irrational fear or phobia through behavioural therapy is to consciously put yourself in an environment which normally would trigger the fear experience.

The only way to make this fear go is to change your E (experience). Over a period of time if T is followed by a desirable E, your R will be favourable.

T= Meeting women =

E= feeling of control=

R=Happiness and Ecstasy.

Now your R which is Ecstasy will propel you to look out for more Ts, and the cycle continues and a time comes when you only remember the favourable E.

If you repeat the above process many times over a period of time, your trigger will no longer remain a trigger but seem like an opportunity. You will internalize the process so much that you will not associate Women with bad feelings. In fact, you will look out for moments where you could meet them and interact with them. So basically, all you have to do is meet as many women as possible and change the kind of experiences from bad to pleasant and eventually start feeling good about it. There will come a day when you will forget that you ever had a problem.'

'Hmm…so it's all up to me, isn't it? I need to have a series of good experiences with women, right?' I said

'Yes! And this extinction of fear will not erase fear conditioning but replace it with new learning. Your Trigger will have no association with fear or danger. It will take some time, but trust me the result is very gettable', Guru said

The things he told me very simple but profound. I felt light in hope of a worry free tomorrow. For my bright future. I tried my best not to display any excitement. I wasn't as carefree in displaying my emotions as Aman.

'Thank you so much Guru. You have shown me the path and I can see myself improving with it too' I wanted to say a lot more but my thoughts were too scrambled to construct proper Thank you sentences. But there was one thing I wanted to know, 'If you don't mind, how do you know so much about all this', I asked him a little hesitantly.

'Anuj to achieve anything in life it's very important to know your obstacles, your enemies inside out. What I have told you can be applied to fear in any form. It's very simple, but to break down the problem in detail gives you a clear picture of what you are dealing with and sometimes in analysing lies the solution'

'That's true. Thank you again!' I said. I wondered why he hadn't answered my question clearly and instead dodged it. *What could be his fears?*

'Now all you need to do is this. Meet as many women as possible. Try and have a bulk of good experiences with women. It's up to you'.

'How come I have never been to this place before, it's so cool', Sandy said.

We were in one of the newly sprung popular pubs in the suburbs.

'Isn't it? The fact is, a couple of months ago I used to come here a lot', I said trying to hide my excitement. Actually I was trying to hide my exhilaration and to behave all cool since the time Sandy had said yes for a meeting. I didn't think of it as a date, I knew I couldn't handle the pressure of dating a celebrity super-model.

I am just going to hang out with her as a buddy! I told myself again and again to feel at ease.

When you want a girl, convince yourself that you don't! Guru had said.

I was meeting Sandy after hanging out with five girls, all referred to me by Guru. The meetings with the last two girls had been decent which gave me enough courage to call up Sandy for dinner.

Anthony and Madhu had also accompanied us. Madhu was impressed with Anthony for having friends who dated models. 'So, yesterday when I woke up at 3.am I saw a cloud of black smoke on my ceiling and..' Madhu was telling Anthony. I wondered how a girl, who with a little grooming could easily look every bit as stunning as say a Sandy be so twisted in her head. But I guess I could only be happy for Anthony. She really seemed a long term deal for him. I looked at Sandy as she sat next to me at the table and I noticed that although she hadn't dolled up as much as that night, she looked prettier. Not sexier or more desirable but she just seemed so serenely beautiful with minimal make-up.

'Anuj I can't thank you enough for getting that pest out of my life. I was literally scared to step out of house alone.' she said. After the ugly episode and then with Bhau warming up to us, Shiva had come up to me to apologize and even assured me that I could go ahead and date Sandy without his interference as his family had had him engaged to a very beautiful Marathi girl from Kolhapur. 'As I look back now.' Shiva had said, 'I guess Sandy wasn't my type. My fiancée is exactly what I wanted from my wife; homely, beautiful and someone who can take care of my house. You go ahead and be with Sandy, I would rather have you date her than anyone else.' After that he had even spoken to Sandy from my phone to apologize to her. It had ended well.

'Don't mention Sandy, what's a friend for?' I said. She then looked at me seemingly thinking about something pleasant and smiled.

Now that's a positive E, I chuckled.

I tried my best not to look too red.

'.....but my favourite is *nothing else matters* and have you heard...' Anthony was saying to Madhu. It seemed that they were oblivion to the world around them, talking like two school kids who were also best friends.

On the other hand I was having difficulty keeping things in flow, 'So how tough is it really, being a model?' I asked. But I realized that she looked a little pensive now and was lost in her own thoughts.

'Anuj, are you hoping that tonight would be a repeat of that night? That since I am a model I would be too free, easy and kiss random strangers?' she said.

'No, obviously not Sandy, I just wanted to hang out, that's all.' I said and she kept her beer glass down after taking a large sip.

'The fact is I don't know why I made out with you that night. I don't know what got into me….I have no idea.'

At that moment I suddenly felt a surge in confidence and reached out to hold her hand, 'Sandy, just forget about it. It wasn't your mistake, if at all, it was mine. I shouldn't have..' and I felt like a man immediately, in control. She smiled at me and things went pretty smooth after the air was cleared. I got to know her better and realized that under all the make-up and glamour she was a very endearing person. Once she dropped her guard she had no airs about her, in fact at moments I found her a bit childlike and funny.

Madhu had to leave early for home so Anthony went to drop her.

After three beers each Sandy and I were sloshed. She told me that she would first drop me in her car. Things had been cool so far but one thing disturbed me a lot.

Everything was going towards one direction: good friends.

I couldn't accept the fact and decided to do something about it. Strangely I could think of only one thing which had worked on her earlier. David's hand gesture! I had in my foolish drunken state thought of it as some magical key to get her. But this time it had no effect on her. She kept on telling me that I was a very good buddy of hers and that she felt that she was talking to a girlfriend. She in fact insisted that I was her girlfriend. Every time she said it felt humiliated. I felt low and became depressed even in my drunk state. I told her to take the car to my friend's house. I wanted to meet Guru and understand why she said what she had. She dropped me and zoomed away. I didn't look back; I didn't want to give her the opportunity to wave at her new girlfriend. I felt I had let myself down. The alcohol had given me the courage to push Guru to let me in at 1 am.

'Anuj just crash in that guest bedroom and whatever it is, we can talk tomorrow, okay buddy.' Guru said being at his politest best.

'No Guru, No. Sandy just called me her fucking girlfriend. What's that supposed to mean? Will I get my periods now? Do you have some whisper or a screamer with you?' I was hurt.

'Hey, what's the matter Guru?' I heard a girl's voice from his bedroom and in seconds I saw her appear at the door of the hall, 'Guru, will you please come back?' she said tiredly. I looked at her and immediately it hit me that I was looking at one of the finest artworks of God. She wore a nightgown which revealed more than it hid. She had the curves which could put a roller coaster to shame and a face so beautiful that your eyes wouldn't ever get tired looking at it. But something was amiss in the whole picture that even my drunken eyes noticed.

'It's nothing Natasha, it's my cousin.' Guru said and then continued in a hushed tone 'Look Anuj, I have company now. Please go to that bedroom and sleep.'

I wasn't listening 'You called that girl Natasha? She is your....', and I realized what didn't fit in the perfect picture.

She wore a *mangal-sutra*. Her name was Natasha.

And what it meant hit me hard.

I went quiet while Guru guided me to the bedroom where I crashed. 'How could you Guru?...you spoke about....ethics...and ..how could you.....', I mumbled while I dozed off to deep sleep lying face down on the bed.

It took me half a minute to realize where I was. I saw Guru talking over the phone to someone, 'You have to do it. The choice is yours.' I walked outside to the hall hesitantly and sat on the couch.

'Okay, call me when it's done.' Guru said and hung up. He then looked at me thoughtfully, 'It was Mohit. He is stuck. Have tea, Anuj.' The tea was ready on the table in a tea pot. I just had to pour it in a cup and add sugar. I smiled and prepared the tea for myself behaving as if I didn't recall anything about last night.

'So Sandy called you her Girlfriend! What's the problem in that?' Guru said.

That's not really the bigger problem now. The more important problem is that I think my role model is a fake, I thought.

'Yes, actually there is no problem. I guess I got very drunk last night. Forget about it.' I said trying to downplay the event as I didn't seek an answer from a man who himself didn't follow what he preached. The girl came out and Guru stood up to hug her.

'Will call you in an hour, baby.' she said kissing him and then she looked at me, 'Hey Mr cousin! Had too much to drink yesterday? Hehe.' she said and left without waiting for my reply. As she walked out of the apartment in her tight jeans and a white sleeveless top, I couldn't help but mentally rate her. I decided she was an 11.

'I know what you are thinking Anuj.' Guru said, 'You know, Love is a bitch. And you can say and advise anything you want to others, but in your own case you get weak.'

'But what about her husband, I know that she is married. Don't you think it's unfair to him?' I asked.

'The real thing Anuj is once you enter this life, you realize that in its soul the game is unfair. To the girls, to their life and to us, the so called Pick-up Artists. Attraction is created but it's not always organic. You just can't keep everyone happy!' He was saying when I interrupted him. 'But all that talk of ethical gaming and propagating its methods? I..I followed every word you said.' I tried not to sound too sentimental about it.

'Anuj you don't have to. I knew that one day I needed to have this conversation with you. But I didn't know when, I guess the time has come.' he said and went over to his mini-bar and made himself a drink. I saw the time, it was 10.30 am.

'There is not and can't be anything ethical about this lifestyle. I got into it because I was naïve and hurt by Natasha. I needed to salvage my honour. Answer questions about myself to myself. I had to learn everything that was known to man about how women think and how a woman is attracted to a man. I watched every possible movie, met anyone who claimed to know, read everything that could possibly teach me anything about attraction. Soon after words I entered the game I realized that I was better than a lot of the others. But there was a problem; I was no longer making the kind of money like I did while doing my job. Luckily for me David gave me an offer where I could make good money assisting him in his workshops. Hence I moved to America with him. But I wasn't satisfied. I wasn't satisfied with the money, the lifestyle and was frustrated. Then came a time when I started missing Natasha again. Yeah, after hundreds of equally hot and hotter women I still missed Natasha, her simplicity and our uncomplicated life. I had to do something. That was also the time I was getting a lot of popularity here. I would get hordes of emails from India requesting me to conduct workshops in India. But I knew our culture wasn't ready for it and yet I knew that this was where the real money was. Thousands of desperate Indian men with no game! It was the perfect playground for me. So I planted this story about my friend making out with my sister which compelled me to come up with ethical gaming. See these days every PUA student comes up with his own workshop, with the same methods. I had to create an USP and a method which would fit into the Indian system first and be gradually accepted worldwide. When you add the word ethic at to something you increase your audience by a huge number. And today I make as much money in India as say any highly successful man anywhere in the world would, minus the slogging your ass part. Besides I have my girl back and I am The Artist as well. What else would I want?' he said. I was repulsed listening to him but I kept my disgust in check.

'But what about your sister? How could you lie about your own sister for such things and spoil her name?'

'Who says I lied? I just created another truth! To spoil her name she should exist, right? I have no sister, my friend.' he said with a wicked smile. For a moment I was scared at how this man's mind works. Although I could see the whole picture now but still I had unanswered questions. 'But you have developed the ethical game. And it works. We all have seen that during the duel. So why do you say there can be no ethics.' I asked him maybe more out of trying to convince myself that he wasn't that evil after all.

'I know that Anuj. No girl is really hurt with this. But you plant a seed in a girl's mind and mostly you do it for a high, not because you love her, not because you really want her. She is just another female for you, another 7 or an 8. After a point it's only to prove a point to yourself that you still have it in you. It's to fill the void every PUA feels within. It's selfish and not ethical. I admit that it's a better method than others but let's face it, it's just a lesser evil, that's all.' Guru paused for a moment and I felt he was pouring out his feelings to someone after a long time. He continued and this time when he spoke he voice was low, 'Anuj, one day you will know. The longer you stay in the game and the more you teach yourself about the laws of attraction, the more difficult it gets for you to feel love. You don't feel the awe of love, the nervousness about what the woman thinks of you. Love is special because it's mysterious. This game just takes the mystery away. You know clearly whether the girl is interested or not by gauging her body language and other indicators. You just don't feel human about love anymore. Life gets shallow and you find your own reflection in the mirror repulsive. That's why I wanted to be back with Natasha because I knew I could feel love only for her and didn't want to live like a sex-machine the rest of my life, loving no one and no-one loving me back.' I heard every word he said and realized he made sense. His method was still light years ahead of some of the others.

'But Guru why are you telling me all this? If I leak this out it could cause your business a lot of damage, and yeah one more thing.. Why did you not charge me for the training?' I asked as I felt since he was in the answering mode I should make full use of it.

'Why am I telling you this? I am 35 years old and have made enough money to last a life time. Natasha has filed for a divorce and we are planning to move abroad. We want to travel the world together and do it now. Not when we are in our 50s. I want to get out of this life but can't throw away everything I have created just like that. And I would need the money as well.' He said and walked closer to me, 'I saw you in the pub that day and admired your courage to tell the girl how you felt. Besides I realized how deeply hurt you were when she insulted you badly. You were so hurt that you decided to follow a complete stranger without knowing why. And the moment I knew you were walking with me, I knew we could channelize that hurt into something big. Like I had. Others have this sadness about rejection too. But you looked as if your soul was taken away from you. In that moment I saw myself in you. Sometimes extreme failure in life is the only recipe for extreme success. And that's when I decided that you would take The School of Thoughts ahead.'

My thoughts were tangled, 'I will take it ahead? I didn't get…'.

'It means that I wanted to give the school to you to run. I would be the sleeping partner. I would still have fifty percent share in the business. Yet that would mean lakhs a month easily for both of us. And before you ask why only you and not someone else from my faculty, let me tell you that Because it's just not knowledge that I am looking out for. You have the desire and you don't look the sort who would be satisfied with anything mediocre. I know it's only you who can replace me!'.

'B-but how can I? I haven't achieved anything yet..why would anyone follow me?', I said as I didn't know what to feel.

'Yes, you are right nobody will, not now. But..' he paused as if to choose his next words carefully,

'But they will, when you become The Artist.'

'I am the screwed man', Mohit told me on the phone. 'She is very smart. She cannot be fooled. Guess what I am doing, I am smoking right now.. its 3 am..and I am smoking..hehe..I am back! At being a loser again!'

'Brother all will be okay..err…can we talk about this tomorrow, it's very late and I am kinda sleepy man', I said and was immediately reminded of my own escapade where I crashed into Guru's house late at night. I decided to be patient and listen to what Mohit was saying. Or at least I pretended to. Besides my mind was already overworked as it still needed time to get around with what Guru had said.

'I will take only five minutes brother…' he said pleadingly.

'No worries brother, go on………' I said

'You know what, I think I made a mistake by calling her. I feel useless again. When I talk to her I am reminded of all the things I am not. Suddenly I feel I am not as handsome or intelligent as I think I am. You with me brother?'

'Yeah I am..'

'Okay..so please repeat all the things I said…the things I think I am not..say them!'

'What? Mohit sir, this isn't your training session…you carry on…'

'Okay. You know how bad she made me feel today. I was again reminded of my days in Delhi. On the first day I had met her she looked the sweet. It was the month of June….'

'What happened NOW? Tell me that. I know what happened that June and the June next year and every June after that. You tell me what happened NOW!' I said. I knew I had to stop him from drifting from the real issue.

'Hehe…You know! I have told you so many times..hehe..I know you know…but I don't know why I feel like telling my story again and again to you guys. I know you get irritated, but I feel better after I tell it someone. I have told mom the same story so many times..and she heard it every time, without blinking. She would sleep listening to me and when she woke up she would hear it again…….Anuj, will you do one thing for me? Please! Don't say no!' Mohit said and his voice was low

'Yeah bro.' I was concerned for him now

'Tell my mom I love her so much. Also tell Anthony and Aman that I love them a lot too. I am pleased that my life had people like the you guys. I love you a lot too.'

'Mohit sir, d-don't say that! Are you going to do something to yourself.. It's not worth it. Are you fucking going to commit suicide man.' I panicked.

'No dude, are you mad?' he shouted in fear, 'Don't say such things man, I am alone...don't scare me..'

'Oh God! So just tell me what happened between you and Pari?'

'Okay..I will..but never say things like that man, it creeps me out! Especially not to a man who is alone in some hotel room, is drunk, has woken the up to smoke at three, is calling a friend to make a decision about getting his ex- girlfriend's attention back who married someone else.. okay?..Never man!..... Anyways, so basically I feel like I am nothing right now. I feel I am empty from inside and can float in the air. I did everything that Guru told me to do. First it was all going a good but later it was all screwed up. She told me never to call her up again.'

'Oops, she did?'

'Yeah she is a bitch. I sometimes think that she is the smartest human being alive. Even Guru's formula failed. However, Guru is also not less haan! He has a back-up plan. But I doubt whether I should do what he suggests.'

'What's that?'

'He told me to sleep with her. According to his plan she will first sleep with me and then fall for me.'

'So what's the problem in that.' I said and for a second I didn't believe I had said it.

'Problem? She is married...I know I want to put my things into her...and it will feel good too..but now I am thinking it's not right... To make her fall for me and make her the realize her past bad karma is one thing but to manipulate Pari by getting physical with her...I don't know..I wanted it to be natural.'

'Oh! C'mon! It is natural. You aren't spiking her drink, you aren't raping her. It will be consensual. Besides you always wanted to get close to her.'

'Hmm..please continue saying things like these..I feel good.'

'Obviously, man! What did she do to you? She slept with that guy when you were dating her. Wasn't that cheating? Did she think about you and how would you feel? Dude, go and grab the opportunity. Take your revenge and fuck off', I said and waited for his response but he was quiet.

'You there?' I asked

'You finished?' Mohit said, 'I feel so good hearing you Anuj. But please continue and say more things like this no?'

'What do you think I am? I am done bro..good night and do what Guru is saying.'

'I will. I have to. But Anuj bro please..'

'Yeah?'

'Say more things like that, no! Please.'

Mohit heard only a click on his phone and he lit up another cigarette.

'I don't think it's possible. I have always believed that you overestimate me.' I said.

'Anuj, you only know yourself as you are now. I know not only what you are now but also what you can be in the future. So no more discussions about it. I would rather you prepared for the duel.'

'But how can it be even possible. It's just been two months since you won. And as far as I know there can't be any duel until you finish at least one year as TA.'

'You are right. But if I step down as TA there will be another duel and I will have the power to choose one competing PUA. Any guesses whom I will choose?' Guru said with a smirk

'But my contender…. he will be chosen by the community and obviously he will be one of the best going around. How will I beat him?' I said

'How will you? Let me put things in perspective for you.' Guru said slowly with a hint of anger in his voice. 'You have me. Do you even realize what that means? You have the best pick up artist in the world standing with you. And a number of people say that I am arguably the best ever. So what do you think your chances are?'

I couldn't answer that. Suddenly the gigantic stature of the man talking to me hit me. In a way I thought it was important that he reminded me who he was.

'So your personal training with me begins, now.' he said and patted my back.

I was the happiest man in the world.

Meanwhile in Hyderabad, Mohit Joseph hadn't given up on Pari. He had finally made up his mind about going ahead with Guru's not so ethical plan.

He waited outside her office. He had reached an hour before it was time for her to leave. Mohit felt uncomfortable doing what he once loved doing for her; waiting. At that point in time the intentions were different. It was pure then. Now, he did this purely for a selfish objective.

He saw her stepping out of her office and going into a nearby ATM. Mohit followed her inside and started using the second machine next to Pari. She saw Mohit, frowned and decided to leave when Mohit called out her name

'Pari! Oh my God! What a coincidence! How are you?' Mohit said with as much excitement as humanly possible

'I am good Mohit.' she said as they opened the door together to come out. Pari saw that Mohit wore a crisp business suit and carried a laptop bag along with him. His shoes shone a dark black and the fragrance of his after shave lingered in the air.

'You look good, Mohit.' She remarked almost helplessly

'Thanks Pari. You don't look bad yourself.' Mohit said when a girl's voice called out his name from a car which stopped close by

'Oh let me introduce you to my colleague.' Mohit said and took Pari to the very pretty girl sitting in the car. The moment she saw them coming towards her she stepped out of the car. Pari looked at her and kept on looking at her for a while. She was around 5'8" inches tall and the prettiest and sexiest girl Pari had ever seen in her lifetime.

What is she doing with a guy like Mohit? Pari thought

'Pari, this is Roma, my colleague and Roma, this is Pari, my ex-colleague.' Mohit said with an air of confidence. Both girls exchanged pleasantries. Pari, however, didn't like the 'ex-colleague' term used by Mohit for her.

'Mohit let's go. Or we will get late again. You know what Pari, today is our last day in Hyderabad and we haven't hung out anywhere so far. It's so stressful to push him out of his hotel room. And you know, he always gets late whenever there we plan to go out for a movie or a dinner. I have to remind him constantly every 15 minutes.' Roma delivered her dialogue perfectly.

'Oh is it? I guess he has changed now. He never made me wait, for anything.' Pari said and Mohit immediately sensed a change in her tone.

'Oh! You guys seem like you were pretty close before. I mean close buddies.' Roma said

'You don't wanna know.' Pari said and looked at Mohit, 'I will let you go now, for your date' Pari said with a smile and went away. Mohit knew Pari well. He knew that it wasn't a happy smile.

Mohit thanked Roma for her help. She lived in Hyderabad and was Guru's friend. At his insistence she had agreed to help Mohit *in getting his love back.*

Within fifteen minutes Mohit received a text message from Pari. He read and beamed immediately.

Mohit you are leaving tomorrow and I don't know if we can ever meet again. Can you ditch that chick of yours and meet me for dinner tonight. Don't get me wrong, just as friends J

Mohit replied in five minutes

Okay, meet me at fever at Paradise Inn in an hour. It is a good restaurant in the hotel I am staying. But only if you promise to behave as friends J

When she arrived in the restaurant, Mohit was already present there waiting for her. She had changed into a long flowing skirt and black top. Surprisingly she had tied her hair back. Mohit always would tell her that she looked better with her hair open. Maybe she was trying to hint to Mohit to not get any ideas.

'Hello, Pari.' Mohit said and got up to pull her chair back.

'Thanks.' she said softly.

'Hope you didn't have any difficulty getting here?' Mohit asked.

'No, this is a very popular place in Hyderabad. In fact I have been here once with Arjun'

'How is he? You could have brought him along as well.' Mohit said. Every word of his was planned to lead him to his goal.

'He is in Germany right now. He always touring. He is very efficient at his work. In fact he is the best at everything. He is in every sense a man, a perfect man' Pari said and Mohit felt as if he was being wounded by her words. How much praise of your love's husband can you bear? Maybe she was punishing him for dating a perfect woman.

'Oh I am sure he is.' Mohit said without a trace of worry.

The waiter came and Mohit ordered whiskey for himself and Pari's favourite vodka for her, without asking her.

'No Mohit I can't. I don't drink anymore. If at all it's only with Arjun', Pari said.

'I insist.' Mohit said sternly but with a smile.

They caught up with lost time after that. Mohit shared scripted stories with her about his success in office and his numerous girlfriends. Pari spoke about Arjun. It seemed she had only him on her mind.

Mohit noticed a speck of food on Pari's hair which she couldn't locate. Mohit walked to her side, sat next to her and brushed it off.

'Thank you Mohit.' she said and their eyes met for a moment and it seemed both were reluctant in breaking the eye contact. Suddenly Pari shook herself out of Mohit's gaze which had taken her back in years. His eyes reminded her of a time when she actually loved him.

'Mohit, please go back to your seat.' she said looking down

'Yes..yes…Lets order dessert.' Mohit said while he walked back to his side of the table.

After the dinner Mohit called a cab for Pari. She sat in the car and moments before the driver could take her away she called out to Mohit.

'Will you drop me home, my friend?' she asked stressing on the word *friend*.

Mohit sat next to the woman who had made him experience extreme emotions. From abundant Joy and happiness to ample sadness and pain! They drove past the clean roads of Hyderabad and Mohit wondered whether he was making a mistake. What if she made him hate this city too?

'Pari let me ask you this. Are you happy in life?

'Yes Mohit. I am.hmmm, actually you can say more satisfied and contented than happy…why do you ask?

'Okay…let's play a game. It will immediately make you happy. You can practise this anytime, anywhere.'

'okay. Sounds like fun.' and she turned towards him with the excitement of a child.

'I want you to shut your eyes and think of the time when you were really happy.'

'Okay.' she said and shut her eyes

'Now I want you to look within you and see in which part of the body that feeling is.'

She didn't speak for a while and then she said, 'It's in my stomach.'

'Okay now I want you to see what the colour of the feeling is.'

'It's violet.' she said and Mohit saw that her face was peaceful. His plan was working.

'Now imagine this feeling to be like a ball inside you.' Mohit said and spoke his next words carefully, 'Now this violet blue ball of happiness will travel through your entire body and spread happiness every-where inside you. Just feel my fingertips and feel it flowing through your body.'

And Mohit began to touch her, only with the faint ends of his finger- tips. She associated his touch with the spread of happiness. First Mohit touched her head delicately and then her forehead. His fingers moved slowly to her cheeks and consciously avoided her lips. Gradually his fingertips moved gently touching her earlobes and then reached her neck and moved towards her soft arms.

She started breathing heavily, 'Stop it Mohit.' she said without opening her eyes. Mohit knew it was fake reluctance.

Mohit took his chance and leaned forward, moving so close to her that he could smell the familiar fragrance of her skin. She felt the warmth of his breath and slowly put a reluctant hand on the back of his neck and held his hair tight. Mohit had to be careful to keep himself in control. He wasn't supposed to make the first move. She opened her eyes and found him close.

'Oh Mohit!' she said passionately and kissed him.

When their destination came, Pari invited Mohit upstairs.

Six months later.........

'Wake up Anuj.'

I heard my mom's pleasant voice and woke up. She and my dad had come back from their morning walk. I walked passed them into the hall groggily and switched on my 50 inch plasma TV. Its 5.1 speakers filled the hall with the news reader's voice on an English news channel. My Mom had stopped being abrasive with me for the past two months as I had made sure that I gave fat checks at home regularly. In the last two months I had given around 6 lakh rupees to them. Although money was important, I knew my mother was at last at peace with the fact that I was doing something reasonable with my life. I had led her into believing that I was a life style trainer in an organisation which had clients from all over the world which explained my odd working hours and frequent absence for days on end.

The newly recruited maid came in with my morning tea. It didn't taste half as good as the tea my mom made but the maid was my gift to my mother. She went into the bedroom with two more cups of tea for my parents.

I looked at the beautiful snow clad mountains they showed on the TV. People were dressed in the warm woollen clothes which covered them from head to toe. And suddenly it struck me. I hurriedly went into my room and took out an envelope I had kept in my drawer last night. I took the envelope and went into my parent's room.

'Mom, Dad, Wish you a very happy marriage anniversary.' I said as I presented the envelope to them.

When they opened the envelope they were speechless. It was a fully paid for, trip to Switzerland for both of them.

My mom came over and hugged me as she wept. I couldn't make out my dad's reaction. I didn't know whether he laughed or cried. Maybe it was something in between.

'Have fun, guys. Dad, don't worry about applying for leaves for the vacation. You can retire now.'

' I will…I will just come back…' he mumbled and went into the bathroom.

He had worked hard for every penny in his life. The stress of working for so many years and not taking time out for himself even once had made him look older. And now his son, who, he had thought would never earn a penny in his life, had told him to retire. My mom and I heard choked sobs from the bathroom.

I had achieved a lot in life. I was a sort of leader to innumerable men; they sought my guidance. I had slept with hottest of women; I had money and could buy anything, however luxurious. I was successful in all aspects of my life.

But I never felt like more of a man than telling my father to retire.

I reached TST at 6 pm. As I walked in swiping my card to open the door, the man wearing the crisp black suit stood up in respect. I walked in and looked once again, like every day, at the changes I had made to the interiors of TST. The bright white walls had given way to dark brown and black. It had gothic paintings, rock posters and painted graffiti everywhere.

I entered a training room filled with students from world over. They seemed completely glued to their trainer's words. Their focus was wrecked by my presence as they stood up quickly looking at me.

'Guys, now let me introduce you to the man, who in fact needs no introduction.' Aman, their trainer and my friend said, 'Mr Anuj Kukreja, The Artist.'

Each one of them walked up to me and personally shook hands. Most of them looked star struck. I took over from Aman and shared my knowledge with the young aspirants who didn't know what to do with their raging hormones. I taught them only as much as they needed to be taught. Guru had shared things with me and trained me in a way that had propelled me into winning the duel and becoming TA. And I couldn't share everything with them

I was sitting in the smoking zone when my phone rang. It was Guru.

'Sorry, I couldn't be reached for so many days. I am in Hawaii and Natasha wanted no disturbance.' Guru said.

'No problems Guru. I have told you before, don't worry about TST. By the way the new batch has commenced today. Their accommodation is taken care of.'

'That's good.' Guru said and paused for a moment, 'I know I am repeating myself, but I can't stress enough Anuj; teach the students only as much as they need to know.'

'Yes.' I said and looked at Aman and wondered if he could hear Guru's voice in the silence of the smoking zone.

'Ok buddy, I am available anytime you need me. Bye.' Guru said and disconnected the call.

'What did he say?' Aman asked as he put the cigarette in the trash bin.

'Nothing much…er….Aman let's go out tonight. Somewhere we haven't been in a long time'

'Okay, but where?

'The Hell…it's been long.'

Aman and I sat on the back seat of my luxurious car as my chauffer began to drive us to our destination. Every time I sat in the car a feeling of calm whitewashed me. I was over - joyed the day Guru had gifted me his car, after winning the duel. 'The Artist needs to look at a higher level than the regular PUA.', Guru had said, 'It will add to your aura.'

But all this showering of favours upon me meant that Vinod, Ankit and other faculty members parted ways with TST. They wanted to work only with Guru and thought it was pointless to be associated with TST without the presence of his a God like figure. They had little faith in my ability to take TST forward as they firmly believed that, if at all, it should have been one of them at the helm after Guru. This had given opportunities for my friends to be inducted as new members of the faculty. Aman and Mohit along with other members took care of the training inside TST while Anthony managed the field activity along with an assistant.

I was hailed as one of the best pick up artistes in the world second only to Guru. I, in turn, passed on the invaluable information to my friends. Although I couldn't teach even my friends everything, it was enough. Together we had picked up hundreds of chicks in the last two months. We no longer were the Screw up artists.

We partied almost every night. We had new girls by our sides every time. Our pockets were loaded with cash and we could afford anything money could buy. We were living the dream

My phone beeped and it was another message from Sandy.

'm out partying and m lukng so hawt! Sending you the picture lucky guy, in a moment!'

She didn't consider me as her girlfriend any more. In fact I had gamed her so much that she had given me subtle hints that she had begun to love me and could consider marrying me. I couldn't care less. I knew love was only a term. I considered it as a euphemism for lust and weakness put together. It automatically meant that I didn't believe in marriage too. My phone beeped again and I saw the picture she had sent me. *She looks adorable;* I thought and immediately felt uncomfortable with the thought. I decided to shift my attention to matters at hand.

As we reached the pub, Aman and I got down from our cars as the chauffer drove it into the basement car park. We waited for the elevators to reach us. As I entered the elevator I prayed for her presence. I knew it was a long shot, but my instinct told me otherwise. Once inside I looked at the interior of the familiar elevator. I remembered how I would take the same elevator in those days and immediately my mind would fill with excitement of seeing her. Today I could just laugh at my naivety.

'Mohit called up. He and Anthony will meet us in two hours.' Aman was saying but my mind was elsewhere.

My body was completely focused on locating a face in the crowd. The bouncer at the entrance stamped my wrist and smirked. He had recognised me from that day, 'After a long time? Haha....be safe don't talk to girls.' and he winked at me. Aman took a step forward to confront him but I held him back, all the time searching for that face. I was filled with so much self-confidence by Guru that such petty remarks had no effect on me. But I had to deal with an old incident, when I wasn't self- assured.

I had to empty my bucket.

We sat there for an hour and yet there was no sight of her. I decided that tonight it wasn't going to be the night and Aman and I left the place and waited for the elevator. I turned left and saw the smoking zone beside us. The very place where she had humiliated me. It was also the place where I first met the man who changed my life forever. I didn't know whether to hate the place or thank it.

The sound of the elevator door opening in front of me broke my chain of thoughts. I took a step inside the elevator and its door shut behind me. Suddenly something struck me and before the elevator could move I pressed a button to open its door again. I felt that I had seen a familiar face. I hurriedly came out and looked in the smoking zone again.

When I saw the face, I thanked my stars. It was Richa. She looked as if she had put on a little weight but still looked as ravishing as the day I had seen her first. She sat in a corner with a girlfriend smoking and talking vivaciously about something.

'Oye Anuj, let's go! What's wrong…' Aman said as he stepped out of the elevator.

'Aman, my brother, just give me five minutes. Wait here. I need you. You will know when.' I said all the time looking at her. It was time for a closure. As I walked toward the smoking zone, unexpectedly my walk became as unsure and awkward as on that night. Fear gripped my heart, again. I became sure this was going to be another screw up. I almost retracted my steps when suddenly I was reminded of a mental exercise taught to me by Guru. I snapped my fingers and all my confidence came back to me. He had made my subconscious associate confident feelings with this gesture.. I had every corner covered. I now knew I couldn't mess it up, even if God wanted me to.

'Hey, girls have you seen a girl around here looking for someone?' I asked Richa's friend. It was an *ex-girlfriend stalking me* opener.

'No..not that we have noticed.' her friend said.

In seconds Richa recognised me. Before she could react or say something nasty, I took over.

I wasn't a novice like our meeting last time. This time she was dealing with the best Pick-up Artist. In the world.

Aman watched me from outside. He knew that I was throwing in routines after routines. He saw me standing at a particular angle near the girls and he could predict every movement I made. I gave him a subtle hint and he walked in. I introduced him to the girls and he engaged Richa's friend in a conversation. He spoke about random things and then threw in a question which would have her opinion on who cheats more; girls or guys? Once she was distracted I took my game with Richa higher. After gaming her for 15 minutes, I left from there.

My next meeting point with her would be the dance floor. She was with her group of friends in one corner of the floor. She moved in a sensuous, erotic manner. I danced close to her with only a horny couple dancing between us. I mostly had my back towards her and once as I turned around to look at her, our eyes met. She didn't break the eye contact. I knew I couldn't take that as a sign of interest in me. I had burnt my hands badly once before, thinking of her stares as a sign that she liked me. Aman in the meanwhile had opened another group and was dancing with a girl from the group. He introduced me to the girl and I asked her for a dance. Aman knew that I would use her as a pawn to attract my main target, Richa. The girl, to my surprise was a terrific dancer. She could match and at moments even outdo me with her terrific dance steps. Guru's advice to me to take dance lessons was paying rich dividends now. We danced with perfect cadence and synchronisation that had everyone's attention. Most importantly, even Richa's. While dancing I noticed a Man waving at me from the bar. I noticed it was my now good friend Shiva. I smiled and gestured at him that I would catch up a little later with him. I couldn't afford any distraction now. As I danced with the girl gradually I found myself feeling a strong attraction for her too. I was lost in her smile when I felt a tap on my shoulder.

'Can I dance with you?' It was Richa. I wasn't surprised.

I nodded and held her hand. She seemed over whelmed with attraction for me. I had gamed her hard outside and now was the hottest man on the dance floor. After ten more minutes she began kissing me.

Don't you have anything better to do then Lech at girls, her cruel words replayed in my head

I didn't respond to her kiss. My game was strong. I wanted her to work hard and crave for every piece of me.

'My boyfriend is about to come. Before he is here, let's go someplace where it's quiet.' she whispered in my ears and I agreed. I was another step close to my goal. I walked past the bouncer who had taken a cheap shot at me. He looked astonishingly at the hot chick who couldn't keep her hands off me. The same girl who had once made me look like a loser. When I looked at him in the eye, he couldn't hold his eye contact with me.

As we walked out hand in hand towards the main door, Richa let out a squeal, 'Oh my god! He is here. I am screwed!'

When I looked at the giant of a man walking towards me, I realized it was the same guy who had confronted and then pushed me that night. I beamed with happiness from inside looking at him. The night was turning out perfect.

'Oh Oh..look who we have here....you don't learn your lessons easily…You wanna steal my girlfriend…' he said with frenzy in his eyes.

'Just go away Sid. I just want to end it with you.' Richa said. She looked scared.

'I will deal with you later, you whore! You…come out with me', he said touching my chest with his finger. Richa and I walked behind him and when we were in a luminous area around the reception, he suddenly turned around and held me by my collar mouthing loud abuses. In seconds a crowd gathered around us.

'You think you are very smart, haan?' and he slapped me so hard with his gigantic hands that I nearly fell down. It took around five seconds for me to regain my balance. Aman came hurriedly and held me. I gestured at him to stay put. It was my fight.

I walked towards the huge monster, 'Touch me one more time, if you have balls, touch me one more time.' I said and immediately he pulled his arm back to have another swing at me and instantly I ducked under his arm. When he missed his shot I immediately jumped as high as possible and came down, breaking a beer bottle on his head. He hadn't realized that I had grabbed a beer bottle from Aman. The impact of the glass hitting his seemingly metallic head was so strong that I couldn't land properly and fell face down on the floor. I looked around for him hoping he would have collapsed next to me, somewhere. But I could only see people's feet around me. I looked and saw the guy still standing. I stood up and looked at him. His head bled but he still seemed okay. I wondered what it would take to take this huge unit down. Now, he grabbed a bottle from someone and paced towards me. He raised his arm to hit me. When the bottle was inches away from striking my head, a hand grabbed the monster's arm. I turned around to see my saviour. It was Shiva. The guy recognised him immediately and took a few steps back.

'You are a new don, is it?' Shiva said, giving him a cold look. From my own experience I knew that this guy could put fear in you. It was Shiva's calling in life.

'I didn't know..er..', he stammered

'Guys take him away. We will deal with him outside.' Shiva ordered his army of men. The manager and the bouncers had reached by now. But they didn't move a muscle. I knew it was a blatant abuse of power. The kind of thing I hated months ago. But at that time power was something which only others had. Today it was mine.

There is nothing ethical about this game, about life!

'Wait!' I shouted while a feeling of invincibility consumed me. I walked up to my now scared enemy, 'Why don't you abuse me again. C'mon give it a shot, let's see what happens?'

'It's his mistake Shiva bhai..he was hitting on my girl..' Before he could finish his sentence, I gathered all my energy and slapped him as hard as I could. Immediately I regretted my decision. My hand hurt more than his face. It felt like slapping a huge piece of rock. But I couldn't show pain and walked closer to him almost touching his body. My head barely reached his chin. I felt the familiar heat of his breath on my scalp.

'What do we do now?' I said, 'Yeah it's my mistake, do you still have a problem with it?' I asked

'No…no problem ,S-S-Sir.'

A feeling of triumph went through me.

SIR! That's right, you bastard, that's how you should address me, that's how the world should address me!

'Shiva let him go. He is nothing to waste our time on.' I said triumphantly.

'Only if you insist, Anuj. Otherwise today would have been his last night.' Shiva said and immediately Richa's ex-boyfriend Sid ran away.

'Thanks Shiva.' I said and hugged him. He smiled and disappeared into the pub with his gang.

'That was cool, Anuj! You have such high contacts! But he deserved it..now he wouldn't come close to me either.' Richa said and laughed heartily.

'I wanna smoke, before we leave, I need a puff.' I entered the smoking zone as Richa and Aman followed me. It was full and there wasn't any place to sit. A group of young guys who had seen the fracas outside immediately got up and offered us their seats.

She kept on talking without much response from me. I only said yes or no in answer to her questions. I finished my smoke and threw the butt on the floor.

'Let's go now....'Richa said and playfully grabbed my arm to pull me up.

'Where?' I snapped

'Aren't we supposed to go somewhere?' she was embarrassed.

'To a quiet place, you mean?'

'Yeah' she said slowly, visibly self-conscious now.

'What's wrong with you.' I howled as I stood up, 'I don't wanna sleep with you.'

Creepy silence occupied the smoking zone now.

'W—what the...why are you screaming.' she said as she took a step backward in horror

'Why are you fucking after my life? Go and fuck around with someone..I am not interested in you...why don't you sleep with... with this guy here...or that guy there.. ' I said grabbing a guy's arm sitting in the couch opposite, 'Sleep with anyone. I am not interested, get on in life you loser!' And I walked out of the room

While Aman and I waited for the elevator I saw the same bouncer standing some feet away. He looked at me and shook his head in disgust. I tried not to give it too much of attention. What he or anyone else thought, I didn't care. I had achieved what I had to.

Before we left, I turned around to look a final time at Richa.

She stood there stunned. The black kohl was smudged, tears had reached her cheeks. Some girls held her trying to console her.

Once outside I looked up in the sky,

Nobody messes with me, God. Not even you.

'I am scared. What if you take advantage of me?' I was gaming her.

'You are so mysterious!' she said and looked deep into my eyes with destructive passion. My eyes scanned her from head to toe. I knew I was looking at the most beautiful girl I could ever see. Every inch of her skin shone through the white glossy piece of cloth that draped her alluring body. She leaned forward and rested her head on my shoulders. I held her soft hands and was worried that they might melt in my hands.

'Do you believe in love?' I asked her. I knew the question was more for myself, 'The incredible power of love, which…' I couldn't finish my sentence. I saw a faint black smoke around my face. In seconds I realised that it came from me, from inside my mouth when I spoke. I was horrified, 'Hey do you see this..see this black smoke', I asked as panic gripped my entire anatomy.

'Yes I do.' she laughed, 'So what? Everyone has black smoke inside them. Don't be such a coward..haha.' she said dismissively.

'No..it's not..it's not normal, nobody has it.' I screamed in horror and ran away in search of water which could drown the smoke inside me. I couldn't find it anywhere. I could now feel the thick smoke coming out from my nostrils; I could feel it inside me. My breathing became quick and I could feel the surge of something dark and unpleasant moving upwards inside me as I fell on knees on the ground. The next second I threw up a bucketful of black liquid on the ground. I kept on retching until I collapsed in my own black puke.

'Hey Anuj. What are you doing?' I heard a faint familiar voice.

I opened my eyes and realised it was Guru. I was relieved that he was here but at the same time embarrassed that he would see me in this sickening state.

'I want you to try this opener.' he said and I saw the beautiful landscaped garden we were in. I looked around and there was no trace of my vomit anywhere on the ground or my shirt.

'Try this. Hey my girlfriend has had a bad reaction to a new shampoo and she has lost all her hair on her scalp. Can you tell me where to buy a wig similar to yours?' Guru said and laughed. He then gestured me to go to a room. I began walking towards the bright white door of the room. Once I pushed it open, an intolerable stench assailed and immediately turned around my head in disgust. I was looking out now and saw a limousine stopping in front of Guru. He had Natasha by his side and both of them sat in the car. They laughed and looked blessed in each other's company. My eyes met Guru's. He smiled warmly at me and zoomed away.

I stepped into the room. I didn't want to breathe but gradually I got used to the stink and it became bearable. The room looked completely empty and it seemed that nobody had entered it for ages except dogs whose poop was everywhere. I wondered why Guru had sent me here. I was about to leave when I noticed a familiar wooden cupboard. Instinctively I walked towards it and pushed it aside. Immediately metal stairs appeared which led to a basement. I walked down the stairs which took me to a room. It was pitch dark. Blindly I touched the walls to turn on any light. My finger noticed a switch and I pushed it. A very bright light filled the entire room. My eyes were dazzled the sudden bright light. As my vision cleared, I took a step back in horror. Hundreds of women occupied the room. I recognised most of them. Suddenly it hit me that I knew all of them. They were all the women I had dated and then later hurt by ignoring their calls, insulting them, abusing and using them. I saw anger in their eyes as they walked towards me slowly. I tried to run away from them but they were just too many to counter or escape from. They begin attacking me with rage. Some kicked, some punched and others pulled my hair. Somehow I broke free and managed to reach a door. Before I could pass through the door a hand pulled me back holding my shirt collar. I turned around and saw that face with black tears on her cheeks flowing from bloodshot eyes. In a split second Richa hit my skull with a hockey stick so hard that trails of blood began to flow from my head. As my head spun I noticed the bouncer from ,The Hell. He looked at me and shook his head. Barely conscious I dragged myself out of there as I heard peals of laughter behind me.

The door opened to a huge lawn in a bungalow. In the distance I could see an old man with grey hair sitting on a chair reading a newspaper with his back towards me. I needed urgent help to stay alive.

'Hello mister! Hello!' I squealed. He didn't move.

I tried again, 'Hello! Sir I need your help.' This time he heard me and turned around. He removed his spectacles and placed them on the table in front of him. He looked at me hard and got up to walk towards me. Once close I realised his face was oddly familiar. I had seen him somewhere but couldn't put a finger on it. He took my arm, put it around his shoulders and took me to the lawn. He made me sit on a chair next to his and offered me water.

'What happened son?' he asked once I gulped down the water.. I knew I had heard the voice too.

'Err Nothing…just a minor accident…' I said and looked for that weird room from where I had come out saving my life. It was nowhere to be seen

'You should call your family, your parents' he said.

'Oh yes, but they are away on a holiday.' I said

'..and your wife?'

'No, I am not married…and I ..I don't think I ever will.'

'Oh is it? I think it's a mistake. You should son. It gets very lonely.'

'Uncle, don't get me wrong, but can I know your name? You seem very familiar.'

He paused for a second and then said, 'My name is Anuj. Anuj Kukreja. What's your name son?'

A bolt of fright went through me. The same features, the same voice. I knew where I had seen him before. In the mirror, all my life.

It was me, talking to my other self.

'This this is ..is not happening with me..man..how could it? You have the same face…..Who are you.' I said as I fell off my chair with tears rolling down my cheek.

'Don't cry Anuj.' he laughed, 'When you cry, I have tears in my eyes too, you understand?' He said and walked slowly towards me,

'You see this huge bungalow? That fleet of cars? You know who gave all this to me? All the luxurious of life? You did. And a big Thank you for that. But you know what else you gave me? Loneliness. The excruciating pain of loneliness. I feel this pain every moment in my old age just because you ..you couldn't love, felt nothing to enter the institution of marriage. Look at me; I live alone in this huge house. I sleep alone. I have no family. I have nobody to pass this onto! I feel like a ghost.'

'No no…this can't be true…' I said all the time dragging away from the old man.

'I don't need this. There is nothing to live for. I will kill myself and finish you along with me.' he said slowly and began walking towards a well close by.

'No..no…don't do that.' I screamed and got up to stop him. But my legs became numb and unresponsive to my efforts of moving. It was too late and I saw him jump in the well.

Immediately I felt short of breath and began gasping for air.

I tried to find my next breath but couldn't. I tried hard, putting in all my strength to breathe. He had jumped into the well and drowned me.

Suddenly a blast of air entered my lungs through my mouth as I got up in panic. I found myself sitting in my bed as my lungs pulled in as much oxygen inside me as they could. I looked around for the well he had jumped into but could only see my cupboard in that direction. I walked slowly towards my door and peeped out to see if there was another freak show happening. But to my relief I could only see the furniture in my dimly lit hall. I wiped the sweat of my face and gulped down a bottle of water. I heaved a sigh of relief and jumped into my bed and began staring at the ceiling. Something inside me didn't want to sleep again.

The terrible nightmare had kept me awake the entire night.

I was taking a shower at 6 am. The temperature outside was very low. Till the time the hot water fell on me, it felt warm and comfortable but whenever it stopped touching my body, a wave of cold would run through my body. But even my shivering body wasn't a deterrent. I had rubbed my body with soap three times already. It was almost an hour since this bath started. I brushed my teeth and flossed over and over again to feel clean from inside. The dream I had three hours ago had made me realise how dirty I felt from within. But before this night, I had never stopped to listen to my conscience. After an hour and half of cleansing myself physically I realised that it wasn't going to be enough.

My mind wandered to the night when I had humiliated Richa. The false high it had given me had lasted ever since. What followed was mindless pick- ups and hurting women consciously. Even if I knew a woman would understand a polite no from me about meeting again, I would be rude and insulting towards her. To smell fear and hurt in women had become an addiction for me. Maybe they bore the wrath of my inability to deal with women while growing up. Maybe subconsciously I blamed women for my pains. My revenge hadn't stop with Richa.

I waited for another hour and started with my phone calls. It was 7 am. First I called up Mohit.

'Mohit Sir, I will not be able to come to TST. You handle it. I will meet you directly at the pub we are going in the night.'

'That's okay.' he mumbled, 'Can't sleep man..something is wrong.'

'Will talk about it later, I have some urgent work.' I said.

I dialled another number.

'Hello. You are calling very early?' Sandy said with a yawn, 'What's the matter?'

'Sandy, I have given it a good thought. I think I- I--I Love You.' I stammered. I didn't care for build-ups.

'What? Are you serious?' Suddenly her voice was alert.

Look at me! I live alone in this huge house. I sleep alone. I have no family. I have nobody to pass this onto! I feel like a ghost' my mind repeated the lines from my dream.

'Yes I am.' I gathered enough courage and tried to inject excitement in my voice, 'Will you—you marry me?' and I closed my eyes. As a young boy whenever I dreamt of saying this to a girl one day, I would plan it all out in my mind. The phone call; when I would tell her to dress in her best, the limousine, the dinner, she would find the ring in her drink and then the most extravagant part; the helicopter ride where we would sit hand in hand and enjoy the panoramic view of the city .

But now I had neither the time nor the motivation of real love to carry out preparations like that. I wanted to put my life back together. Now.

'W—what the fuck?' she said.

That too wasn't the answer I would visualise.

'What? you don't want to? But you-you said t..that... .' I stammered.

'No..no not like that...I had a different concept of a proposal. But you are saying this at 7 am and I haven't even brushed my teeth. I mean I can see my vomit on the floor from last night....'

'Sandy, yes or no?'

'It's Yes, you asshole!' and she giggled with happiness.

I was relieved. I tried to sound excited, 'Wow! I can't believe it! Thank you Sandy.' I paused, 'We will meet tomorrow. Let's celebrate this. I will give you surprises like taking you to spa, movies and I will invite all your friends for a party.'

'What the f...' before she could finish, I disconnected the call. I knew when it came to romance, I was still a novice.

My final and the most important call was to Guru. My fingers hesitantly dialled the numbers.

'Hello Anuj. Tell me?' he said. There were no superfluous exchanges of pleasantries with Guru.

'Hey Guru! How's Moscow?' I said.

'It's good Anuj. But let's get to the real deal here. You obviously haven't called to know about Moscow when it must be 7 in the morning in Mumbai. Tell me.?'

'Guru..err.. I need to ...I need you to give TST..to me.'

'What?' he said in disbelief.

'Hear me out....It's just that, right now, I don't get the feeling of complete control over things. You know..er...but what I have thought is perfect for the both of us.'

'And what's that, Anuj?' he was surprisingly calm.

'See, what it would mean is a minimal, almost negligible cut in income for you. We can decide on a fixed amount that I can send you every month. However, if in the future I choose to step down or decide to part ways, you get TST back. It's more like a lease but I need complete power over decisions. How d-does it sound to you?'

'Hmmm.....' he paused for a while, 'Anuj, it doesn't sound bad. I am sure you have something constructive in your mind. If what you are saying can be done, I don't have a problem. Fax me the papers.'

I was relieved. Over the months Guru had gauged every move I made, closely and I knew by now he was satisfied with my decision making ability. But I only had a faint hope that he would agree to this. Now I had spoken to Guru about the offer without offending him. I didn't want to upset Guru not because he was my mentor but because I looked at him as a brother.

'Okay I will. In fact I will send it to you by afternoon today.'

'Okay Anuj. Cover everything in the papers.' and I heard a click.

My afternoon passed with my lawyer and CA as we drafted the final clauses of the agreement. It didn't take as much time as I had expected. They were good at their work.

'Anuj, should we pick you up or well you come on your own?' Aman called me in the evening.

'I will reach directly. But Aman, promise me! No gaming women today.'

'Same page bro! Even I need a break. I feel all this is too much. Anyway, see you at the pub.'

Promises don't matter, not when it comes to girls I thought looking at Aman and Mohit with the girls.

'Bro, how is it going?' I asked Anthony who seemed immersed in texting his girlfriend.

'All cool re. She just keeps on telling me that she trusts me and all. She says this stuff more when I am partying.' Anthony said and he paused for a while,

'Bro..check that chick out on your left, man..Awesome…!' he said looking at a girl in a denim mini skirt.

Suddenly his phone beeped and his focus shifted from the girl to his phone. He showed me the message from Madhu.

'How's the music there, my loyal boyfriend?'

'See, what I mean? I don't get why she puts so much pressure on me. Check out some of her other messages....'

'Oh okay... What are you drinking, my dependable man?'

'Hmm...I am feeling very lonely. Pity can't be out late nights with my faithful baby.'

'I am having dinner now. I have made pizza for everyone, my trustworthy sweetheart.'

'She really wants to trust you bro!' I said with a smirk.

'Don't worry man; I love her. Can't ever cheat her.' Anthony said as his eyes fell on the hot chick again, 'Madhu will be on my side forever man. True love is hard to find. These other chicks are a waste man. They just wanna have fun. It's all cool but why should we dedicate our lives to impress them? Madhu has seen me when I sometimes I look like shit, she was with me when my pockets were empty, she has smelled my stinkiest of farts, but bro she loves me more every day.'

I could just look back at him in respect. He had said something so insightful in his own simple way.

A minute later Madhu called up Anthony and told him to go to the bathroom to take a leak so that he didn't get very high.

'Hey! My reliable friend, carry on..come soon and we will wait for you here.' I said and Anthony went out to go to the washroom.

Minutes later Mohit and Aman walked towards where I sat. They didn't seem particularly excited with the fun they had with the girls.

'You takin'em home with you?' I asked both of them.

'No.' Mohit replied, 'Don't feel shit these days. Feel like taking a break from all this. Don't get sleep these days.'

'Yeah Anuj.' Aman said, 'It's become more of a habit. Even if I don't want to..I just end up gaming. It's like smoking. Don't feel any better while smoking or after smoking, but still can't quit.'

'It's good you guys feel this way. I am happy.' I said and paused for a moment. 'But don't quit TST, not just now, give it at least three months. However, quit gaming women, at least for a while.. Money is good here, can't leave it just like that. I have something on my mind.' I said. My doubts were confirmed, my friends didn't have the motivation to continue here for long. Just like me. But we couldn't let go the financial independence it had given us. I couldn't think of getting my parent's lifestyle back to ordinary. After all I had told my father to retire. The whole night after the nightmare I had jumped deep into my subconscious. I tried to analyse what my inner self wanted to tell me in the form of a dream. What I really thought about what I had become. I knew that I wanted to get out but at the same time not forgo the money I was making. I then did what I always do when in a corner; think how would Guru get out of this, what he would do.?

And when I had got an answer, I was amazed at how I could not have known it earlier. The answer was there in front of me, all the time.

I decided that doing what I intended to do would mean lesser income which again I had to share with my friends. And yet my income would be in lakhs every month; It was enough. I would live with dignity, with peace of mind.

I stood on the steps alone smoking a cigarette. My friends had gone back inside but I decided to stay back, lighting the second cigarette.

'Hey, I wanted to ask you something?' a tall, lanky guy asked a girl in a group. I watched them keenly from the top of the stairway.

'Yes?' she said sharply as all her friends turned in to watch the conversation.

'I..I…err..can you come to one side…not here, I can't ask here!' he said shyly.

'Hello! Whatever you want to say, say it now, here..or else please leave.'

'I wanted to..err..I kinda like you..and was wondering if we could go out on a date…' he said looking down. I felt amused at the guy's weak approach. I knew who he reminded me of.

'No….look at you..ewwww….just go and find someone of your own level.' she said as her entire group began laughing at him and giving each other high fives. The guy looked down and was almost in tears. He went back to his friend who looked equally unsure of himself. He stood there as everyone from the girl's group passed by him mocking him one by one. When everyone left he came and sat on the stairs as his friend tried to cheer him up.

I finished my smoke and smashed it under my boots. My mind was in turmoil. My heart was weak. I took my first step, I wasn't sure.

You gave me loneliness. The excruciating pain of loneliness. I feel this pain every moment in my old age.

I took another step.

I didn't want to live the rest of my life like a sex-machine, loving no one and no-one loving me back.

I kept walking and now was standing only a step behind him. I had decided. I put an arm around him which startled him.

'Hey…er..who are…'

Life gets shallow and you find your own reflection in the mirror repulsive.

I stood in front of him. Our eye contact was strong. I knew he wouldn't refuse. My lips wanted to say it but my heart stopped me. Then suddenly it came out of my mouth,

'If you don't want to feel like this ever… follow me.'

Srishti's all time bestsellers ₹ 100 each

- A Dilli-Mumbai Love Story
- A Feeling Beyond Words
- A half baked love story
- A Life that you knew..
- A Little Bit of Love...
- A Little Love Incident
- And then it rained....
- Anyone Else but you
- A Roller Coaster Ride!
- As Long as I Love you...
- A thing beyond forever
- A Walk Down the Lane...
- Because you Loved me..
- Beep you! you BeepHole
- Belong
- Boundless Saga of Love
- By the River Pampa I...
- Careful what u Wish for
- Coming up on the show..
- Corporate Atyaachaar
- Crazy Bloody Thing LOV
- Dancing with Maharaja
- Everything you Desire
- Few things left unsaid

- From Cubicles 2 Cabins
- Heartbreaks & Dreams!
- I am Broke....! Love me
- I am Still Committed..
- If God Had A Desk Job..
- If God went to B-School
- If I Pretend I am Sorry!
- It Happened that Night
- In Course of True Love
- I too had a love story..
- It's all About Love...
- It Should Be u!! My Love
- It wasn't Love at First
- I will Love Once Again!
- Jab se you have loved me
- Journey of two Hearts
- Just Like in the Movies
- Life is What you Make it
- Love Happens Like that
- Love, Life & A Beer Can!
- Love, Life and Dream on
- Love, Life and Lust...
- Love Life & all the Dots
- Love, me and Bullshit!

- Love Power Politics!!
- Love a Rather Bad Idea
- Love & Urban Melodrama
- LUV is a Dirty Business
- My Love Never Faked...
- Nothing for you my Dear
- Nothing Lasts Forever
- Of Tattoos and Taboos!
- Oops! 'I' fell in Love!
- Ouch! that 'Hearts'..
- Patyala Down De Throat
- Plz.. Kiss me or Kill me
- Reality Bytes 'Bites'
- She is Single I'm Taken
- Simple Things Make LUV
- Something in your Eyes
- Sumthing of a Mocktale
- 34 Bubblegums and Candies
- That Kiss in the Rain..

- The Dev-D Syndrome...
- The Equation of my Love
- The Funda of Mix-ology
- The Idiot-Dudes.....
- The India I Dream of
- The Journey of Rock...
- The Journey to Nowhere
- The Lost Scraps of Love
- The Off-Site Tamasha
- The Other way Round
- The Quest for Nothing!
- The Thing Between U & Me
- Those Small Lil Things
- Three Times Loser....
- To Whom it May Concern:
- When Life Tricked me..
- What... if not I.I.T.?
- Will you Marry Me Cupid

- Brain Building for achievement
  Herbert N. Casson

- Cheiro's : Language of the Hand

- Winning Personality:
  The Magic key to success
  F. Oss